T0041236

Reluctantly Home

ALSO BY IMOGEN CLARK

Reluctantly Home

IMOGEN
CLARK

Text copyright © 2021 by Blue Lizard Books Ltd
All rights reserved.

Published by Lake Union Publishing, Seattle

www.apub.com

Amazon, the Amazon logo, and Lake Union Publishing are trademarks of Amazon.com, Inc., or its affiliates.

ISBN-13: 9781542021203
ISBN-10: 1542021200

Cover design by Lisa Horton

Printed in the United States of America

Reluctantly Home

1

2019

She was going to be late for court.

She had been cutting it fine anyway, leaving chambers when she did, but Dominic had said it would only take half an hour to get there once she was through the worst of the central London traffic. Now, however, she was sitting in a stationary queue of cars watching the clock on her dashboard click over from minute to minute.

She couldn't be late. The judge would crucify her in front of her client. He might even refuse to give her audience and then she'd end up slinking back to the office with her tail between her legs.

She could feel her heart beginning to race and her chest grew tight as her panic rose. She didn't even know where this court was, or where she could park. And she still had some papers to read before the hearing. The whole thing was a disaster before she'd even begun. What had she been thinking, leaving so late?

Then, mercifully, the traffic began to clear, and the stream of cars sped up. She let out a slow breath. The situation might be salvageable. If she didn't hit any more slow patches between here and there, she'd arrive with time to spare. She could feel the tension slip from her neck and shoulders as she relaxed. She began to run through her opening address, speaking it out loud as she drove; her voice sounded clear and confident. Years of court experience brought with them a certain self-assurance. She was good at what she did, she knew she was. She would win the hearing this morning and then . . .

She didn't see the boy until he was already on her bonnet, his face distorted first by shock and then the impact with her windscreen. And then he was gone, rolling away from her and out of sight.

Where was he? She was going to run over him as well as knocking him down. Her instincts took over and she slammed on the brakes, the car shuddering to a stop. The driver behind was surely going to smash into her now. She braced herself for the impact, but it didn't come, the car managing to brake in time. She could see the driver, a woman with silver hair, in her rear-view mirror. Her eyes were wide, her mouth open in horror.

But where was the boy? She should get out and see if he was all right, but she couldn't make her legs move. All communications between her brain and her muscles seemed to have been cut. Her breath was coming in short snatches, as if something had sucked all the oxygen out of the car and she couldn't get enough to fill her lungs. Her heart was banging so hard in her chest that she could barely hear anything else. But there was something, a little sound in the distance that she couldn't quite focus on. It was a voice, she worked out. Someone was shouting at her. She tried to concentrate, listen to what they were saying, but it sounded very quiet and far away.

'Are you hurt? I'm calling an ambulance. Stay where you are.'

It was the woman from the car behind, now out on the road next to her window, mobile phone in hand.

'Ambulance, please. And police. There's been an accident. A boy. He just ran out into the road. He didn't look. He ran out and a car hit him . . . No . . . I don't know . . . No, it wasn't my car. It was the car in front of me, but it wasn't her fault. There was nothing she could have done. He just ran out . . . Yes, I think so. Hang on.'

And then the woman was talking to her again through the window, her voice muffled.

'Are you all right? Are you injured in any way?'

Suddenly she had to get out into the fresh air. The space was too small. She couldn't breathe. She scrabbled for the seat belt, clicked it loose and flung the door open, pushing her way out. There were cars everywhere, all stopped and pointing towards her as if she was the main attraction. It felt surreal to be standing in the middle of the road surrounded by cars but without the sounds of engines around her.

But where was the boy? She dropped her eyes, searching for him, and there he was, lying across the opposite carriageway, the wheels of another car stopped just inches from his supine body. The first thing she noticed was that his leg was all wrong. It shouldn't be at an angle like that. She wanted to bend down and straighten it for him. And then she saw his face. His eyes were wide open and sightless. That was when she knew, without a shadow of doubt, that he was dead. That she had killed him.

And then she woke up.

2

'It's okay. It's over. It's just a dream,' Pip whispered to herself, repeating the mantra she had been desperately clinging to for the six months since the accident. Slowly, inch by inch, she pulled herself round to consciousness as her breathing levelled out and her heartbeat began to return to normal. She could feel her pyjama top sticking to her shoulders. The damp sheets beneath her were already growing too cold and clammy to sleep on.

Was this her life now, Pip wondered, being woken every night as her mind replayed the accident on a never-ending loop? It had been six months, and yet the dream was still as vivid as if she had hit the boy yesterday. And each time, she woke at exactly the same moment. It wasn't the shock of the impact that ricocheted her from sleep into consciousness, although she could still feel the thud of the boy's body as he hit her bonnet. No, the last thing she saw before she snapped awake was always his eyes, wide and staring at nothing. Those eyes haunted her, day and night.

Gradually Pip started to focus on the familiar space of her childhood bedroom. How had she ended up back here, after all those years trying to get away? She had been gone for over a decade, but the room still looked as it had done when she was eighteen. The baby-pink walls were speckled with dark Blu Tack marks where photos and pictures cut from magazines had promised her a life beyond the farm, and her bookshelves still bowed under the weight of teenage paperbacks and folders stuffed full of A level notes. When she was here, it felt almost as if she had imagined the life she had created in London, or that it had happened to someone else. It felt as if it was floating further away from her with every passing week.

She heard a door creak open and then the soft pad of footsteps on the landing.

'Pip? Are you okay?' her mother asked in hushed tones through her closed door. 'Can I get you anything?'

Pip cursed under her breath. Why couldn't her nightmares be silent so she could keep them to herself? She imagined her mother lying awake in the dark next door, just waiting for her terrors to make their nightly visit, her father snoring gently next to her, oblivious.

'I'm fine, Mum,' she said, trying to sound reassuring and not irritated. 'Go back to bed.'

She heard her mother creep away, the bedroom door opening and then not quite closing behind her. Was this what her future looked like now, with her unable to make it through a night without reliving every moment of the accident, and her mother watching over her like a hawk? How was that a future?

But what did she expect? Pip had taken a life, and for that it was only right she should forfeit her own. The inquest had found her to have no legal responsibility for the boy's death; it had simply been a tragic accident, but that made no difference. She knew what had happened was her fault, and she couldn't imagine ever being able to forgive herself. Guilt was her constant companion, never once leaving her side, so she couldn't forget, even for a second, what she had done. And her life, destroyed by panic and guilt, seemed a fair price to pay. A life for a life.

She settled herself back into the cold, damp sheets, ready to lie awake until morning.

Pip must have dropped off to sleep at some point, because she woke to the smell of burning. The acrid air stole into her nostrils and her eyes snapped open. What was on fire? Should she run? Then she remembered where she was. Her parents' house. The smell currently filling her room would be the toast her mother was making for breakfast. Some things never changed. The ancient Aga that sat in the farmhouse kitchen had been there since Pip was a baby and making toast on it was simply a question of timing, but somehow it always burned.

She got up, threw a dressing gown around her shoulders and headed downstairs, the smell getting stronger the closer she got to the kitchen. Once there, the air was thick with smoke and her mother was standing over the bin trying to scrape the worst of the charring off with a knife. Her father and his farmhand, Jez, were tucking into their breakfasts at the scrubbed pine table and barely seemed to have noticed.

'Morning,' said Pip.

Her mother looked up and then back down at the blackened piece of bread in her hand.

'I burned the blessed toast,' she said. 'The cat brought a mouse in and . . .' She shrugged sadly by way of further explanation. 'It was the last of the bread, too, until I get to the shops.'

'Nothing changes, eh, Pip?' her father said, cheerfully biting into his sausage. 'There's plenty of bacon left. Sit down and have a bite with us before we head out.'

Jez was wiping the remains of his egg yolk up with a piece of bread, but he looked up and then shuffled his chair across a little to make room for her to sit down. He gave her a smile, wide and friendly, but Pip ignored him, or rather, pretended she hadn't noticed. The two of them had been close when they were kids, and he kept trying to talk to her, but she didn't have the strength for conversation and, if she was honest, she wasn't that interested in rekindling their friendship. Jez was part of her past, and she didn't need him in her present. What would be the point? She wasn't planning on being around for long enough to get to know him again, and anyway, they'd have nothing to talk about. They might have been close as teenagers, but she doubted they had much in common now. He was still here, for a start, content to work on a farm a few miles from where he'd grown up, whereas she had built a fabulous life for herself in London, and although she liked him well enough, investing time in their erstwhile friendship would take more than she had to give.

'Never mind,' she said to her mother. 'I'm not that hungry. I'll just have a cup of tea.'

What she really wanted was coffee, decent coffee made with hand-ground beans and filtered to a rich smoothness, but all her mother could offer was an old jar of instant that had lost any tempting aroma it might once have held through sitting on the window sill for months, possibly years. No one drank coffee here and so this jar was reserved for visitors. After two or three cups of the filthy stuff, Pip had resorted to drinking tea instead.

'Oh, Pip,' her mother replied, and in those two words Pip could hear the worry that was so clearly etched into her face. Pip was tired of being the cause of so much heartache, but she couldn't summon the energy to change that, either.

'You can't go to the shop on an empty stomach,' her mother continued to object. 'Let me make you some porridge. Or a boiled egg at the very least. . .' She looked at the charred slice of bread in her hand and then opened her fingers and let it fall into the bin. 'But there's no toast for soldiers,' she added, her mouth twisted into a wry smile.

'Honestly, Mum,' Pip said, filling the kettle and setting it to boil on the hot plate. 'There's no need. Tea is fine.'

Her mother made a noise somewhere between a tut and a harrumph, but she didn't push the point.

'I thought we weren't calling you Pip any more,' her father chipped in, and Pip cringed.

'Have you heard this one, Jez?' he continued. 'Our Pip's only gone and changed her name to Rose. We didn't know a thing about it until her chap Dominic came to stay. When he called her Rose, I was looking round to see who he was talking to.'

'It's just my work name, Dad,' said Pip, anxious not to get caught up in the discussion around what she called herself yet again. She had tried to get her parents to call her Rose when she first came back to Suffolk. Her mother had made an effort initially, but had given up. Her father, however, seemed tickled by the suggestion and still wouldn't let it drop.

'Pip was christened with two names,' said her mother patiently. 'It's up to her which one she chooses to use.'

Pip gave her a grateful smile, but she had already turned away and Pip glimpsed the tail of her hurt look as it crossed her face.

'Well, I still can't see what's wrong with Pip,' her father muttered under his breath.

Pip thought she could sense Jez staring at her, but she ignored him. She didn't need him judging her on top of everything else.

The men finished their breakfast, the chairs scraping across the tiled floor as they pushed them away from the table. After one last, noisy slurp of his tea, Jez took his plate and mug and placed them neatly by the sink, ready to be washed. Her father kissed her mother on the cheek and then they were gone to put their boots back on and head out to the fields.

Pip pulled a tea towel from where it was hanging on the Aga and began to dry the dishes her mother had already washed. She stacked them neatly in the cupboards, moving around the kitchen instinctively, although it hadn't been her home for a third of her life. It was disheartening how easily she'd slipped back into life on the farm. She'd spent ten years trying to escape the place, had grabbed hold of her dreams and turned them into reality, and yet now she was right back where she'd started, helping out in a charity shop and having her breakfast burned by her mother.

Her mother was busy decanting eggs from a bucket into cardboard egg boxes. The family had always sold what they couldn't eat by way of an honesty box at the end of the farm track, and as a child, taking the little key down to the road, opening the coin box and emptying its contents into her waiting hands had been a highlight of Pip's week. Sometimes she had been allowed to keep a coin or two to buy sweets or a comic from the corner shop. More than once her friends had encouraged her to syphon off a little of the egg money for themselves, assuring her that her parents would 'never know', but Pip had always refused. Partly, she liked to think, this was to do with the inherent integrity that had steered her towards a career in the law. Truthfully, however, she could never be sure that her mother wouldn't know exactly how much should be in the box and catch her stealing. A fear of being caught and causing disappointment was the greatest deterrent of all.

'Will Dominic be coming this weekend?' her mother asked, without looking up from her task.

The question was lightly posed, but Pip could hear a thread of tension in her voice.

'I'm not sure,' she said, even though she wasn't expecting him to come. 'He's very busy, Mum. You don't get to be a QC by sitting around on your backside, you know.'

'No,' her mother said quickly. 'No. I'm sure you don't.'

Pip was pretty sure her mother didn't know that QC stood for Queen's Counsel, nor what a prestigious position that was to hold, but she had given up trying to explain how the bar worked a long time ago.

'And his diary is full with non-work stuff, too, things that I would have been doing if I wasn't stuck up here. You do realise, Mum, that we're big news, Dominic and me? We get invited to all kinds of events, parties, shows, gallery openings. You name it. He can't just drop all that because I'm not there to go with him.' Pip sounded petulant, childish, but she didn't care.

'No, no, of course not,' said her mother. 'But you have been quite ill, Pip. I'd have thought he'd try to make a little bit more of an effort to come and see you. I hear him ring sometimes . . .'

Pip bristled. Did she have no privacy, even with her mobile? It was like being a teenager and having to sit on the stairs to use the landline whilst her mother earwigged.

'. . . but a phone call isn't the same as actually coming to visit.'

But she knew her mother was right. Dominic's trips to the farm had tailed off, and she missed him, missed the glimpse that he gave her of her old life. And when they did speak, she could feel him floating further away with every conversation. He seemed to struggle to find a connection with her when she wasn't in London, as if a link in the chain that held them together had broken. He told her his news, but when she had almost nothing to say in return, the conversation fell flat. Pip knew she should trust that everything would work itself out when she got back home to London, but that was getting harder to do with each passing week.

'No. Well, sometimes we all just have to make do with what we've got,' Pip snapped.

Her mother seemed to recoil at the sharpness of her tone, and she felt guilty. Again. It wasn't her mother's fault she was in this situation, so it was hardly fair to take it out on her, but somehow Pip just couldn't help it.

'Are you going into the shop today?' her mother asked in a voice not much louder than a whisper. She didn't look up as she brushed a little straw and mud off the last of the eggs and popped it into a box.

Pip muttered a yes. What else would she be doing?

'Audrey says you're doing very well. I bumped into her in the Co-op yesterday.'

Pip could hear the pride in her mother's voice, and she had to swallow her anger down even deeper. She was working in a charity shop. Of course she was doing well. It was hardly difficult. This time last year she had been appearing in the European Court of Human Rights and now she was folding other people's cast-off clothes in a scruffy second-hand shop in Southwold. And which of these jobs did her mother seem to hold in the highest esteem?

Pip swallowed hard. 'That's nice,' she managed. 'Right. I'd better be going,' she added, anxious to get away before the conversation descended into another argument.

'But you still haven't had any breakfast,' she heard her mother objecting to her disappearing back.

3

It was a bright, fresh morning as Pip cycled along the narrow lanes to the Have a Heart charity shop. The zinging electric yellow of the rapeseed crop was just starting to bloom in the fields and birdsong rang out from the hedgerows, but Pip barely noticed any of it. She was entirely focused on getting herself from A to B without falling apart.

Obviously driving herself to the shop was not an option. She hadn't driven anywhere since the accident and couldn't imagine ever getting behind the steering wheel of a car again. Her father had suggested that they dig her old bike out of the shed, where it had lain quietly rusting for the last ten years. He had spent time lovingly cleaning it up for her, oiling its creaking chain and gears so it was almost as good as new. The frame was a shocking pink, a colour that felt so alien to her freshly minted London persona that Pip couldn't quite believe she'd ever chosen it, and it had a creaking wicker basket that hung from the handlebars and made her feel even more provincial.

There had been no helmet with it, though. When she'd asked her father where it might be, he had looked first surprised and then incredulous.

'The shop's only down the road, Pip,' he'd said. 'What on earth do you need a helmet for?' But then he remembered why she needed to use the bike and not her car and he'd shuffled uncomfortably from one foot to another. 'But I'm sure we can get you one if you'd feel safer,' he added, placing a large, rough hand on her shoulder and squeezing.

So a helmet had been duly purchased, in black, not pink, and Pip could now get herself into town and back without the humiliation of having to ask for a lift.

It had been a struggle at first; any encounter with a road made her heart rate soar. But gradually, she had got used to it, and now she could just about deal with the country lanes without too many panics, although she often got off and pushed when the traffic got heavy.

The Have a Heart charity shop sat on the main shopping street in the town, and was run like a military operation by a distant friend of the family. Volunteering there had been her mother's idea to try and 'take her out of herself'.

'It'll do you no end of good, Pip,' she'd said. 'Getting out of the house and meeting people is probably just what you need. And it'll give some structure to your days, too.'

Pip was less sure. She had barely even been in a charity shop, let alone contemplated working in one. But her mother was right; she did need something to do, and it began to feel, to a small degree at least, like a way of giving something back. Of course, it went no way to appease her guilt, but she hoped it might send a message to anyone who was watching that she was trying to atone.

The shop work was remarkably unchallenging, which was exactly what she needed, and it kept her mind busy, so she didn't spend all day thinking about the accident. Its main benefit, however, was that it got her away from the claustrophobic atmosphere at the farm.

As she approached the shop door, she saw the usual pile of abandoned black bin bags disgorging their contents across the doorstep. It was the same most days. Audrey had placed a laminated sign in the window kindly requesting that people deliver their donations when the shop was open, but nobody took any notice. Pip wondered whether this was a matter of simple convenience, or whether it was really just embarrassment at being associated with their cast-offs. Some of the items that people left were barely fit to be used as rags, let alone sold on for future wear.

Pip locked her bike to a drainpipe and dropped her helmet into the basket in full confidence that it would still be there when she returned at the end of the day. Then she went to sit on the bench opposite to wait for Audrey to open up. A couple of minutes later her boss came bustling down the pavement towards her. Head down, she walked fast, as if she were carrying out a vital but rather tiresome mission, sidestepping anyone in her path without raising her gaze. When she reached the shop, she stared at the pile of donations and shook her head vehemently, her grey perm barely stirring. Pip could see her lips moving with muttered curses.

She stood up and moved to the edge of the pavement. Some days merely standing this close to the road would be enough to trigger a panic attack, but today she was fine, and she crossed without incident. There was no predicting how she'd be from one day to the next. Some days, the road posed no problem at all, but on others it was all she could do to stand within ten feet of it. Not knowing how she was going to react made her more anxious still. The whole thing was a downward spiral that she couldn't seem to crawl out of.

Audrey was still muttering under her breath, her consonants spiked and vicious, when Pip reached her, her heart sinking. It was going to be a long shift if her boss was in a bad mood before the day had even begun.

She girded her loins and mustered a smile. 'Morning, Audrey,' she said as brightly as she could manage.

Audrey looked up and rolled her eyes heavenwards.

'I don't know why I bother putting up a sign. I really don't. Do they think we have nothing better to do than carry their stuff around for them?'

In fact, they didn't have anything better to do. It was a matter of a few feet from the door to the room where they sorted the donations, and Pip couldn't understand the hardship that Audrey seemed to feel so keenly, but she knew better than to pass comment.

'I'll bring it all in,' she said instead. 'You go and put the kettle on.'

Audrey gave her a tight little nod, but no smile, and kicked a plastic bag out of the way so she could open the door and step inside.

Pip began to shift the bags from the door to the table one at a time. So little happened here that any study of time and motion was irrelevant, and if she made five journeys and the task used up five times as much time then that was a bonus. The contrast between this and her life in London couldn't have been more marked.

She opened the neck of the first bag and peered in. Its contents were neatly folded, which boded well. Audrey would be pleased. She liked to get decent-quality stock, although dresses like these from Marks & Spencer or Next weren't Pip's idea of decent. Her mind flew to the racks of designer labels that were hanging, unworn, in her wardrobe in Dominic's flat. Rose had far more sophisticated tastes than she allowed Pip to have, and none of her London finery had made its way up to Suffolk. Now she was here, she had adopted a bland and anonymous style: jeans paired with high street tops just like everyone else wore and, as the weeks rolled by, she could feel herself slowly morphing from Rose back into Pip.

She hoisted the final bag on to her shoulder and prepared to carry it inside, but then she saw that there was a small cardboard box hidden underneath. Boxes tended to be filled with knick-knacks, the sort Pip had rarely seen before and which fascinated and repulsed her in equal measure. Mass-market moulded glass-ware; cheap plated jewellery, the base metal showing through and destroying any illusion of authenticity; and badly chipped and mismatched cups and saucers, fit only for landfill, that someone had thought others might be prepared to pay good money for. The whole enterprise continued to astound Pip by its very awfulness. But emptying boxes filled with ugly things was infinitely preferable to sorting through overwashed (or in some truly revolting cases, underwashed) garments. Plus, there was always the outside chance of uncovering some treasure.

Audrey was still in the back room with the kettle, so if she was quick, Pip might manage to go through the box herself. With a burst of speed, she lifted the box and rushed inside with it.

It was heavier than she'd expected, and nothing shifted about inside as she walked. It must be books. Books were her favourite find. Second-hand books didn't turn her stomach in the way other possessions did. Their history was intriguing rather than something best not thought about. Generally, the donations were thick paperbacks, the sort you bought at an airport and then left on a swap shelf before flying home, but occasionally there would be an ancient hardback covering some antiquated skill or a biography of a long-forgotten star of the silver screen. Pip liked those best. It felt good to read about other people's lives, lose herself in them for a while and have her mind taken away from her own troubles.

She placed the box on the table and cast a quick glance in the direction of the staff room, such as it was, but there was no sign of Audrey. The pleasure of going through its contents would be hers alone.

4

Pip lifted the lid of the cardboard box and peered inside. She had been right. It was full to the brim with books. She plucked a couple from the top of the pile. Judging from their covers, with the unfamiliar fonts and yellowing images, they were at least fifty years old, if not older, and she didn't recognise any of the titles.

She dug a little deeper and pulled out a selection of paperbacks with the distinctive orange and white jackets of vintage Penguins. Again, there was nothing amongst them that she had heard of, and her excitement began to wane. Boxes of books, it seemed, weren't always as much fun to open as boxes of knick-knacks. Eventually, she reached the very bottom and her fingers touched something that felt different to the thumb-worn paperbacks. It was hard and smooth with rigid edges and corners and, her curiosity piqued, Pip drew it out to examine it.

It was clear at once that this wasn't a printed book. She peered more closely at the cover. It was an appointments diary for 1983. Pip sighed. This was just like the bin bags full of unsaleable clothes. What did people think the shop would do with an old diary? Maybe Audrey's grandchildren could use it for scrap paper, she supposed, but they could hardly sell it.

She started to flick through the pages; but rather than being blank, as she had assumed, every available square inch of space was filled with a neat flowing script.

It fell open on a date in February, inviting her to read but Pip knew she shouldn't. Diaries were private, personal; everyone knew that. Reading another person's diary was one of life's most heinous offences. But it was also one of the most tantalising, and this one was almost forty years old and had been discarded in a box full of charity donations. Whatever rights to privacy there might have been once had surely been forfeited. Pip let herself read.

Friday 25th February

Sometimes I really hate Joan. I know we're stuck here together with nowhere else to go and we have to make the best of a bad situation, but I swear she makes every-thing ten thousand times harder than it needs to be. And she's such a cow to me. She does it on purpose, I'm sure she does – I can picture her sitting in her bedroom just thinking up new ways to torture me and poor little Scarlet, as if any of this mess is her fault.

But today her vileness reached new depths. Scarlet's blanky disappeared. I know it's only an old cot blanket and almost worn to rags, but Scarlet adores it. She car-ries it round with her all the time and she won't go to sleep unless she's holding it and rubbing its satin edge up against her darling little cheek.

Anyway, it was her nap time but there was no sign of blanky anywhere. She cried as if her tiny little heart would break. I tried comforting her but she was having none of it. I gave her no end of other things to hug but nothing else would do. And the more tired she got the worse state she got herself into. So I asked Joan if she could help me find it, but she refused and kept going on about how it was irresponsible of me to let Scarlet get so attached to one thing. She couldn't have been more cruel about it. And all this time poor darling Scarlet was screaming and screaming as if someone was trying to murder her. In the end, she got beyond herself and just cried herself to sleep in my arms. She was completely exhausted by the whole ordeal.

Then later, I found blanky in the kitchen bin. When I fished it out it was filthy, with teabags and potato peelings stuck to it. I asked Joan about it. I mean, there are only the three of us here, and me and Scarlet didn't put it there. Joan just said that Scarlet was too old to have something like that and it was about time she threw it away. So the entire time that I'd been searching, with Scarlet breaking her little heart, Joan had known exactly where it was – the heartless bitch.

I can't believe how horrible she is to us. Sometimes I lie awake at night just wondering how I could get my own back, or even get rid of her somehow. Of course, I'd have to make sure I wasn't caught, because if I had to go to prison then poor S would have no one.

Even though I'm Joan's sister and Scarlet is her niece, I don't think she loves us at all. If I could live anywhere else in the world I would go. I swear, you wouldn't see us for dust. But I know I can't. We're stuck here, in this godforsaken house in this tiny town, whilst my old life just disappears down the Swanee.

The last sentence chimed so loudly with Pip's own position that it brought her up short. It was uncanny. She could have written the entry herself. Looking up from the diary for a moment, she checked that Audrey was still occupied elsewhere and then read on.

Saturday 26th February

I've been quite low today. It's probably because Joan was so horrible yesterday. I kept thinking about how things might have been. It's the injustice of it all that really irks me. The pregnancy, losing the best job I've ever had, being forced to move back here. It's all so unfair. Plus, the second series of Into the Blue *is coming out soon, which is just the icing on the stinking cake! I saw a trailer for it today and, annoyingly, it looks fantastic. It breaks my heart that the role should have been my big break and yet here I am, no longer an actress – no longer anything at all except a single mother. I know that's a really important job and I wouldn't be without my darling S, but I don't see why I couldn't have had the job and the baby. I'd have made it work if I'd only been given the chance. But no. I had to up sticks, leave it all behind and just accept that's the way things work.*

And what makes it worse is that Joan is so obnoxious. She never misses an opportunity to say something nasty. She obviously thinks I should be ashamed of Scarlet – she even called me a trollop this morning. And she said it in front of S! Of course, S had no idea what it meant, but

*she asked me afterwards and I had to make something up.
I was biting back the tears. I'm sure poor little S noticed
that I was upset. It can't be good for her growing up in
this toxic atmosphere, but what choice do I have? That's
how J gets away with it. She knows that I've got nowhere
else to go.*

*I almost asked Ted if we could live with him last week but
I know that wouldn't work. I've got no money and I can't
ask him to support us. People will think that S is his child
and that would just make his life difficult as well as mine,
plus it would break his mother's heart and I couldn't do
that to him. I know he wants to help, but there's not much
he can do from down there. At least when I ring him if
Joan goes out, he's happy to listen to me rant. Bless him.
He's been so good to me. I really miss him.*

*And (now I really am ranting) on top of all that, I'm a
much better actress than the one they replaced me with.
I know that sounds a bit arrogant but it's true! Rory
MacMillan will never know what he's missed.*

Pip's mind was all questions. Who was the diary writer, and her
horrible sister? What had happened between the two of them to
so damage their relationship? There was clearly a child involved,
Scarlet, but where was the father? Ted was mentioned, but it wasn't
him. And who was Rory MacMillan? The whole thing read like a
soap opera.

Pip had never heard of a programme called *Into the Blue*,
although if it was on the television in 1983, seven years before she
was even born, it was unlikely she would have done. She itched to
do a quick Google search, but if Audrey caught her on her phone

in shop time she'd be in trouble. Rose wouldn't care, but Pip knew that shop life ran much more smoothly if she didn't break any of Audrey's rules. She would look it up later.

Away in the back room a teaspoon chinked on china as Audrey stirred sweetener into her drink. She would be coming back in to check up on her at any moment.

Pip had too many questions to leave the diary with the rest of the books. She'd take it back to the farm and have a flick through in peace. Then, if it contained anything that might identify the writer, she could bring it back and discuss what to do next with Audrey. If it turned out that the writer was a famous actress then it might even have some value, which would please Audrey no end. And if, as she suspected, it proved to be of very little interest, she would just put it back with the day's donations and pretend it had only just arrived.

Quickly, she stuffed the diary into a plastic carrier and hid it in her bag, but as she did so she could feel her conscience pricking her. Was it theft to take the diary without paying for it? And what about the thorny issue of reading someone else's private thoughts? Pip weighed the arguments in her head, but found her integrity to be intact. She wasn't doing anything wrong, not really. The diary had been given away so the owner clearly wasn't worried about what happened to it now, and if she was able to identify her, she could always return it. But actually, it was the prospect of spending an evening or two lost in someone else's life that was too enticing to ignore – anything to escape the horrors of her own. This was the first time Pip had felt anything approaching excitement since the accident, and she liked it.

She began restacking the books in the box. It felt like such a pointless waste of time, but time was all she had. If her London colleagues could only see her now, she thought wryly.

'How are you getting along with those donations?' came Audrey's shrill voice.

Pip jumped guiltily as if Audrey could see straight into her thoughts.

'I'm working through them now,' she replied, her smile painted on brightly for Audrey's benefit. 'Just the usual stuff. Nothing special.'

Audrey bustled over, looked in one or two of the bin bags with her nose wrinkled. Then she flicked open the lid of the cardboard box and tutted loudly.

'Books. We've no space for more books. I don't really know why people send them. But then again, I suppose they sell.'

Pip tipped the contents of the bag out on to the sorting table and tried to focus on the job in hand, but in her mind she was with Scarlet and Joan and the writer of the diary.

5

1979

Evelyn Mountcastle leaned back against the headboard and closed her eyes. Her head was thumping. She focused on the orangey glow of the inside of her eyelids and breathed deeply, but the pummelling in her head continued. Drinking cheap champagne always did this to her. The pale bubbly liquid was so prettily innocuous that each time it passed her lips she seemed able to convince herself that this time it wouldn't ruin her. It always did.

Groaning quietly, she felt the fountain pen slip from her fingers. For a moment, she let it lie as she concentrated on the pain in her head before realising, a moment too late, what the consequences would be. Her eyes snapped open and she scrabbled to retrieve the pen, but not before a bloom of purple ink had seeped from the nib on to the yellowing sheets.

'Damn,' she said as she swept the pen up and began searching for the lid. She would write her diary later when she could give it her proper attention. Hopefully by then her head would have stopped pounding.

The telephone began to ring in the corridor outside her room, and Evelyn sagged deeper into the pillows. She hoped that her flatmate Brenda would be there to pick it up, but as it rang on and on, she knew she was going to have to go. Swinging her legs out of bed, she moved as quickly as her nausea would allow, shivering against the freezing cold and worried that whoever it was would ring off before she got there, rendering the trip from her warm bed entirely futile. However, she got there in time and snatched up the receiver.

'Hello,' she said. 'Evelyn Mountcastle speaking.'

'Were you in bed? It's virtually lunchtime, you know. The early bird and all that . . .'

Evelyn recognised the drawling voice of her agent, Julian, and her heart lifted a little. Julian never rang unless he had something to tell her, and that generally meant work.

'Anyway, now that I finally have you, I have good news!' he said, without waiting for an answer to his first question. 'Come into the office later, darling, and I'll fill you in.'

Evelyn wished he would just tell her now, but she knew he wouldn't. Julian was all about the drama, and he wasn't going to waste any opportunity to let her see how very indispensable he was to her.

'Is it the *Into the Blue* audition?' she asked hopefully.

'See you at two,' was all he would say, the old tease, and then he was gone.

At least she had time to get herself together before then. She scampered back to her room and hopped into bed, pulling the covers up around her chin against the ravaging cold. Her hangover felt a little better already. It must be the *Into the Blue* thing. She wasn't up for any other parts at the moment, and anyway, she had a good feeling about it. It had her name on it.

She had met the programme's producer, Rory MacMillan, at a rather tawdry New Year's Eve party a few weeks before. He had cornered her and talked at length about his various projects, his head close enough to hers that she could smell the whisky on his breath, his hand planted firmly in the small of her back.

'I have this one project in the pipeline,' he said conspiratorially. 'It's very new. A TV cop drama, but the thing about it is, get this, the lead role is a woman.'

He emphasised the last word, his eyes open wide at the shock of it all. Evelyn had mirrored his expression to encourage him to keep talking, but all she could think was, 'I could do that.'

'Think emotion and brains rather than car chases and beating up suspects,' he continued. 'It's a very modern concept.'

Evelyn's heart started to beat faster. She could see herself in the role already. Move over John Thaw and Dennis Waterman. It was her turn. This was the cusp of the 1980s, after all; change was blowing in the air.

'Although you might be a little too young,' Rory MacMillan continued. 'I don't know how long it takes to climb the ranks in the police.'

Considerably longer for a woman than a man, Evelyn thought, but as pointing that out wouldn't help she didn't say it out loud.

'I can play older,' she said helpfully, and gave him her most winning smile.

'Actually, there's a junior sidekick too,' MacMillan added thoughtfully. 'Feisty, smart, attractive . . .' His hand slipped from the small of her back to her bottom and he gave it a little squeeze. 'You'd be perfect,' he concluded. 'Get your agent to ring my secretary after the holidays and we'll fix something up.'

◆　◆　◆

Evelyn reached the offices of Coleman, Travis & Scott, Theatrical Agents (Julian was the Travis, having inherited his part of the business from his uncle) just before two o' clock and made her way up the stairs. The reception desk was manned by a succession of bright-eyed young actresses who had come to London to seek their fortune on the stage but had been forced to take an office job to tide them over. Evelyn always wondered at their choice. It seemed unnecessarily cruel to work in a place that employed actors when one couldn't get employment oneself.

The receptionist this time looked even younger than usual. She was putting letters in envelopes, but things seemed to have become muddled and Evelyn, having watched for a moment or two, wasn't convinced that the right people would be receiving the right missives with their morning paper.

'Evelyn Mountcastle for Mr Travis,' she announced in a clear, confident tone. Evelyn lived in hope of one day turning up and being recognised without having to give her name, but that had yet to happen. It wasn't as if she was a total unknown. She had had bit parts in *Upstairs Downstairs* and three episodes of a drama set in World War I, but she was hardly a household name. That was her ambition, though. She knew that fame could be a double-edged sword, but she was perfectly prepared to take that risk.

The receptionist, who looked as if the muddle with the post might actually reduce her to tears, nodded and then cocked her head in the direction of Julian's office.

Julian was on the phone. Evelyn could hear him before she entered his room, his languid tones floating out along the corridor.

'Yes, I see that, darling, but look at it from my point of view. She's no spring chicken and she's not getting any younger. If we don't give her this then it might be last-chance saloon time.'

Evelyn tried not to listen, but she couldn't help but wonder which of his clients Julian was discussing and, more worryingly, how old she was. Older than her, of course. She was just thirty which was no age, was it? She could still pass for a character in her twenties with no difficulty, and could even play a schoolgirl with the right hair and make-up. But it always bothered her when she heard Julian talking in this vein. They were both aware that time was ticking by.

Julian looked up when she came in, gave her a grin, pulled a face at whoever was on the other end of the phone and then flapped an arm feebly in the direction of the chair opposite his desk. It was piled high with cardboard files, which Evelyn lifted carefully and placed on the floor at her feet.

'Of course,' Julian was saying, with a gesture that told Evelyn he was trying to wind the conversation up. 'Well, do your best, darling, and let me know how you get on. Yes. And love to everyone at your end. Toodle-pip.' Then he put the phone back in its cradle with an exaggerated flourish and turned his attention to her. 'Evelyn. My dear girl. How delightful it is to see you.'

He said it as if her arrival was entirely impromptu and not to attend a prearranged meeting. In days gone by, this would have unsettled Evelyn, but now she knew his vagueness was just a conceit and Julian was entirely in control of every aspect of his life.

'Hi Julian, darling. How are you?' she said. 'You look well.'

'Lord knows how,' he replied as he indicated the piles of files, but Evelyn could see that he was pleased to have been complimented. 'It's been bedlam around here for weeks. I'm never off the phone these days.'

She gave him an indulgent smile. 'Come on, Julian. You wouldn't have it any other way.'

'Too true, too true. Now. This Rory MacMillan project,' he said, switching effortlessly to the matter in hand. For all that Julian liked to play his part as fuzzy and abstracted, he was actually as sharp as a sea urchin's spine and knew exactly what was what at all times. This was precisely why he was Evelyn's agent. 'They're thinking of you for the part of Detective Constable Karen Walker. Lots of screen time for her, as she's generally trailing after her boss. Not heard who they're seeing for the boss yet, but I think we can expect it to be someone that the public will know. And that all bodes well for you, Evie, sweetie. Assuming you can pull it off.'

'Do they want me to read?' she asked.

'Yes. Read for the director first and then, if they like that, a meeting with Mr Rory MacMillan himself,' replied Julian. 'And as you already know him, that should be a breeze.'

Was it Evelyn's imagination, or could she detect something in his tone that suggested he was impressed? It was hard to tell, but Rory MacMillan was a big name. Even Julian, with his 'I've seen it all before, darling' attitude might be a little bit excited by the opportunity that had presented itself to her. She wondered about confessing to him that she didn't really 'know' Rory MacMillan; it had been one conversation at a party, but she decided against. It would do her no harm to let Julian think the acquaintance went deeper than that.

'They're serious, then? About me, I mean,' Evelyn asked, hardly daring to believe it. When she'd gone for other parts, she had only ever seen the casting director, never the producer, but then she had never been up for something as big as this before.

'It seems so,' Julian drawled. 'And so they should be. This is well within your range. They'd be mad to miss you.'

Despite his optimism, Evelyn tried to keep a lid on her excitement. This still felt like a lot of hoops to jump through.

'And is there anything else in the pipeline for me?' she asked hopefully, thinking of her bare kitchen cupboards and the freezing cold flat.

'Not just at the mo, darling. These perishing strikes are putting the wind up everyone. People are nervous about committing to things just now whilst the country is going to hell in a handcart, but don't you worry. If you manage to bag this one, then you won't have time for anything else.'

Evelyn bit her lip. It was a ten-part series with the chance of a second if things went well. A part like this would be the making of her.

6

The audition was at the film studios in Wembley. Evelyn had been once before, which reduced her nerves just a little, and she tried to look confident as she marched up the drive to the reception desk. She wondered how many other hopefuls would be there. She assumed dozens, possibly even hundreds of people, all as desperate as she was to get the part, but as she drew closer there were only a handful of other actresses waiting. She checked her watch and then the date, but she had both things correct. Her heart, already pumping hard, started to work a little harder still. Were they only considering so few people? Maybe she was in with a real chance.

Her initial anxiety switched to excitement. This was what she did. She performed. And it didn't matter what it was or who to. When the time to shine arrived, Evelyn Mountcastle shone. She straightened her skirt (dark, pencil, worn to give the subliminal impression of a policewoman), took a deep breath and stepped into the reception. Every pair of eyes turned to look at her. Unperturbed, Evelyn walked as confidently as she could to the desk.

'Evelyn Mountcastle,' she said clearly, and handed over her portfolio.

The receptionist took it from her and put it on a pile with the others without even glancing at it.

'Take a seat,' she said.

Evelyn chose a chair nearest the door, rearranged her skirt and then, when she was sure she was sitting in the most flattering position, lifted her chin to take a look at her rivals. She immediately wished she hadn't. There were five other women sitting there. All of them were older than her and at least two were, if not quite household names, then certainly someone who would turn heads in a restaurant – 'Isn't that . . . ? You know. The one from . . . ?'

Evelyn refused to be intimidated. She had just as much right as they to be there and just as much chance of being spot on for the role. Plus, she had inside information. Mr MacMillan wanted her. How many of these others could say that? As she thought all this through, a door opened, and the first name was called. Evelyn crossed her fingers and prepared to wait.

The hands on the wall clock made their steady way around the hour as Evelyn waited. Eventually it became apparent that she would be last to go in. The others had all emerged looking calm and collected, although one had been in the audition room for less than two minutes, which couldn't bode well for her but was a positive thing for Evelyn.

'Evelyn Mountcastle,' the receptionist called finally, and even though she had been waiting for this moment, Evelyn still started at the sound.

'Yes,' she said, and stood up so quickly that her head felt momentarily woozy. She made her way to the door through which the others had disappeared, her hands clammy and her stomach full of butterflies, but ready to show them everything she had.

The corridor was dark, but there was a door open at the far end and she made her way towards it. It took her into a studio, one wall mirrored and with a grand piano in the far corner. Three men sat behind a table positioned in front of the mirror, so that as she approached she could see her own reflection. She tried not to be distracted by it.

'Good afternoon,' she said confidently to the man sitting in the middle of the panel who she deduced to be the more senior and consequently more important, although really, she had no idea.

'Hello, Evelyn. Very nice to meet you.' He was incredibly quietly spoken, and Evelyn strained to hear him. He handed her a script. 'Page sixteen, please. Can you read Detective Constable Walker?'

'Of course,' she said. 'How would you like me to play her?'

The man on the left answered her. 'She's a bit rough,' he said. 'Keen as mustard but without any nuance about her. Calls a spade a spade, if you know what I mean.'

'All right,' replied Evelyn smoothly, her brain running ten to the dozen as to how to portray this. She turned to page sixteen and considered it. DC Walker had about half a page of script and she read it quickly so she had some idea of what was coming. And then she began.

When she'd finished, she looked up and smiled. 'How was that?' she asked. 'I can make her more aggressive if you like, or more thoughtful. Whatever you think. She strikes me as having more common sense than is perhaps expected of her, wise beyond her years, if you know what I mean?'

The man in the middle was nodding at her. 'Go on,' he said.

Evelyn wasn't sure she had anything to add, but she carried on anyway. 'I think she'd be very loyal, the kind of officer her boss can rely on in a crisis, so that even though she doesn't have much experience, she still makes a valuable contribution to the team.'

More nodding, which Evelyn chose to interpret as a good thing. She smiled and turned her head a little to show off her best side.

'Okay, thank you, Miss Mountcastle,' said the one who had yet to speak. 'We'll be in touch.'

And then it was all over. Evelyn collected her portfolio from the disinterested receptionist and made her way back outside to catch her bus.

7

'There's no bread,' announced Brenda when Evelyn appeared for breakfast the next day. 'And there's only a splash of milk, so use it carefully.'

'Shall I pop to the shop?' asked Evelyn helpfully.

'Don't you watch the news, Evie? There's no bread, full stop. There's nothing. The lorry drivers have been on strike for weeks, or hadn't you noticed?'

Evelyn was put out. She didn't really follow the news. It was so dull and nothing ever seemed to happen other than people complaining, which brought her mood down. But she wasn't stupid.

'Of course I've noticed,' she snapped. 'So, there's no bread in the shop either?'

'Nope,' said Brenda, raising her hand, which held a cream cracker slathered with raspberry jam. 'I'm using my initiative. It's not too bad, actually.' She turned her attention back to her newspaper. 'They're saying Monday was the worst day of industrial action since 1926,' she added. 'And the gravediggers are out in Liverpool. You can't get a body buried for love nor money, apparently.'

'That can't be very hygienic,' replied Evelyn, pulling a squeamish face. 'Won't there be diseases and what have you? Typhoid or the plague or whatever?'

Brenda shook her head. 'Too cold,' she said simply.

Evelyn pulled her thin robe more tightly around her slender shoulders and suppressed a shudder.

'Well, it's certainly freezing in here,' she said. Ice had traced patterns on the inside of the window, like the whorls of so many fingerprints.

'Mr O'Malley rang,' Brenda replied. 'Apparently he's worried that the gas bills are going to be too high, so he says we have to ration our heating to two hours a day.'

'But that's ridiculous,' complained Evelyn. 'Does he know how cold it is?'

Brenda shrugged and Evelyn noticed that she seemed to be wearing almost every item of clothing she possessed. The inadequacies of her own glamorous but totally impractical coverings were suddenly writ large for her. It was turning out to be the coldest winter she could ever remember. It had been cold sometimes at home in Suffolk when she was a girl, but nothing to compare to this.

'Right then,' said Evelyn decisively, determined to put a positive slant on their predicament. 'Black coffee it is.' She flicked the switch on the kettle and reached for a mug and the jar of Nescafé.

'Actually, Evie,' Brenda began. She sounded tentative and unsure of herself, and Evelyn stopped what she was doing to listen. 'There was something I wanted to talk to you about.'

'If it's about your shampoo, I'm sorry that I've been using it. I'll replace it, I promise. It's just that there hasn't been much money coming in since Christmas.'

'It's not about the shampoo,' said Brenda kindly. 'Come and sit down.'

Evelyn abandoned her drink and pulled up a chair obediently. She looked at Brenda, waiting to hear what she had done wrong this time, her heart filled with trepidation.

'So,' Brenda began. 'Jim has asked me to marry him and . . .'

She got no further before Evelyn was up on her feet again. She flung her arms around her flatmate and squeezed her tight. 'Oh, Bren. That's fantastic news. Congratulations! Have you got a ring yet? Have you set a date? Did he get down on one knee?'

It didn't matter how modern Evelyn considered her attitudes to be. In the face of a good old-fashioned proposal, she reverted to the values she'd been brought up with – traditional ones.

Brenda shrugged. 'It's a bit of a farce if you ask me,' she said. 'We're as good as living together as it is, but his mother has this idea that we're not a "proper"' – she made air quotes, her fingers laden with sarcasm, and rolled her eyes – 'couple unless we're married.'

Evelyn shrugged. Even though it would be very chic and Bohemian for Brenda and Jim to live together without the sanctity of marriage to protect them, she had some sympathy with Jim's mother's point of view, not that she would have said as much to Brenda. And there was the added delight of a wedding for her to attend.

'Well, I think it's lovely,' she said enthusiastically. 'Congratulations.'

'Thanks,' replied Brenda with another little eye roll, and Evelyn thought that maybe a little soupçon of excitement wouldn't go amiss from the bride-to-be. 'Anyway, that wasn't what I needed to talk to you about, exactly. The thing is, I'll obviously be moving out. Are you okay to take the flat over on your own?'

Evelyn's panicking mind was going into overdrive. She could barely afford her share of the rent on this place as it was, but she could hardly tell Brenda that she couldn't leave her, not when she was getting married.

'Of course,' she said with a beaming smile. 'That's absolutely fine. Don't give it a second's thought.' Evelyn wasn't an actress for nothing.

Brenda, happy with her response, thanked her profusely and then left her on her own at the kitchen table. Well, thought Evelyn, she was going to have to get the part now. She was down to the last few coins in her purse and all out of options. If some money didn't come in, and quickly, then she might have to admit defeat and go back home to Southwold.

Actually, no, Evelyn corrected herself. Things would have to get a whole lot worse than this for her to contemplate going back. Southwold had never felt like home, even when she lived there. The youngest of three children and by far the most flamboyant, Evelyn had been born to strict Presbyterian parents who had actively disapproved of her life choices. They had both died young, however, leaving Evelyn's elder sister Joan occupying the family home; the home that the three of them had inherited in equal parts but that Joan had commandeered. It ought to be an option for Evelyn to demand her share of the funds, but to do so would be to admit to her sister that she needed the money, and that was something Evelyn couldn't bring herself to do. Her inheritance would come to her eventually. At least this way Joan had somewhere to live, and Evelyn could enjoy the warm glow that came from having done something nice for her sister, despite everything horrible Joan had done to her.

Joan was a spinster, which was of little surprise given her terse and truculent personality traits. She professed that her single status was by choice, but Evelyn suspected her sister was deeply bitter about her failure to find a husband and so felt able to make allowances for Joan's general unpleasantness. Their brother, Peter, weak-chinned and lily-livered, had found himself an equally feeble wife and together they had created a neat 'one of each' family, which seemed to work well for them but which was Evelyn's definition of hell. Peter, however, was also unlikely to stand up to Joan on the question of their inheritance, and so the status quo rolled on year on year.

Sometimes Evelyn almost felt sorry for her sister, but it never lasted for long. Joan had picked up the mantle of disapproval of Evelyn from where their parents had let it fall and, if anything, was even more vociferous in her objections to Evelyn's lifestyle than they had been. On the list of things about Evelyn of which Joan did not approve were: living in London; living in a flat share; being an actress; being single at thirty (the irony of this one seemed to pass her by); and failing to stay in Suffolk to be near their parents and thus leaving the responsibility for them and their home to her. And this was why Evelyn would have to be destitute or desperate or, more likely, both before she would even consider going back home.

The *Daily Mirror* was lying on the table. Brenda's chap must have left it there. Evelyn began to flick idly through it. They were calling it the 'Winter of Discontent', and the country was starting to feel very jumpy, edgy almost, as more and more trade unions called their members out on strike. These were strange times indeed. And Sid Vicious was dead, apparently. That was a shame, she thought, but not really a surprise.

If she got this part, she would be a success, maybe even a household name. Then Joan would no longer be able to scoff at her and accuse her of wasting her life on a pointless whim. In fact, Joan would have to congratulate her and admit that she had been wrong all along.

And how Evelyn was going to enjoy that moment.

8

Evelyn sat in the chair opposite Julian and grinned as she waited for him to give her the news.

'Well, you certainly impressed them,' he said. 'They thought you showed' – he paused, running his finger down his notes until he came to the right place – '"remarkable insight" in your reading of the character.' He looked up at her, his eyebrows raised and a quirky smile on his lips. Then he dropped his gaze back down. 'Apparently you brought an "added dimension" to the character that even the writer himself hadn't considered.' He sat back in his chair and laced his fingers behind his head. 'Well done, Evelyn. Very well done indeed.'

Praise as fulsome as this was rare, and Evelyn could feel heat rising in her cheeks. She gave a modest smile. 'And DC Karen Walker features in every episode?' she asked, even though she already knew this to be true, having clarified it several times since the audition.

Julian put his stockinged feet up on the desk as if he were in his living room rather than his office. Evelyn found this state of undress a little disconcerting, but she tried to ignore his scarlet socks and focus on his face, which was now smiling broadly at her.

'Yep,' he said. 'It's a big part, Evie.'

Evelyn nodded, but then a wave of anxiety twisted in her gut. It was all very well them liking her, but as yet they hadn't formally offered her the part.

'What's your feeling, Julian?' she asked him. 'Do you think it's mine?'

Julian examined his nails and gave them a quick buff on his trousers. 'I think quite possibly. From what they said to me, anyway, darling, but it all depends on MacMillan. If he likes you then you're in. But then he does like you, or so you said. So it shouldn't be that hard to convince him that you'd be perfect.'

Evelyn's stomach hit the floor. What if she had imagined it all? What if MacMillan had said exactly the same thing to every young actress at the party? She swallowed hard and tried to push the thought out of her head. She needed this job. Her life in London was depending on it.

'And the meeting with him is at four thirty tomorrow afternoon at the Hilton? On a Sunday? Are you sure?' she asked doubtfully. A meeting on a Sunday didn't seem right to her.

Julian checked his notebook, running his pen down the indecipherable scrawls until he found what he was looking for. 'That's right. Sunday. He's a busy man, our Rory. They don't work nine to five, you know, these television executives. Just go to the hotel reception and ask for him and they will direct you. Now, off you scamper. I do have other clients apart from you!' He fluttered a hand to shoo her away.

Evelyn stood up, rushed round to the other side of the desk, bent down and planted a kiss on Julian's cheek. 'Thank you, Julian,' she said breathlessly.

'I'm just looking out for my ten per cent,' he said in a matter-of-fact tone, but he was grinning at her. 'And Evelyn,' he added as she reached for the door handle, his voice a little more serious now, 'don't blow it.'

Sunday arrived and Evelyn dressed carefully in a skirt and blouse and a pair of unladdered tights that she'd stolen from Brenda's room, fully intending to replace them the following day. The doorman opened the door for her as she approached the hotel and then smiled at her as she passed by him.

'Good afternoon, miss,' he said.

'Good afternoon,' she replied. She sounded like a schoolma'am. Or a policewoman. The thought made her smile.

She walked straight to the reception desk, feeling as if every eye in the place was on her. She was going to have to get used to that, she thought. The turned heads, the nudging and whispering as she walked into a room.

'I'm here to see Mr MacMillan,' she said, hoping that the slight shake in her voice was only audible to her.

The receptionist looked at the book in front of her, running a manicured finger down the columns. 'Mr MacMillan is in suite 507,' she said. 'Fifth floor,' she added, pointing to the lift.

'Thank you,' replied Evelyn, and set off in the direction of the lift hoping that she looked nonchalant and as if she went to meetings in hotel suites every day of the week, but inside her stomach was churning with nerves. She was so close to this that she could almost taste her success. And this final part of the process would surely be easy. The casting panel liked her and she had already impressed Rory MacMillan at the New Year's Eve party. Talking to him now was just a formality, a getting to know each other a little better.

She wondered who else would be there. The quietly spoken director from her audition, she imagined, and maybe whoever they had cast as the inspector. Evelyn ran through a list of possible actresses in her head, hoping that whoever it was was already famous. But even if they weren't yet, she supposed they soon would be. They both would be.

Suite 507 was at the end of a long corridor and Evelyn knocked lightly on the door.

'Come in,' someone said. It sounded like the Glaswegian lilt of Rory MacMillan, but she couldn't be sure. She opened the door.

A short corridor opened out into a sitting room. It had windows to two sides and views out over Hyde Park, although dusk was falling outside and she couldn't see far. Lights twinkled on the inky horizon.

Rory MacMillan was sitting on a sofa, dressed casually in slacks and an open-necked shirt, the telephone receiver wedged under his chin. He was twisting the cord round and round his fingers in a continuous movement as if it were an executive toy. He looked up as she came in and nodded at the sofa opposite him. Evelyn couldn't make much sense of the conversation, which was mainly yeses and nos, peppered with the occasional uh-huh.

Whilst she waited, she looked about for signs of the others, but there was nothing to suggest that anyone else had been there. One whisky tumbler sat on the glass coffee table beside one plate, dirty with the remains of a club sandwich. Maybe the others would be coming soon, she thought, or maybe it was just going to be her. Evelyn considered how she felt about this for a moment. Did the prospect of a one-to-one meeting make her any more nervous? No. She was fine with it. Hadn't they spent almost half an hour chatting on New Year's Eve? And to have the ear of someone as senior as MacMillan wasn't something that usually happened to a relative unknown like her. She would be able to get a real insight into what he was hoping for the series as a whole. Julian would be delighted when she told him. She could almost hear her agent in her ear, urging her onwards. 'Find out what's next, darling. Make sure there's a part for you in that one, too.'

Evelyn started to relax. This was the lifestyle she was going to have to get used to once she'd got the job and made a name for herself. And a British television drama was just the start. Who knew what doors it might open? She allowed the idea of Hollywood to cross her mind, if only for a moment.

But she had to stay focused. She hadn't actually got this in the bag yet. She mustn't go running before she could walk.

MacMillan was winding his conversation up. 'Yeah, fine. I'll ring Dougie next week, make sure he's lined up. Yeah. That's all fixed. It is. Trust me. Right, speak next week. *Ciao.*'

He replaced the phone in its cradle and turned to face her. He was a big man, bigger than she had remembered, his chest broad and his limbs strong and athletic. She could see the fabric of his slacks straining over his muscular thighs.

'Evelyn!' he said. 'So great to see you again. Sorry about that. No rest for the wicked, eh?' He winked at her. He was quite attractive, she thought, in an 'older man slightly rough around the edges' kind of way. 'Would you join me for a drink?'

He picked up his empty tumbler and Evelyn deduced that he was offering alcohol and not tea, even though it was only four thirty in the afternoon. That was fine. She was open-minded about these things. She wasn't sure what to ask for, though. She had never been in a hotel as smart as this one before. Would he have to ring room service if she asked for something that wasn't in the mini bar? She didn't want to do anything that might be irritating. She could ask for champagne, but she hadn't got the part yet and didn't want to jump the gun.

'I'll have one of those,' she heard herself say, even though she had only ever had whisky at her Uncle Roger's funeral and hadn't liked it that much.

MacMillan smiled. 'A girl after my own heart,' he said as he made his way to the drinks tray. 'Ice and soda?'

Evelyn knew enough about whisky to know that Scots like him didn't drink it with ice, and she didn't dare try it neat. 'Just soda, please,' she said. 'Plenty of soda.'

He prepared the drinks, giving himself a far bigger measure than he poured for her. That was a relief, at least. She could just sip it politely and leave what she didn't want. After all, it wasn't as if he was paying for it himself. This would all be on expenses. Again, a little shiver of excitement went through her. This could be her soon. Drinks on expenses, meals out, the high life. All she had to do was not blow it.

He sat back down and then leaned back in his sofa, spreading his legs expansively across the space.

'Mike tells me you did a great audition and he wants to give you the job,' he said.

Evelyn could feel a blush flood her cheeks, which irritated her. She was a grown woman, not a wet-behind-the-ears girl.

'Thanks,' she said simply.

'So now you just have to impress me,' he continued. 'But don't look so worried, Evelyn. I'm sure you'll be preaching to the converted.'

'What would you like me to do?' she asked. She wasn't sure what he was expecting of her. Did he want her to run through the lines again? She could have a go, but without the script it would be tricky to make it sound convincing.

'Tell me something about yourself,' he said. 'Just who is the real Evelyn Mountcastle?'

This was worse than trying to remember the script. What did he want to hear?

'Well . . .' she began cautiously.

'I mean, what makes you tick, Evie?' he continued, using the name usually reserved for those who knew her well. 'What drives you forward? What keeps you awake at night?'

The thought of not being able to pay my rent, she thought, but she couldn't say that. She was driven by a desire for fame, but she couldn't say that either; it would make her look shallow when she wanted to seem intriguing and interesting. Maybe she should just make something up, but then again, it was the real her that he wanted to know about and there was nothing wrong with a bit of ambition.

'I want to be a star,' she said. 'I want people to turn and look at me when I walk into a room. I want them to ask for my autograph. I want to have success in the UK, but then I want to go to Hollywood to do a big feature, work with some of the great directors, Scorsese, Spielberg, Altman.' She suddenly panicked that she was suggesting television was somehow second-rate, but he was smiling at her and nodding encouragingly.

'I love to see that kind of ambition in my actresses,' he said, taking a large slurp from his glass. He belched lightly. 'I want girls with fire in their belly.'

Evelyn was hardly a girl, but she didn't feel she should correct him.

'So, Evie,' he said, patting the sofa next to him. 'Why don't you come over here and tell me just how you think I can help you get there.'

9

Pip watched the clock impatiently, the hours crawling by in a way they had never done when she had been working in her busy office in London, until it was finally time for Audrey to declare the day done, switch off all the lights and lock the door behind them.

'See you on Monday,' said Pip as they parted ways. 'Are you doing anything nice this weekend?' she added as an afterthought, although she really had no interest in the answer.

Audrey's face set hard and she rolled her eyes heavenwards. 'Bring-and-buy sale at the church hall,' she said grimly. 'No one else stepped up so it's left to yours truly to organise. Could you tell your mother to bring the baking over by eight thirty? There's bound to be a queue. It's ridiculous, really. They'll barge the doors down for a bring and buy, but not set foot in this shop.'

'Well, I hope it goes well,' Pip replied quickly, keen not to get volunteered into helping, and then sidled away to unlock her bike before the thought could occur to Audrey. Even though she wasn't fit enough to be holding down her proper job in London, this parochial little life with its unimportant problems was driving her mad. How did all these people not die of boredom, tucked away out here in the middle of nowhere? A bring-and-buy sale, for God's sake.

With the plastic bag containing the stolen diary wedged into the bicycle's basket, Pip rode back to the farm down the narrow leafy lanes, planning out her evening as she went. She would escape from the kitchen as soon as she could after supper, run herself a deep, hot bath and then have an early night with the diary.

What was happening to her? Rose would be horrified at the prospect of such a dull evening. But Rose wasn't here and Pip was doing her best to hold things together in whichever way she could. She could hear Dominic scoffing at her plan, too, but she didn't care. She felt a weird connection between herself and the diary writer, and she needed to investigate it. The writer appeared to be stuck in the wrong place just like she was, although Pip hadn't yet worked out why. She needed to read some more.

But it wasn't just the puzzle of the situation that was sucking her in. Spending a few hours lost in someone else's life would also be very welcome, giving her mind a chance, however fleeting, to break free from the horrible loop that played constantly in her head – guilt, fear, recrimination, grief and then back to guilt.

On her brighter days, Pip could convince herself that it hadn't all been destroyed, that the world she had painstakingly built for herself before the accident was still there, just waiting for her to step back into it. All she had to do was get well enough to pick up where she had left off.

If only it were as simple as that.

Her parents, delighted though they had been to welcome her back to the farm, didn't seem to understand why she had had to leave London in the first place. She had tried more than once to explain it to her mother, who, whilst sympathetic, struggled to follow.

'I had a panic attack, Mum,' she told her, unable to keep the frustration out of her voice. 'Well, I had loads of them, but I had a really big one at work.'

'But surely they should have made allowances for you, Pip, after what happened.'

Nobody would say the words, Pip noticed. The fact that she had killed a child was so washed in euphemism that it came out if not clean, then certainly less bloodstained.

'They'd already made plenty of allowances, Mum, but I let them all down. I collapsed in the middle of the Supreme Court with everyone watching me. I didn't even know my own name. They couldn't let me carry on working after that. They have their reputation to think of, and mine.'

'But that wasn't your fault,' said her mother indignantly. 'You were ill.'

Pip suspected that her mother had read that panic attacks were a symptom of mental illness and whilst she struggled with the concept, was determined to embrace it for her daughter's sake.

'But that doesn't make any difference, Mum. Clients pay a lot of money for me to act for them. If I can't do that without breaking down and making a show of myself, then they just won't give me any more work.'

Her mother nodded as if she could understand this. 'That doesn't seem fair,' she added. 'It wasn't your fault.' She was quiet for a moment or two and then, twisting the tea towel she was holding in her hands, she said, 'Can I ask you something personal?'

Pip nodded, worried about what was coming but unable to come up with a reason to avoid it.

'What does it feel like?' her mother asked. 'Having a panic attack, I mean. I've tried to imagine it, but I can't, not really.'

Pip didn't want to have to explain in case the mere description triggered one, but it had clearly cost her mother a lot to ask her.

She took a deep breath. 'It's horrible, Mum. I feel completely out of control, and you know how much I hate that.'

Her mother nodded. They could both agree that Pip liked to be in control.

'It kind of starts with my scalp,' Pip continued. 'And then my neck and my cheeks go numb. That's when I know it's coming and I can't do anything to stop it. It's like I can't get any air, like there's a band squeezing my chest so I can't breathe. Then my vision goes wobbly and in the end I just black out and . . .' She stopped. She didn't know what happened after that. She glanced up at her mother. There were tears rolling down her cheeks.

'Oh Pip, love,' she said, her voice cracking a little. 'My poor baby.'

Pip had no tears. They just wouldn't come. It was as if her emotions had been sliced away from her. 'It's okay, Mum,' she said. 'You get used to it after a bit.'

But that wasn't true. She had lost count of the number of flashbacks and panic attacks she had had since the accident, and yet she still couldn't come to terms with it. And that was why she couldn't believe she would ever be able to pick her London life back up. She was starting to forget what it was like to be Rose.

In fact, she'd been so wrapped up with what was going on inside her head that she barely looked beyond her own problems these days. But now, the more she thought about the diary and what it might contain, the more excited she became. And this curiosity was something new.

By the time she wheeled the bike into the farmyard, she was buzzing. She looked to see if the light was on in the kitchen. If her mother wasn't in there, then it would be child's play to sneak the diary in without anyone noticing. But of course the light was on, warm and welcoming. Briefly she considered leaving the plastic bag with the bike and going back to retrieve it later, but who was going to be interested in whatever she was carrying? She tucked the bag under her arm and headed into the warmth of the kitchen.

'Hi, Mum,' she called as she opened the back door.

'There you are at last,' replied her mother, her voice a little strained and unnaturally bright. 'You've got a visitor.'

Pip peered past her mother and saw the broad back of a dark-haired man in a smartly cut suit sitting at the table. It was Dominic, and Pip was surprised to find herself mildly irritated that he should have shown up unannounced and spoiled her date with the diary.

But that wasn't right. She was supposed to be delighted he was here, and she was really, she told herself. It was just that she hadn't been expecting him. The shock of it had thrown her and she wasn't good with surprises any more. Finally, she got to the place where she should have been at the outset: pleased to see him.

'Dominic!' she squealed. She dropped her handbag and the diary on the dresser and almost ran the short distance across the kitchen with her arms open wide. 'What are you doing here? I didn't know you were coming up this weekend. You never said. But it's lovely to see you,' she added breathlessly, just in case there was any doubt.

Dominic stood up and, opening his own arms to greet her, smiled.

'Surprise!' he said, and Pip pushed herself against his torso and buried her face into his lapel, the citrusy scent of his aftershave putting her in touch with a part of herself that had, until that second, felt vague and blurred. She felt his arms close round her, but there was no accompanying squeeze. Immediately she felt wary, anxiety rising in her like cold, dank floodwater.

'That party in Bristol was cancelled,' explained Dominic. 'So, as I had some unexpected time on my hands, I thought I'd pop up here. I hope that's all right with you.'

'Of course,' Pip replied as she tried to push her own doubts away. It was fine, she told herself. Everything was fine.

'And I'm sorry to descend on you with no notice, Rachel,' Dominic added, turning to her mother.

Her mother waved a hand dismissively, as if an additional person at the farm was not even worthy of mention, but Pip knew she would be fretting about the contents of her fridge and how she could transform it into a meal of the appropriate standard for her sophisticated house guest. She would be worrying about the state of the sheets, too. The Appleby family really didn't deal well with impromptu.

'Supper won't be for an hour, though,' her mother said, 'so why don't you two go and make yourselves comfortable in the snug and I'll bring you a drink through in a few minutes.'

Pip released Dominic and held him at arm's length whilst she considered him. His hair was slightly longer than usual. He must have missed his barber's appointments without her to nag him to go, but apart from that he looked just the same; a little more tired, perhaps.

She found his hand with hers and pulled him out of the kitchen and away from her mother. She felt him following behind her as they made their way down the dark corridor to the snug. A cheery fire was burning in the grate, as it did most days, no matter what the season. The farm's old tomcat was stretched out luxuriously on the hearth rug and didn't stir as the two of them entered the room,

Pip pulled Dominic down on to the sofa and leaned in to kiss him. He kissed her back, but with a chaste little peck rather than anything more passionate. He perhaps felt a little awkward, being not much more than a stranger here, Pip thought. And they hadn't seen each other for a while. They would need to reconnect, but there would be plenty of time to relax. They had the whole weekend ahead of them.

'So, Rose,' he said. 'How are you doing? You still surviving up here in the arse end of nowhere?'

It was strange to hear her London name used here in Suffolk now. It was already starting to jar in her ears.

'It's bearable – just,' she said. 'But I think I'm getting there. I mean, no huge leaps or anything. It's a slow process, but I do think I'm a bit better.'

Was this true? She wasn't sure, but she knew it was what he wanted to hear. He was impatient for improvement, and so she needed to feed him something.

'But enough about me,' she added. 'What's going on at home? What's the gossip? God, I wish I'd known you were coming. You could have brought me some different underwear. And shoes now it's getting a bit warmer. I've only got boots here. It's so weird to have all my things in London and me stuck . . .'

Her sentence trickled to an end and he let it, without attempting to address any of her questions. Something wasn't right here, but Pip wasn't sure what it was.

She tried again. 'And how's work going?' Work was the one subject that could be guaranteed to get him talking. 'Are you busy?'

Dominic nodded, pulling at his earlobe in a way Pip had always found endearing, but that she now suspected might be a tell of some sort.

'Yes,' he replied. 'We're all pretty pushed. It's all decent stuff, too. Some high-profile instructions.'

Pip felt her heart tug a little. She missed her old life, the competitive edge that cut across everything, even between the two of them. But at the same time, having Dominic here and thinking about work was starting to make her chest constrict. She took a deep breath to calm herself. The last thing she needed was an episode now, just as she was trying to convince him that she was getting better.

'Who's picking up my cases?' she asked, though she really couldn't bear to hear the answer.

'Priti,' he said. 'She's doing well, actually, catching on quick.'

Another stab to Pip's heart. Priti was junior to her and, worse than that, had been sniffing around Dominic for some time, always there with a ready smile and an offer of help when the opportunity arose. The last thing Pip needed was her colleague filling her shoes, on either score.

Dominic shuffled a little in his seat and cleared his throat.

'Listen, Rose, I didn't come here to talk about work,' he said, and Pip felt herself relax a little. She didn't want to confess to Dominic just how anxious this talk was making her feel. It was much better if their conversation drifted away from the subject of work to something less tricky, even if it was a little mundane. She smiled at him and moved across to lean her head on his shoulder, but he pulled away from her.

'Look—' he said, and then stopped.

He chewed at the inside of his lip and Pip waited, her heart starting to pound again. Had something gone wrong at work? Was she going to be in trouble when she got back?

'The thing is . . .' he continued. Another pause. He ran his hand through his dark hair. 'Shit, this is hard.'

'What's hard?' she asked. 'What's the matter? Is there something wrong? Are you ill?'

'It's not that,' he said.

Pip was at a loss now. There was nothing she could think of that would justify this nervousness.

'Whatever it is, Dom, I'm sure we can sort it out,' she said softly.

He swallowed hard.

'I think we should split up,' he said.

His words hit Pip like a spray of bullets, but she couldn't tell which part of her was bleeding.

'I know you're struggling with everything and the timing is crap but it's just not working out for me. It wasn't working before you . . .'

Before I killed a child and had a nervous breakdown, she thought, but could not say out loud.

'But—' she began, but he cut across her.

'I'm sorry. I don't want to hurt you, Rose,' he said. He couldn't meet her eye and seemed to be repeating the speech he must have pre-prepared. Pip listened, hearing his words but not believing them. 'I truly don't,' he said, 'but I can't carry on like this. Who knows how long it will be before you're back to normal? And it's not fair on either of us to let things drag on, to let you think that everything is fine when it isn't.'

'But Dom . . .' Pip put her hand out to touch his cheek, as if by making that physical connection she could stop this chasm opening up between them, but Dominic pushed it away, his action gentle but firm.

He got to his feet. 'So that's why I came up here. I wanted to tell you face to face rather than over the phone.'

For a moment he looked as if he was expecting to be congratulated for his noble behaviour, but when she didn't speak, he added, 'But now I should go. I'm sorry, Rose. It's been fun but I think we're at the end of the line. We both need to move on and get on with our lives.'

Pip couldn't move. Her mouth fell open but no words came. She felt numb, but then she always felt numb these days. She'd felt numb ever since the accident.

Maybe she always would.

She tried to summon a response of some sort, but all she could think of were the practicalities. He couldn't leave her. He was all she had left, the only thing connecting her with her other life, her real life. If he walked out now, then she would be trapped in this new, fake world forever. She searched inside for the emotional response that she knew was expected of her, but there was nothing there – just a void.

Dominic reached the door then turned to look at her, his hand gripping the handle tightly.

'I'm sorry, Rose,' he said again. 'I really am. I'll let myself out. Say goodbye to your parents for me. I'll be in touch about your things.'

And then he was gone, leaving by the farmhouse's front door rather than going back through the kitchen.

Pip just sat there, staring at the space where he had been.

'Pip?' her mother's voice came from the kitchen. 'Was that Dominic crossing the yard? Has he gone to get his things from the car?' She appeared in the doorway, her cheeks pink, a smear of tomato purée across her chin like a vivid scar.

'Pip?' she asked. Pip stared at her blankly, not really hearing her. She spoke again. 'Pip? What's the matter? What's happened? Where's Dominic?'

Pip felt very calm. In fact, she couldn't ever remember feeling this calm before.

'He's gone,' she said. 'It's over and he's gone.'

10

'Oh, my sweet girl,' sighed Pip's mother, immediately coming to join Pip on the sofa. She settled down next to her, sliding her ample frame in so the sides of their bodies were touching. Pip hadn't been so close to anyone other than Dominic since the accident, and it felt odd to feel the sudden heat of her mother's body seeping into her own. Surprisingly, though, she didn't pull away, her long-forgotten instinct to gather warmth from her mum in moments of distress taking over.

She couldn't seem to work out how she was feeling. It ought to have been a shock, but if she was honest, really truly honest with herself, she'd known it was coming. The clues had all been there: their stilted phone conversations, the diminishing number of visits to the farm and the gap that she had felt opening up between her and his life in London. They all pointed in the same direction.

At the start, she had assumed she could rely on Dominic to see her through this nightmare; that he would stick by her until she got herself back on her feet, even though the situation was difficult.

But maybe he just didn't have it in him. He couldn't give her what she needed, or perhaps he just didn't want to. That was possibly closer to the truth. If she were to believe what he had just told her, then he'd wanted to finish things for some time before the accident, and had merely been biding his time until a decent period had elapsed so it didn't look as if he had deserted her when she was at her lowest. Pip wasn't sure she did believe that. They had been strong back then, with no cracks in their relationship at all. He must simply have convinced himself that things were rocky before in order to justify leaving her now.

That was what hurt the most. Whilst she had been clinging on to the plans she'd made for their future together once she was back home, he had been working out how he might get rid of her for good. Who had he talked to? How many of their friends knew he was planning to leave? Perhaps they even felt sorry for him – poor Dominic, standing by Rose because she's too broken to abandon. She could hear them now, twittering at the dinner parties she had missed, the drinks dos that Dominic had attended without her whilst she'd been stuck in Suffolk.

'He's trapped, you know. Apparently, the whole relationship had run its course before she killed that boy, but then she had the breakdown and there was nothing Dom could do but sit it out and wait for her to get better so that he could ditch her.'

'But it's been months.'

'Indeed. As I say, poor Dom.'

Maybe that was it? Had he only stayed until he was sure she was stable enough not to harm herself? Pip couldn't believe he'd think like that. At no point since the accident had she been suicidal. But did Dominic know that? She wasn't sure he knew her at all.

'Pip, sweetie, are you all right?' her mother said, interrupting her thoughts. She laid a hand gently on top of Pip's and the touch of her skin brought Pip back to herself. They were still sitting side by side, jammed together with nowhere to move. Suddenly it felt too close. Pip needed to get out, to create a space round herself, to bring down her own personal forcefield to protect herself. She shuffled forward on the sofa until she could stand up and escape.

'I'm okay,' she said. 'I think I'll go upstairs. I just need to . . .'

Without elucidating further, she slipped from the room. She felt as insubstantial as a waft of smoke, as if she were so fragile it would just take one sneeze and Philippa Rose Appleby would be gone.

'Shout if you need anything,' she heard her mother call after her.

Pip took the wooden steps to the first floor two at a time, barging into her room and banging the door shut behind her just as she had done many times before; so many stairs flounced up, so many doors banged. Sometimes it felt as if the last ten years of her life, what she had become, what she had achieved, had all just melted away. No one here really understood her life as a barrister. Her father was as much in the dark about what she did as her mother. She had once heard him telling someone that she defended murderers for a living, his chest puffed up as he spoke and his eyes casting round the room, making sure everyone was listening to him. She had lost count of the number of times she had tried to explain that there were different kinds of barristers and that neither she nor any of her colleagues were involved with criminal law. To start with, she had been frustrated that her father took so little notice of her other life, her real life, that he couldn't explain it properly to others, but when she had seen the look of pride on his face as he recounted the particulars to the enquirer she had had to reconsider. Did it really matter that the details were muddled as long as the main points were correct? Her father was proud of her life in London, even though he didn't understand it. Wasn't that enough?

What was there left for him to be proud of now? Who was she any more? No sharp suits, no strutting in and out of the Inns of Court, aware of ordinary people watching her and wondering how important she was, no status-enhancing boyfriend with all the trappings he had brought with him.

A life for a life.

Now all the trappings were gone, she wasn't sure what was left. She had always defined herself by what she did rather than by who she was, by what she wore on the outside instead of what was happening on the inside. Status had shaped each part of her, moulding her into what she had become. So where did that leave her now it was all gone? Drifting with neither rudder to steer her nor anchor to hold her safe. It was terrifying.

Pip climbed into her bed, but instead of burying herself beneath the covers she propped herself up against the headboard and stared at her childhood, preserved shrine-like in this room. She felt eerily calm. In the space of six months, every aspect of a life she'd thought was secure and stable had collapsed or evaporated. So why wasn't she crying? Where were the howling tears of anguish, the breast-beating and lamentations that she might have expected to follow such a catastrophic turn of events? Her eyes were dry. Apart from a pivot towards the philosophical, which had taken her by surprise but was not upsetting in itself, she felt fine.

But that couldn't be right. She must be in shock or something, or maybe her precarious mental state had rendered her incapable of processing what had just happened. It was true that feeling numb had become something of a habit with her recently, but this felt different. This wasn't a lack of emotional engagement due to trauma, like before. This was something closer to acceptance. Pip probed her emotional depths and found that she was okay. In fact, she was more than okay. She actually felt relieved. She now knew exactly where she stood. With Dominic gone from her life, there was absolutely nothing left.

She was empty, a vacuum, a void.

11

Pip didn't sleep that night; she didn't even try. She stayed where she was, propped up against the headboard, staring out at the dark night sky through her narrow window. It had been early evening when she retreated to her room, the faded chintzy curtains not yet pulled against the night, and so she had followed the progress of time by watching the colour of the sky slide through orangey-pink to midnight blue and back to pink again. Stars twinkled and then disappeared, and the moon, wafer-thin, slinked past on its inexorable path to the west.

At not long after three she heard the cockerel start up. When she had first come back to the farm he had woken her every morning. In London she slept through revellers and sirens and the clarion cries of endless burglar alarms without even stirring, and yet the plaintive crowing of one cockerel had cut through her sleep like a knife.

'Call yourself a farmer's daughter,' her father had teased when she had complained about the bird and she had thought to herself, 'Well, no, actually. I don't call myself a farmer's daughter – not to anyone that matters, anyway.' But of course, she hadn't said this to him. Whilst Pip didn't want all and sundry knowing about her humble origins, the last thing she wanted to do was to hurt her father.

And now it was Saturday morning and the weekend was spread out in front of her like a fresh page in a notebook. Or a diary. The diary! In all the calamity of Dominic's unexpected visit and its aftermath, she had totally forgotten about the diary. She'd had a plan for her weekend that had been temporarily blindsided. But now Dominic was gone – in all senses of the word – and so what better way of distracting herself from unwelcome thoughts about him than returning to Plan A and losing herself in someone else's life for a while?

She flicked the duvet back and slipped her feet out of bed. She would sneak downstairs, retrieve the diary and bring it back to her room. But as soon as she opened her bedroom door, she could hear her mother's voice calling out to her.

'Is that you, Pip?'

Pip felt the familiar irritation grow. It was so claustrophobic. She couldn't even breathe here without somebody noticing and wanting to make sure that she was doing it properly.

The voice was coming from the bathroom, where the door stood wide open. Her family had never had much of an issue with privacy, something that hadn't worried Pip when she'd lived there and didn't know any different, but it now felt overfamiliar.

'I brought a plastic bag back with me last night. Do you know where it went?' she asked, heading for the stairs.

'With an old book in it? I put it in the dresser. I didn't want Dom . . .' Her mother stopped mid-sentence as she emerged from the bathroom, a threadbare towel barely covering her torso and her sandy-coloured hair hanging in dripping tails around her face. 'I didn't want the place looking untidy,' she continued, her ruddy cheeks a shade pinker than usual.

'It's okay, Mum,' Pip replied reassuringly. 'I'll be all right. Honestly. And it's probably for the best. We'd been drifting for a while, and what with me being stuck here . . .' She paused, changed direction. 'Please don't worry about me. I'm not about to fall apart or anything.'

The irony of this sentence almost made her laugh.

'Good,' replied her mother, although her expression was sceptical, as if she didn't really believe what Pip had said. Pip wasn't entirely sure she believed it, either. Could she really dismiss Dominic walking out on her quite so lightly? But then again, this wasn't really her, was it? This was the shell of her, but her vital parts – her heart, her soul, the essence of who she was – had been placed in frozen suspension by the accident, leaving her incapable of normal responses.

There was an awkward pause as both women stood on the landing, each waiting for the other to speak.

Pip broke the moment. 'Right,' she said. 'I'll just go get the bag.' And then she headed down the stairs before her mother could question her any further.

In the kitchen, Jez was at the table filling his flask from the huge teapot that her mother kept full for whoever might need a cuppa. Pip hovered in the doorway. She was still in the clothes that she'd spent all night in, her hair unbrushed and what was left of yesterday's mascara no doubt smudged in black shadows beneath her eyes. It didn't really matter what Jez thought of her, but something held her back. She didn't want him to see her looking so dreadful.

It was too late, though. He had heard her, and he looked up and gave her a grin.

'You look rough,' he said, and then pulled a face as if he'd remembered why she was back at the farm just too late. 'God, Pip, I'm sorry,' he said. 'I didn't think.'

She put a placatory hand up and shook her head. 'Don't worry about it,' she said. 'I know. I look bloody awful. Didn't sleep much.'

'Right,' he said. There was a pause and then, 'Well, I'd better get off. Your dad's waiting for me. Nice to see you though.' He stared straight at her, his eyes locking with hers and holding her gaze until she looked away.

'Have a good day,' she said to his retreating back.

Something about the exchange whisked her back to her teenage self, and she suddenly felt very aware that for all the time she'd been back at the farm, she'd made no effort to connect with him. There had been a period in their lives when the two of them had been as good as joined at the hip. They'd basically grown up together: same school, mutual friends, shared experiences. At one point, they had been really close. As close as it got, in fact – a passionate, urgent desire for sex pushing them together, even though they had always considered themselves friends rather than a couple.

But then she'd gone off to university and he had taken a job on the farm with her dad, and they had drifted away from one another. Or, more truthfully, she had put up her sails and sailed purposefully in the opposite direction towards something new. Then she'd come back, and whilst he must have known what had happened to her – didn't everyone? – he had decided, or possibly been instructed, not to pry.

Pip realised now that she wished he would pry, just a little. It might feel good to talk to him; he might understand how she felt more than her parents could. He'd always known her better than anyone else in Suffolk, maybe better than anyone anywhere, and she suddenly felt a nostalgic yearning for his slant on her life. Perhaps she would ask him out for a drink one night, for old times' sake. Her mother had said there was a girlfriend on the scene, but surely two old friends going out for a quick drink wouldn't upset anyone.

She watched Jez through the window as he hopped into the waiting Land Rover. Yes, she really would like to spend a bit of time with him.

But right now she wanted to read the diary and so she crossed the kitchen to the old Welsh dresser, opened the cupboard and peered in. The plastic bag was there, thrust unceremoniously to the back. She retrieved it carefully so as not to dislodge the precarious pile of underused utensils. Then she opened the bag and peered inside. The diary was still there, although where else would it have got to? Her mother would have had neither the time nor the inclination to read it. She would simply have stuffed the bag out of the way so Dominic wouldn't think the family untidy, as if such things could possibly matter. Pip closed the dresser and padded quietly back up the stairs.

'Did you find it?' came her mother's voice.

Pip sighed. She really couldn't move without being tracked. 'Yes, thanks,' she called back.

She opened her bedroom door and closed it firmly behind her. Maybe she should invest in a bolt if she was going to be here for a while, but then she reprimanded herself. That wasn't fair. Her mother was just concerned for her well-being, and Pip had to allow her that.

She slipped back into bed, pulling the covers up around her, and took the diary from the bag.

12

1979

The part was hers. Julian had rung to inform her that the role of DC Karen Walker was in the bag. Filming would begin in the summer with the programme airing after Christmas in the prized 'dark winter evenings' slot. It was wonderful news. Everything had gone exactly as they had hoped.

Evelyn was recording the moment in her diary, but had stopped writing to brush the tears from her cheeks. Instinctively, she shielded the pages. She didn't want spotted rainbows of smudged ink across this particular entry. It would mean that she would never be able to read the page again without asking herself why she had cried when she wrote it, and then remembering.

It didn't matter. That was in the past, and now she had the part she didn't need to dwell on what she had gone through to get it. This was going to be the start of her success, she could feel it, and that was a good thing, something to be celebrated. The role of DC Karen Walker in the groundbreaking, women-led police drama series would be the making of her as an actress. By the time the credits rolled on the final episode, anyone who mattered would recognise her face. There would be photoshoots for the cover of the *Radio Times* and they were bound to want to interview her and the instantly recognisable Maggie Booth, whom they had cast as the inspector, on *Parkinson*. Only those who didn't watch television would fail to know who Evelyn Mountcastle was, and, to be honest, who cared about them?

So why was she crying?

Why indeed.

Evelyn dropped the diary on the bed and pulled the covers up under her chin. She would continue writing later, when she had got her emotions under better check. It was all too raw right now, the shock of the day before juxtaposed with the elation of the news just received. Evelyn didn't quite know what to do with it all.

At this precise moment she felt stupid. Stupid and naive. She had been so ill prepared, when looking back, it was entirely obvious what MacMillan had had in mind. A hotel room on her own on a Sunday – how did she expect that was going to pan out? But when Evelyn examined her conscience, she could honestly say the thought that he might want more from her than mere conversation hadn't occurred to her until it was too late.

When he had patted the sofa next to him, she had resisted. She had heard of this kind of thing; of course she had. The casting couch and all that. Everyone knew someone with a story. But this wasn't that kind of scenario, she thought to herself as she steadfastly refused to move closer to him, and she definitely wasn't one of those actresses. She would get the part on her own merits or she didn't want it.

He had been fine with her resistance, had smiled at her as if he didn't mind what she did one way or the other, and she had felt pleased with herself. She had shown him that she was serious about her career and had no intentions of sleeping her way to the top, and he had understood that and respected her for it.

After that, he had taken the lead in the conversation, talking about his job, the famous people he knew, the contacts he had in

Hollywood who he could put her in touch with. Evelyn's head had spun with it all – although that might have been the whisky. After the third time he'd topped up her glass, she had stopped counting. She was only taking sips, but it was impossible to keep a tally when he kept spoiling her gauge.

And then, when it was quite dark outside, he had stood up and flicked off the overhead lights.

'No need for those,' he said. 'It's much more relaxing with just the side lights, don't you think?'

He had come to her sofa then and settled himself down beside her. She had wanted to move away but she didn't want to appear rude, so instead she crossed her legs and tried to make herself as small and neat as she could. He had laid his big, manicured hand on her leg, stroking her thigh through the fabric of her skirt with his thumb. The skirt rode up a little and she had tried to shuffle it back down. She was no prude, but this really wasn't what she wanted. She had hoped he would get the signals she was sending him, but apparently they weren't fit for purpose because he missed them entirely.

By the time he leaned over her and pressed his lips on to hers, she had known what was going to happen next and had already considered her options. There were only two – to allow matters to progress as he clearly intended them to, or to object and leave. And then she thought about her dreams, and the part that was so tantalisingly close, and her unpaid rent and the horrifying idea of having to go back to Joan with her tail between her legs, and she realised there really was only the one option after all.

And so she had closed her eyes and let him kiss her. She had felt his large hands paw at her neck and her breasts, the buttons on her blouse giving way under the pressure of his fingers, and she had gulped down her fear. It was just sex. She had had sex before. She knew what to do. And she was prepared to go through with it if that was what it was going to take for him to give her the part. It wasn't such a big sacrifice, she thought, as he rucked her skirt up around her waist and pulled at her tights so that they bunched first at her knees and then around her ankles.

She tried to appear to enjoy it – she was an actress, after all. She could not bring herself to speak, but she made noises that suggested desire, hoping that they might encourage him to a faster outcome. The little intake of breath that she uttered when he entered her was genuine enough, although not a sign of rapture as he appeared to assume. She tried to relax; she had read somewhere that it hurt less if you were relaxed, and she moved her hands up and down his back in a parody of pleasure. It was very wide, she noticed, and covered with wiry dark hair. She was curious about the hair. It was almost like a pelt. She had never seen anything quite like it before, she thought, as he thrust into her. If she thought about the hairs it was easier not to think about what was happening. As he pushed himself into her, she ran her fingers across them, noticing how they were thickest down his spine, petering out a little where his ribs curved round.

And then it was over.

He groaned and slid off her.

'Thanks, darling,' he'd said, as if she had been doing him a favour. She had almost said, 'You're welcome,' as an automatic response.

She sat up, businesslike, pulled her tights from round her ankles and righted her skirt. The buttons on her blouse were trickier as her hands were shaking so violently, but somehow she managed. He stayed where he was, sprawled in a post-orgasmic state of bliss she imagined, although she didn't look at him too carefully. She just wanted to leave, to get away.

But first, she had to make sure. 'So, you'll tell Mike that you want me for the part?' she asked, making her voice as steady as she could. She was going to be bold. She owed that to herself, at least, but she hardly dared listen for the answer.

He opened his eyes and looked up at her. For a moment, he seemed confused about what she was asking, but then it came back to him.

'Oh, *Into the Blue*. Yes, darl. That's yours.'

He closed his eyes again. Evelyn stood rooted to the spot, not knowing if she was dismissed or whether there was more expected of her, but then she heard his breathing deepen. He was asleep. She straightened her hair, slipped her bare feet into her shoes and retrieved her bag and coat. And then she left the suite.

Now, back in her room in the tiny, freezing cold flat, the only thing that mattered was that she had the part. The rest of it would fade in time. She had done what she needed to do. There was no point dwelling on it. She wasn't the first and she certainly wouldn't be the last. She should consider it to be merely a part of the job and move on, and hopefully it need never happen again. It was simply the way to get her foot on the ladder, that was all, her kick-start. She repeated this to herself as the tears trickled down her cheeks.

A noise on the landing outside the flat brought her attention back to the present. She heard a key turning in the lock. It would either be Brenda or their landlord who, despite their protestations, seemed to consider it perfectly acceptable to come and go as he pleased with no concern for the privacy of his tenants. Evelyn's heart gave a little flutter in her chest. She hoped it wasn't him. She would have to skulk around in her room until he had gone, as she owed him rent that she currently had no means of paying. He wasn't an unreasonable man and would give her more time if she asked, but she really couldn't face having to throw herself on his mercy – not today, not now.

But then Brenda called out. 'Evie? Are you here?'

Evelyn straightened her spine and sniffed back her tears. She leaned over to check her face in the age-spotted mirror, to straighten her hair.

'Yes,' she replied. 'Give me a mo. I'm just . . .'

But then the door of her room opened and Brenda's face appeared, a heavy plaid scarf wrapped several times around her neck so her head appeared to have been planted on the top like a pineapple.

'Hi, Evie. Only me. I was just . . .' Brenda stopped mid-sentence and eyed her perceptively. 'Is everything okay?'

For a split second, Evelyn considered telling her flatmate exactly how she was, what had happened and how she felt. Brenda was a good listener. She wouldn't condemn her; she would understand that Evelyn had had no choice and what she had done had been the only path open to her. And it would feel good to talk to someone, wouldn't it?

But then she thought about the rumours, the stories that might start to circulate about how she had got the part, and she decided against it. She pulled her face into a wide, bright smile, just like she had on stage countless times, and said, 'Yes. I'm fine. I've just woken up, that's all. And guess what? I've got some incredible news.'

13

Evelyn loved a wedding. Weddings were just like a stage performance, with everyone knowing their role, their lines and their cues. Never having starred in one herself, Evelyn was happy to sit with the other extras, looking lovely and reacting as required as the main players acted out their parts at the front. It was, she felt, a lovely way to pass an afternoon.

This ceremony was taking place at Camden Register Office. Evelyn much preferred a church wedding and that was definitely what she would have chosen if she were getting married, but Brenda and Jim were only doing this to appease their parents, and so long white dresses and bloom-adorned pews were not on their wish list.

It was, at least, a bright March day. The perishing cold of winter was slowly being replaced by something less bone-numbing but Evelyn, taking no chances, was wearing a maxi dress. It was an old favourite – she didn't have the budget for anything else just yet – but she didn't think she had ever worn it with Brenda. It had felt a little tight when she'd struggled into it this morning, however. She would need to keep an eye on that. Everyone knew that the small screen added at least ten pounds.

Evelyn reached the building and skipped up the steps. It was a challenge, being at a wedding without a plus one, but she was pretty sure she could pull it off. She just had to smile and look confident, and wasn't that just what she had been born to do?

She followed the signs through the building until she found the right place. Guests in hats with flowers attached to their outfits mingled with others in bell-bottom jeans and platform shoes, making it clear which were friends of the parents and which of the bride and groom. Evelyn decided that her dress placed her in the no man's land between the two, which was no bad place to be.

A minute or two later the doors opened and the guests filed into the official room. As a friend of the bride, Evelyn made her way to a chair on the left-hand side of the room and chose a seat about ten rows back. The dark wooden panelling was imposing and, she was prepared to concede, added a certain solemnity to the proceedings, but it wasn't a patch on a church. Jim was standing at the front with a man Evelyn thought she recognised from a night out with Brenda. He was shuffling from one foot to another as if the floor were hot, and kept turning around to peer at the door.

The conversation around her began to drop and then hushed completely. Brenda must have arrived. Evelyn spun in her seat to try and get a glimpse of her. As she did so, a man in a brown pin-stripe suit sneaked into her row and took the seat next to her.

He grinned wildly. 'That was close,' he whispered, one eyebrow raised. His eyes were a warm toffee colour that seemed to match his hair exactly, as if the same paintbrush had tinted them both.

'Talk about cutting it fine,' Evelyn whispered back. 'Any later and you'd have been following her down the aisle, or whatever it's called here.'

She smiled at him to show that she wasn't being critical, and then turned her attention back to Brenda. She could see her now, waiting by the door with a round man who had what was left of his mousey hair combed over the top of his pate. He must be Brenda's father, Evelyn decided, although she couldn't see any family resemblance. He nodded to Brenda reassuringly and she nodded back, and then they set off towards Jim. The pulsing rhythm of Sylvester's 'You Make Me Feel (Mighty Real)' filled the room, and half the guests jumped visibly whilst the rest looked at one another and grinned. Evelyn wasn't sure what she thought. It made a change from Mendelsohn, but she could sense a general feeling of disquiet in those around her.

'Brave choice,' whispered the man with the toffee-coloured eyes. 'I like it.'

Evelyn smiled and nodded back. She wished he would stop talking to her. It wasn't appropriate, but she was too polite to just ignore him.

Brenda looked lovely, dressed in a halter-neck jumpsuit in a delicate primrose yellow. Again, it lacked that weddingy feel that Evelyn might have preferred, but Brenda, whose smile was enough to light up the room on its own, was clearly delighted. Evelyn was thrilled for her. Jim looked as if all his Christmases had come at once as he watched his bride make her procession towards him, a bounce in her step as if she were actually crossing a dance floor. The man next to her was tapping along to the song with his feet, a hand beating out the offbeat on his brown stripy trouser leg. The wedding was starting to have a positive party vibe about it and Evelyn could see that the registrar looked anxious, as if the ceremony was running out of his control.

After Brenda finally reached Jim, the tape was turned off, and the older guests visibly relaxed as the service then followed more traditional lines until the final vows were taken and the deed was done. Evelyn stood and applauded the happy couple as they made their way out of the room. The man next to her pushed his fingers between his lips and gave an ear-splitting wolf whistle that almost deafened her. Automatically she put her hands to her ears to protect them.

'Sorry. Bit loud,' he said with a sheepish grin. 'Name's Ted, by the way. Ted Bannister.'

He held a slightly grubby hand out for her to shake. Evelyn took it, hoping that her reluctance wasn't written all over her face.

'Evelyn Mountcastle,' she said.

'Are you going to the bash at the pub?' he asked her.

She nodded and he looked around with extravagant enthusiasm, his head turning comically from left to right.

'No Mr Mountcastle?' he asked. 'No beau waiting to take your arm?'

He had what Evelyn considered to be a real London accent, all 'born within the sound of Bow Bells'-ish.

She shook her head. 'No. Just me, I'm afraid,' she said in her best RP. She had managed to lose her East Anglian burr and was now proud to be unplaceable, by her voice at least.

'Then would you allow me to accompany you?' he asked.

He was starting to remind her a little of Dick Van Dyke in *Mary Poppins*. She wasn't sure it was entirely proper to pick up an escort for a wedding at the ceremony itself, but arriving with a total stranger had to be better than arriving alone.

'Thank you,' she said. 'That would be lovely.'

Ted held out his arm for her to loop hers through. This felt horribly intimate, but he was grinning as if the whole thing was one jolly jape, so Evelyn decided to go with the flow. She gave a little curtsey, bowed her head and accepted his arm. Then the pair of them followed the other guests out on to the street to head to the George and Dragon, where there was to be a finger buffet and dancing until closing time.

The pub wasn't far from the register office. Evelyn had tried to memorise the route from her A to Z so she wouldn't have to ask anyone, but as it turned out there was no need. Ted had it covered.

'Come on,' he said as he led her along, their arms still linked. 'I can get us there.' He pointed down an alley that was stacked with wooden packing cases and empty apple boxes. 'There's a shortcut down here.'

Evelyn eyed the narrow alley with suspicion, but Ted added, 'Don't worry. It's perfectly safe. I know this part of town like the back of my hand. I have to do deliveries round here for my boss.'

'What do you deliver?' asked Evelyn, curious to learn something of her new companion.

'Oh, this and that,' he replied non-committally. 'Trust me. Sneaking down this way cuts a good five minutes off the walk.'

Without waiting for her to object, he pulled her down the alleyway and for the first time Evelyn began to feel uncomfortable. She could hear her sister Joan's voice in her head, warning against going off down dark alleyways with strange men, and for once she knew Joan would be right. It was madness to follow him. She should say something, refuse to go that way and insist on sticking to the main roads, but it felt rude to object when he was being so kind as to escort her. And anyway, Ted felt like someone she could trust, and she considered herself to be a good judge of character. Then, before she could get too cocksure about her own perspicacity, her tricksy mind pulled her back to the Hilton Hotel. She had been wrong then, totally wrong.

There was nothing she could do about it now, however, so she allowed herself to be led along, all the while trying to make a mental map of where she was in case she had to retrace her steps at speed. But there was no need. Soon enough they emerged back on to a bustling main road and found themselves right outside the George and Dragon.

'There you go,' Ted said, grinning like the cat that got the cream. 'Told you. Like the back of my hand.'

He opened the wooden swing door and held it for her so that she could go in first. She shuffled inside, pausing after a few feet whilst her eyes adjusted to the gloom. The pub was full of men, all nursing pints and cigarettes. The stench of stale beer, stale tobacco and grime wafted up out of the semi-darkness, making her feel queasy. She thought she might just retreat outside for some air, but Ted was at her back and guiding her steadily towards the bar.

'Just over here,' he said as he steered her forward. 'The function room's up those stairs.'

Upstairs the air was a little clearer and Evelyn immediately felt better. The room was about half full, and she recognised a few of the outfits as belonging to other wedding guests, although none of the faces were familiar. Then she saw Jim, looking too hot in the suit that must have been his one concession to his parents. She gave him a little wave.

'Evelyn!' he called over to her, and one or two people looked round. This pleased her. She imagined that Brenda and Jim might have told some of their guests that the actress Evelyn Mountcastle would be coming to the wedding.

'And you've met our Ted, I see,' Jim added as they got closer to him.

Our Ted? Evelyn wondered if the two men might be related, but then Jim went on to explain.

'Ted and me was at school together,' he said. 'He was a bit of a rascal.'

Out of the corner of her eye, Evelyn saw Ted pull a face, objecting to Jim's description of him. He must have been trying to make a good impression on her. It was sweet, really.

'But he's pulled his socks up since then,' Jim continued, eager to correct any misapprehension, 'and now you couldn't hope to meet a finer citizen.'

'No need to lay it on with a trowel, mate,' said Ted. 'Evelyn and me are getting along just fine without your introductions.'

He winked at her, and Evelyn again had the slightly discombobulating feeling that she was walking directly into the lion's den.

'Fair enough,' said Jim. Someone was waving at him from across the room. 'Looks like I'm needed over there,' he said, his smile wide at being the centre of attention. 'I've got no idea where the missus is.'

'That's not a great start, mate,' laughed Ted. 'You're going to need to keep her on a tighter leash than that.'

Evelyn could just make out Brenda, swamped by a group of well-wishers, the only clue that she was buried amongst them a flash of her yellow jumpsuit.

'She's over there,' she said helpfully.

Jim nodded but then headed off towards the other group, which pleased Evelyn. Brenda and Jim might be married now but they were still independent people.

'Would you like a drink?' Ted asked, and she refocused her attention on him. 'Babycham, maybe?' he suggested.

Evelyn generally liked a Babycham if there was no chance of the real thing, but in the slightly stuffy, smoky atmosphere of the room over the pub, the idea of the fizzy little drink somehow didn't appeal. She was still feeling queasy, and alcohol really wasn't going to help with that.

'I'll just have an orange juice, please,' she said. 'Fresh, not cordial.'

Ted raised an eyebrow but headed off towards the bar, leaving Evelyn on her own, but he wasn't gone long, soon making his way back across the crowded room carrying a glass of Britvic Orange and a pint.

He nodded at an empty table to his right. 'Shall we sit down?'

Evelyn hesitated. If she sat down with him now, then she would probably be stuck with him for the rest of the reception as the other tables would start to fill up when the buffet was served. But would that be so awful? Ted seemed pleasant enough. He was a childhood friend of Jim's so his credentials were verified and, from what she had garnered so far, he was fun. She could probably do a lot worse and as long as she was careful not to give out the wrong message, spending time with him would be preferable to having to infiltrate other more established groups of guests.

'That would be lovely,' she said after what she hoped wasn't too long a pause.

They sat down and Ted placed her drink in front of her. The tables were decorated with paper tablecloths in a yellow that was more Bird's Custard than the delicate primrose of Brenda's outfit, and jam jars sprouting daffodils were dotted about the place, too. It all looked very attractive for a room above a pub.

'Doesn't the room look lovely?' she commented to Ted, more for something to say than anything else. And then, 'When do you suppose they'll serve the food?' She was suddenly and unaccountably ravenous.

Ted shrugged. 'Not got a clue,' he said. 'While we wait, why don't you tell me something about yourself? How do you know Jim?'

'I don't,' admitted Evelyn. 'Well, not really. I share a flat with Brenda. Well, shared. She's moved out now that she's married.'

'So you're on your own?' asked Ted.

'Yes,' replied Evelyn with a sigh. 'I am. Not sure for how long. I suppose the landlord will get someone in. I certainly can't afford to pay two lots of rent.'

In fact, she could barely afford to pay one lot until she got paid, something that she usually kept carefully guarded so as not to splinter the slightly skewed reflection of her life that she presented to the world at large. But in this room full of people she neither knew nor wanted to get to know, she wondered whether she couldn't open up a little to a stranger about the precariousness of her current situation. What harm could it do?

'If the truth be told, Ted,' she said, 'Brenda moving out is going to send me up the creek without a paddle. I'm not at all sure how I'll cope.'

Ted looked at her appraisingly. He had a kind face, she thought, when it wasn't joking and messing about.

'I know how that one works,' he said quietly. 'Been there myself. Have you got a plan?'

'Not in the short term,' she admitted. 'I do have a job in the pipeline, quite a good one as it goes, but I'm not quite sure when that will get going.'

'And in the meantime, you're not answering the door or opening any post?' He winked at her and it made her smile.

'Yep. That's about the size of it,' she said. 'But less of me and my woes. How about you? What do you do?'

Ted's eyes dropped to his pint and he shuffled in his seat. 'Bit of this. Bit of that,' he said, without meeting her eye.

It didn't sound very honest, whatever it was, but Evelyn found that she didn't mind. She was more intrigued than anything else. 'Sounds fascinating,' she murmured.

Ted shrugged. 'Pays the bills,' he said. 'Most of the time, anyway.'

He finished his pint and gestured to their empty glasses. 'Another?' he asked her. 'Do you want a real drink this time? Can't have me drinking on my own.'

Evelyn wasn't at all sure that she did, but she didn't want to seem ungrateful. 'Gin and tonic,' she said.

'Ice and a slice?' he asked as he stood up, and she nodded.

A straggle-haired DJ was just setting up in the corner of the room, his boxes of records all set out on a table next to his turntables. He was playing an Abba hit from a few years before by way of background music, and Evelyn caught herself humming along with the melody. The party would probably become less sedate as the evening drew on, she thought. Brenda and Jim knew how to enjoy themselves and the voices in the room were getting louder and louder as the alcohol flowed. She decided she would probably leave before it got to that point. She would wait until the food had been served – she couldn't afford to turn down a free meal – and then quietly slink away without anyone noticing. She could explain to Brenda later if she seemed upset that she had gone without saying goodbye, but to be honest she suspected she wouldn't be missed.

Ted had been to the bar for a third time when the buffet was declared open. He and Evelyn were at the front of the queue, after the bridal party themselves of course, and they both came away with plates piled high. Ted had to hold his sausage rolls in place on top of the mountain of finger rolls so they didn't tumble off. He didn't seem to think any comment on his apparent greed was called for, so Evelyn didn't comment either, and just tucked into her food with relish.

'So how come you're not hitched, then?' Ted asked her as he licked the salty crisp crumbs from his fingers. 'Nice-looking lady like yourself, I'd have thought you would have been snapped up years ago.'

Evelyn shrugged. 'Where to start?' she said. 'Never met the right man. Always busy at work. Wrong time, wrong place. Take your pick.'

'But you do want to get married, have kids and all that?' he asked.

No one had ever asked her that before. She was thirty, so perhaps people now assumed she wasn't interested in a conventional married life. But she was. In fact, the idea of never having any children made her unloved heart beat harder in her chest. She had always assumed that it would just happen when the time was right and she found it distressing that it was beginning to look like it might not.

'I do,' she replied. 'I really do. But I have things to do first.'

At this point other people would probably have sucked their teeth and shaken their heads and made some unhelpful comment about not leaving things too late, but Ted just nodded as if this was a perfectly sensible way to carry on, and Evelyn felt herself warming to him for his understanding.

'And what about you?' she asked. 'Anyone special in your life?'

There was a pause in which Ted seemed to close down. His smile faltered and he cast his eyes low to the floor before he spoke.

'There was someone,' he said. 'Anni-Frid.' He paused, swallowed. 'But it didn't work out.'

Evelyn watched him carefully, dying to ask questions but worried that it might scare him off. In the end she just said, 'I'm sorry,' and he shrugged.

'It was a tragedy, really,' he continued, his gaze still firmly on his pint glass. 'But she went off with a bloke she worked with. Benny. He wasn't much to look at – short, beardy. I told her she should take a chance on me but in the end, she picked him. Suppose that's the name of the game.'

He looked up now, his playful eyes peeping out under his lashes, and then he grinned and Evelyn realised she'd been had.

'Oh, for goodness' sake,' she said in mock anger. 'I was building up some proper sympathy for you then.'

'Sorry,' he smirked. 'Couldn't resist. Actually, I was married once but it didn't work out. We were both too young. Amicable split. No hard feelings, but I'm not looking to make the same mistake any time soon.'

Was he marking her card, Evelyn wondered? Not that it mattered. Despite her overall life plans, Evelyn wasn't looking for a husband, or even a boyfriend just at the moment. She was going to be far too busy for anything like that.

At that point, the disco burst into life with a Boney M. song and immediately people headed for the space in the middle of the floor. There was to be no 'first dance', then. If Evelyn ever got married, she would definitely want to be whisked around the dance floor by her new husband with all her friends and family watching her.

She realised that she felt suddenly and inexplicably weary and she stifled a yawn, but Ted saw.

'Boring you, am I?' he asked, but he was smiling.

'I'm sorry, Ted, but I'm so tired all of a sudden. I think I might head off home.'

'Well, let me walk you back,' he said, and she appreciated that he didn't try to persuade her to stay. She felt almost overwhelmed by her urge to be at home in her bed. It wasn't like her to pass up a social occasion but then again, she had been in an oddly pensive mood all day.

'No funny business,' he added. 'Scout's honour, but we can't have you wandering about London in the dark on your own.'

Could Evelyn trust him? She thought so. They had been together for hours and he hadn't as much as touched her knee.

'That would be very kind,' she said. 'If it's not too much trouble.'

'Should we say goodbye?' he asked her.

Brenda and Jim were bouncing up and down in the middle of a bunch of revellers and looked like they wouldn't be stopping for some time. Evelyn shook her head.

They stood up, Ted downing the last of his pint, and then skirted round the dance floor, down the stairs and out into the street. The air was chilly now, but the sky was clear and one or two determined stars were twinkling.

'When I lived in Suffolk,' said Evelyn as they set off towards the flat, 'there were millions of stars. You could even see the Milky Way on a good night. I always feel a bit sorry for all the Londoners who have no idea what's right above them.'

Ted shook his head. 'I don't need to know what's out there,' he said with a shudder. 'And the countryside's not for me. Far too much air.'

They laughed, and Evelyn let Ted slip his arm through hers as he had done when he'd escorted her to the pub earlier that day. Now, though, there was a kind of understanding between them and the rather frantic mood of before had been replaced by something akin to friendship.

'Thank you for your company this afternoon,' Evelyn said when they reached the door to the flat. 'I very much enjoyed it.'

'You are most welcome,' he replied. 'I had a nice time too. Could I have your phone number? Maybe we could meet again one afternoon, find another pub to waste some time in?'

Evelyn thought for a split second and then rattled off the number, which he wrote down on a till receipt using a stubby pencil that he pulled out of his coat.

'It's incoming calls only, though,' she said with a wink, 'so don't be expecting me to ring you back.'

He left her at the door without even trying to kiss her and Evelyn found, to her surprise, that she was a little disappointed. She didn't suppose he would ring. Men like him never did. Still, it had been a lovely wedding.

14

At last there was some progress on *Into the Blue*. The weeks since she had been given the part had dragged by and so, finally giving into the inevitable, Evelyn had been forced to get herself another job to tide her over; but as there was no need to be racing off to auditions she had found herself a civilised position temping in an estate agent's office. She whiled away her time, between bouts of filing and sending out property particulars, fantasising about the house she would buy for herself once she had a steady income. Working in an estate agent's was the perfect way to hone your dream life, it seemed.

When she left the office at half past five, Ted was waiting for her in the café over the road. They had taken to meeting up like this for a cup of tea at the end of their working days. As good as his word, Ted had rung her after Brenda's wedding, and they had met up for a drink and a chat. There had been no suggestion that it was a date of any kind, and this suited Evelyn. It appeared to suit Ted, too, because things had quickly switched from pub to a contemplative cup of tea before heading off to their own lives for whatever their evenings held in store. This tended to be very little for Evelyn. She was finding the daily grind of an office job surprisingly exhausting, and was fit for nothing by 6 p.m. She wasn't sure how Ted spent his evenings, but she tried not to be too curious if he didn't want to tell her. The mutual benefit of their arrangement appeared to be good conversation and friendship.

Evelyn sidled across the road, dodging between cars without waiting for the little green man, and went into the café. Ted was at their usual table next to the window, two mugs of tea and a plate of malted milk biscuits set out before him. Sometimes they were shortbreads, or Rich Tea and, on one red-letter day, chocolate digestives. It all depended on what Sanjeet, whose café it was, had left over after the day's trading.

Today Ted was wearing jeans and a T-shirt. On other days he wore a jacket and tie, and occasionally the brown wedding suit. Evelyn assumed his clothes reflected the duties of his day but she never pried, asking simply, 'Good day?' as she sat down, to which he invariably replied, 'Fair to middling.' Generally, when she arrived he would be scouring the small ads in the London *Evening Standard*, and today was no different.

'You never know what you might pick up from the small ads,' he'd told her when she asked why he scrutinised the back pages of the paper so carefully. 'It's like a whole microcosm of London life right there in those little boxes.'

They had shared more of the detail of their lives with one another now. She knew that he lived with his mother in a flat on the seventeenth floor of a tower block in Hackney. He seemed to be her only carer.

'Mum's not as young as she was,' he'd told Evelyn. 'She can't manage the stairs like she used to and the lift is always out of order. I've told the council to move her somewhere more suitable but of course, nothing's happened. Lord only knows what would become of her if I wasn't there to do her shopping, but no one seems bothered about that.'

The council's failings, many and varied, made a regular theme for his complaints, but Evelyn now knew that Ted was devoted to his mother and would happily spend the rest of his days fetching and carrying for her.

It was a far cry from her relationship with her own family. This was also a subject they had covered at length over their cups of tea.

'What I don't get,' Ted had said vehemently whenever the vexed subject of Evelyn's relations had come up, 'is why they couldn't just accept that you wanted to be an actress and then help you get there. To my way of thinking it makes no sense, driving you away like they did.'

'They didn't exactly drive me away,' Evelyn said. 'I left of my own accord.'

'But only because they weren't there for you. If I had kids I'd make sure they knew that I'd back them to the hilt, no matter what they wanted to do,' he replied, angry on her behalf and without any hint of a doubt about his own parenting skills, notwithstanding his distinct lack of children. 'And,' he'd continued, warming to his theme, 'why Pete and Joan have continued in the same vein now that your mum and dad are dead is a total mystery to me. I mean, who are they to dictate to you how you should or shouldn't live your life?'

It tickled Evelyn that Ted would talk so freely about her siblings, even shortening their names, without ever having met them. Her brother Peter had never, ever been a Pete. She also loved the outrage Ted seemed to feel about the injustices done to her, not least because it was unique.

'Well, you can't really blame them,' replied Evelyn, although she did. 'They never understood me, any of them. But it's okay, because I don't ever have to go back.'

'And when this new TV programme hits their screens they'll see that you were right all along and have to eat their words.'

Ted had sat back in his chair, triumphant, and Evelyn hadn't had the heart to tell him that her sister Joan didn't even own a television set and so would probably never see the show.

'How did it go with Julian?' Ted asked her now, shutting his newspaper and folding it up.

'Really well,' replied Evelyn, nodding enthusiastically as she nibbled on a biscuit. 'Rehearsals start next week.'

'Finally!' Ted said, but Evelyn shook her head.

'Actually, it's all happened quite quickly for television. But yes, it will be good to get started.'

'And then you'll meet all the cast. You've met the director bloke already, haven't you? What about the producer?'

Evelyn felt her stomach turn over at the mention of Rory MacMillan. 'I've met them both at various stages,' she said briefly.

Ted picked a bit of biscuit out of his teeth with a fingernail. 'What are they like?' he asked. 'I've always imagined TV types to be a bit pleased with themselves.'

Evelyn paused as she decided which line to take. For a moment, she considered telling Ted what she really thought, and why. It would be so wonderful to have someone to tell about the afternoon in the hotel suite, about how it made her feel. But if she did that then she wouldn't be able to put the whole episode in a box in her head and forget that it ever happened. As soon as she told someone else, the whole ugly situation became real.

'Oh,' she said in as light a tone as she could muster. 'They're all right really. You just have to know how to handle them.'

'Oh, hark at her,' laughed Ted. 'Miss Worldly Wise over there.'

He was teasing her and that was fine, but she wasn't sure when she had ever felt less worldly wise.

15

2019

The diary was dated 1983 and immediately Pip's curiosity was piqued. Was the author a regular diary-keeper? Was this one of a set and if so, how come it had been separated from its companions? Maybe whoever had donated it made a choice to dispose of that specific year. She pictured a set of diaries on a shelf and someone selecting the year that they wanted to eradicate. This seemed an unlikely answer to the conundrum of why the diary had wound up at the shop, but the idea pleased her. What if it were that easy to remove the last six months from her own life? Would she do it? In a heartbeat, she decided. In a heartbeat.

However, it was far more likely to be by unhappy accident that this volume had ended up in the donation box. Well, unhappy for the owner, perhaps, but happy for her.

The diary was A5 in size and the cover was printed with tiny orange daisies, bright and cheerful-looking, and each with a yellow dot at its centre. Pip ran the pad of her finger over the embossed 1983 and tussled with the ethics of what she was about to do, concluding yet again that the contents of the diary couldn't be that private if its owner had given it away.

In her heart, though, she knew this wasn't right. No one would give away a diary on purpose. If you didn't want it, then you'd destroy it somehow. The fact that this one had ended up in a box of books in a charity shop could only mean it was there by mistake. But, she reasoned, it was a mistake she might be able to rectify if she just read a little of its contents to see if she could identify the author. As ethical arguments went, this was thin at best, but what did it really matter? This wasn't a court of law.

Satisfied, after a fashion, with her ragged logic, Pip lifted the cover. And there was the answer to her question on the very first page. Alongside the printed words, 'This diary belongs to . . .' was written in neat block capitals EVELYN MOUNTCASTLE.

Pip's heart sank. That was it then. Mission accomplished. It belonged to one Evelyn Mountcastle and she had discovered this without having to read a single private word. Now all she had to do was discover the whereabouts of the owner and return it. Job done.

But that was no good. Pip was ready for an exploration of someone else's world just for a little while, for a heathy dollop of escapism. Didn't she deserve that, at least? Her own life was broken, possibly beyond repair. Surely someone up there should be cutting her some slack.

She shelved her carefully nurtured integrity and turned the page.

The writer's expansive, cursive handwriting flowed over the creamy paper, gushing forth like water from a spring, all bubbles and effervescence. Even without reading the words, Pip could see the enthusiasm with which they had been written by the short, punchy sentences, the frequency of exclamation marks. There weren't bubbles over the 'i's but there might as well have been.

You could tell a lot from someone's handwriting, Pip knew, and this suggested a person with a zest for life, a natural exuberance. Pip's own writing was neat and easy to read, but also rather boring.

As a girl she had longed for a more distinctive style, even trying out various options with a view to switching to something with a little more personality, only for her writing to slip back to type whenever she stopped thinking about enhancing it.

But this was totally different, and from her handwriting alone, Evelyn Mountcastle looked like someone that Pip might like. She tried to calculate how old Evelyn might be now, but without any details of her life it was hard to work it out. Pip's analytical mind began whirring. In the entries she had already read, Evelyn had a daughter, Scarlet, who seemed to be very young. So, say Evelyn had been thirty in 1983, she would be somewhere in her sixties now. That meant that there was a good chance she was still alive. The books and diary could have surfaced through a house clearance after her death, but it seemed unlikely.

Pip took a deep breath and then made a conscious decision to begin reading.

January 1st 1983

Happy birthday me!

In my life before Scarlet (B.S. if you will), I would probably have been at some sensational party as the clock struck midnight and time slipped me into my birthday. I'd most probably have been leaping about, making sure everyone knew that it was now me and not the turn of the year that required their attention. Honestly, I can barely remember those carefree days now. They feel like they happened to someone else, and in a different lifetime.

As 1983 began, I was tucked up in bed rather than celebrating at a party (although I wasn't asleep – I do still have some vestiges of fun left in me and the turning of the year is something that should be marked, no matter how quietly). There was a party going on down the street somewhere and I could hear the revellers as they barrelled past the house on their way home. I also heard Joan open her window and bellow at them to be quiet because decent people were trying to sleep. Ironically, Joan probably woke more people with her caterwauling than the revellers had done. Now there's a woman who doesn't understand the concept of fun!

And then, a few short, sweet hours later I was woken by Scarlet who snuck into my room and my bed, pushing her cold little feet against my warm ones. She'd even remembered that it was my birthday, which is very impressive for a three-year-old. But then she is a very impressive child.

So, there is no better time than the start of the year to take stock of where you are and where you want to be. I am here and I don't want to be! Well, that was easy. Not so easy is the task of changing things, but I'm going to make it my mission for 1983 to get back on track. Scarlet will start at school next year, but there will be playgroup before that so I should start to get a few precious hours to myself. I might even be able to get some kind of job, so I wouldn't have to be beholden to Joan for absolutely everything. She makes it so obvious that she begrudges every penny she has to spend on me and Scarlet. But if I can work when Scarlet starts playgroup, then at least I could contribute a little, or even get some savings behind me ready for my escape!

When we move back to London, Ted says it will be easy to find someone to have Scarlet after school. So I'll be able to go back to work properly. I am literally counting down the days . . .

By the time she heard her father's Land Rover driving into the yard, Pip had reached the end of February 1983. From what she could gather, Evelyn Mountcastle lived a very small life with her daughter Scarlet and her sister, Joan. She seemed to have been in Southwold, which made sense given that the diaries had shown up at the shop. There were a couple of references to places that Pip could remember from her own childhood, although she hadn't found anything specific enough to pinpoint where their house was.

She reached for her phone and googled 'Evelyn Mountcastle actress', but there was very little there, just a listing for a part in some seventies drama called *Upstairs Downstairs*, but all it gave was her name and date of birth, and confirmed that she had been born in Southwold, Suffolk. There was no photograph.

If Evelyn was from Southwold, though, then surely someone would know something about her, perhaps even her own mother. Southwold wasn't a very big place and her parents had lived there all their lives. Quickly, she pulled on some jeans and a sweatshirt and went downstairs to join the others for breakfast.

Her father and Jez, having already done a couple of hours on the farm, were seated at the table, and her mother, polka-dot apron tied tightly round her waist, was serving sizzling strips of bacon on to buttered muffins. Jez looked up when Pip walked in and gave her a tentative smile. Her father eyed her quizzically, which Pip found disconcerting until she remembered that he would know about the drama with Dominic and would be worried about her state of mind.

'Morning Pip, love,' he said. 'How are you?'

She could hear the concern in his voice but knew he would never ask her outright about the state of her love life. That kind of talk was definitely reserved for the women of the household.

She gave him her best smile. 'I'm fine, thanks, Dad.'

He held her gaze for a second or two longer, as if trying to satisfy himself that she was telling the truth, and then returned his attention to his breakfast.

Pip lifted the teapot and pressed the flat of her hand to the china to test the temperature.

'Would you like some bacon?' her mother asked, but Pip shook her head. She had lost her appetite for huge farmhouse breakfasts. In London, fruit, yoghurt and granola, or smashed avocado, were more the order of the day. Or just coffee. God, she missed coffee.

She wanted to ask her mother about Evelyn as casually as she could and without referring to the purloined diary. It felt like her secret and she didn't want to share it if she didn't have to.

'Oh Mum, I meant to ask,' she began as lightly as she could, 'do you know someone called Evelyn Mountcastle?'

Her mother pursed her lips and furrowed her brow as she searched her mind for the name. 'Evelyn Mountcastle,' she repeated, but then she shook her head. 'Can't say I do? Why? Who is she?'

'Oh, no one,' replied Pip a little too quickly. 'I just overheard something in the shop, that was all, and I wondered if you knew her.'

'Sorry, love. Do you know an Evelyn Mountcastle, Roy?' her mother asked her father, but he too shook his head.

'Never mind,' said Pip. 'It's nothing important. I was just curious.'

Disappointment seeped into Pip's fragile good mood. It had been a long shot that her parents might know something about Evelyn, but not out of the way impossible. It seemed, though, that in this as in so many other things recently, she was to be unlucky.

Maybe Audrey would know her. Pip might even recognise her herself, if she was a regular in the shop. She would do some careful sniffing around at work and see what she could unearth.

Jez swallowed his mouthful of bacon, took a slurp of tea and wiped his mouth with the back of his hand. 'I know Miss Mountcastle,' he said, without looking up from his plate. 'Mum used to clean for her. Well, not her but the other Miss Mountcastle. Her sister. She lives on the seafront in one of those big houses that looks out on the prom. Or at least she used to. Mum's not worked there for donkey's years. But I remember her because she was a right cow. Not Evelyn. The other one.' Then he took another bite of his muffin, rendering further conversation inadvisable.

The other Miss Mountcastle must have been the Joan from the diary, Pip thought, excited that she was starting to piece things together.

'But you don't know if she's still living there?' she asked, ignoring her mother's curious expression, but Jez just shrugged and shook his head.

'And how did you say you knew her, Pip?' her mother asked.

Pip needed to backtrack fast. The last thing she needed was her mother getting involved. This was her adventure.

'Oh, I don't,' she replied breezily. 'I just heard her name, that was all.'

She tried to feign insouciance. She could tell from the way her mother had stopped washing the dishes at the sink that she wasn't convinced by her explanation, but it would have to do.

Taking a piece of toast from the toast rack, Pip began buttering it with measured concentration. Then her father started talking about the wheat crop, and the conversation moved away from Evelyn Mountcastle.

16

Monday rolled round again. Pip had spent most of her weekend engrossed in Evelyn's world and was slightly resentful that she had to break off to go to work. When her mother had first made the arrangement for her to help Audrey out, it hadn't been anyone's intention that it would be a full-time position, just a little something to get her away from the farm, to help with her rehabilitation, but over the weeks Pip had just started to turn up at the shop every day and no one seemed to object. If she didn't make her way there each morning then she would be stuck with nothing but the contents of her own mind for company, and that wasn't a healthy place for her to be.

Of course, she was fully aware that by failing to face the darkness in her head she was simply prolonging the time that it would take for her to recover, but that was the best she could manage at the moment. The thing with Dominic was a classic example. He had been her partner for well over two years before the accident. She had moved into his swanky flat, learned to like his friends and share his extravagant taste in cashmere jumpers and silk handkerchiefs. His life had become her life, and she had even dared to think that they might have a long future together.

And now he was gone, evaporated from her world like the steam from his Gaggia coffee machine, and she had barely wept a single tear. She was astute enough to understand that her lack of reaction was not a reflection of how upset she was about the break-up, but more to do with her overall state of mind. She had become an emotional wasteland. Nothing seemed to touch her any more, nothing could pierce the carapace that she had enclosed herself in because no emotional hurt could be as terrible or as devastating as the one she was already dealing with. Or not dealing with.

When she did allow herself to think about the accident, gingerly, tentatively, like a tongue touching a mouth ulcer, it felt as if she would never get back to the way she had been before. She hadn't had a full-blown panic attack for a month now, so that had to be a good sign, but flashbacks still haunted her. A blast on a car horn, the screech of tyres on tarmac, the wailing call of a siren could all trigger her fear. Other things made her heart race, too: a car pulling out from a side road, pedestrians standing too close to the pavement's edge as they waited for a gap in the traffic to cross the road. Any one of these was enough to prompt a vivid rerun of the accident in her mind's eye.

And then there were the children. Even though she no longer drove a car and was unlikely to do much harm with her bicycle, just seeing children near the road was enough to make the whole terrible incident as raw and real as it had been on day one. Women who carelessly pushed their buggies out in front of them as they tried to nip between the cars, boys with footballs or skateboards or anything that might put them in harm's way. She wanted to scream at them, to warn them of the perils they faced in showing such wanton disregard for their own safety. Pip hated headphones and ice cream vans and gangs of teenagers and other bicycles – basically anything that might distract a child and cause them to run out into the road and under the wheels of a passing car, just as the boy had done to her. She felt that she needed to save their lives because she couldn't save his. And whilst technically, morally and legally Pip might be blameless, of course she wasn't really. She had killed a child. It had been her. No one else. And it was something she would carry with her every day. Forever.

The only solution she had found was to keep herself busy. And at the moment, being busy meant going to the shop.

When she arrived that morning, the front door was already wide open and business was, if not brisk, then at least under way. A woman with hair an unlikely shade of auburn was stalking through the rails of clothes like a wildcat, searching for anything new, and another couple of women were rummaging through everything with careless fingers, chatting to one another as they moved. Until she had begun working in a charity shop, Pip had had no inkling of how many people made a quick flick through the rails a regular part of their days. In fact, she didn't even know where there were charity shops in her part of London. Working here was proving to be a very edifying and humbling experience.

Pip hung her coat up and went to tell Audrey that she had arrived. She found her at the till, chatting to a customer as she folded her purchases, popped them into reused plastic bags and then took the few coins that the shop charged. Not wanting to interrupt, Pip busied herself straightening the books. She knew better than to stand still doing nothing on Audrey's watch.

Once Audrey was free, Pip sidled over to her.

'Morning,' she began. 'How did the bring-and-buy sale go?'

Audrey gave a little toss of her head, a knowing smile flickering across her lips, and Pip knew at once that not only had the sale been a success, but that Audrey was sure all credit for this should go to her.

'Very well indeed,' she said proudly. 'Another heathy chunk of money towards the church roof fund. And how about you? Did you have a nice weekend?'

Pip's thoughts skipped to Dominic, to his face as he told her was leaving, but she closed the images down as soon as they popped up.

'Pretty quiet,' she said. Her mind raced as she tried to think how to get the information she wanted without arousing any awkward cross-questioning, but in the end she just said, 'Audrey, do you happen to know someone called Evelyn Mountcastle?'

Audrey was rearranging a selection of notelets, moving the less popular designs to the front of the stand. 'Evelyn Mountcastle, the actress?' she asked, without looking up. 'Not to speak to, although I'd recognise her if I saw her in the street. Not that you're likely to see her in the street.'

There was so much tantalising information in this reply that for a moment Pip was thrown off course as she decided which part to chase first.

'I didn't know she was an actress,' she began, although of course she did.

'Oh, yes,' replied Audrey, drawing out the syllables and thus revealing that there was a story to tell. 'Quite well known in the seventies, I gather. But there was a scandal of some sort and she came back to Southwold and then . . . Well, it was so tragic.' Audrey shook her head mournfully.

'What happened?' asked Pip, trying not to sound like a rubbernecker, but desperate to know all the same.

'That house was full of misfortune,' Audrey continued. 'It's no wonder she went a little doolally. I mean, you would, wouldn't you? Send anyone a bit mad, something like that.'

Something like what? Pip was bursting to ask, but then a customer called over from the back of the shop needing some help with a zip and Audrey bustled off, leaving Pip with half a story.

As the day wore on, Pip tried to create opportunities to ask Audrey more about Evelyn Mountcastle, but without success. She was reluctant to just come straight out with her questions in case she somehow gave away that she had taken the diary, which she knew Audrey would take a very dim view of.

On the other hand, Pip thought as she sorted clothes into piles, Audrey seemed to know everything about everybody in the town. And if she didn't know, she made it her business to find out. Pip might do better not to delve any deeper with the inquisitive Audrey, instead she should try to find the information she wanted from another, less curious, source.

She immediately thought of Jez. He clearly knew a little about the family, and Pip was pretty sure he wouldn't care why she wanted to know. Plus, it would give her the chance to spend some time with him. After their encounter in the kitchen, she thought she might be ready for that, enjoy it even.

As the day drew to a close, Pip decided that she would spend the evening in her bedroom with the diary. She wasn't really up to sitting with her parents. They would ask how she was after Dominic's departure and she didn't want to get into that.

When she arrived in the kitchen for dinner later that evening, though, there was something in the air. Her parents exchanged glances as they sat down, and Pip knew at once there was something they wanted to say.

She didn't have to wait long.

'Your dad and I have been talking,' her mother began as she served the fish pie on to three plates.

'Oh yes?' replied Pip shortly, without looking up.

'Well . . .' her mother continued doubtfully.

She paused, and a heavy silence hung over the table. Pip waited for her to spit whatever it was out. She hated the fact that they must have been talking about her when she wasn't there, hated that there was anything to talk about.

'It's just,' her mother tried again. 'We were thinking that, maybe . . .' Her mother's eyes found Pip's father's, and she gave him an imploring look.

He seemed to take the hint and picked up the baton. 'What your mum's trying to say is that we were wondering whether now would be a good time to have a bit of a chat about your plans. For the future,' he clarified.

What plans? Pip had no immediate plans, other than to retreat to her room and read the diary.

'It's just that with . . . Well, with everything that happened at the weekend, we thought maybe we should go down and collect your things, bring them back home. Obviously you could move back to London, if you wanted to, eventually.'

'Of course I'm moving back to London,' Pip snapped. 'I can't stay here.'

Her words came out more harshly than they ought to have done, and Pip saw hurt cut across her mother's face.

'No, no. Of course you can't,' her mother agreed, pivoting on the spot and following Pip's lead. 'We know that. But just for now, just whilst you're getting better.'

'We don't want you having the stress of finding a new flat, not at the moment,' her father added. 'How about me and Jez go down in the van, collect your bits and pieces and bring it all back here for now?'

'It's not fair to leave all your things with poor Dominic,' her mother said.

Pip pressed her lips together to stop herself from screaming at them. Poor Dominic? Poor Dominic! Would this be the same Dominic who had kicked her when she was at her lowest ebb, who had abandoned her without a second thought for all her hopes and dreams?

But what would be the point of exploding at her parents? They were trying to do what they thought was best for her, and she was going to have to retrieve her belongings sooner or later. It might be less painful if her father did it for her.

So she swallowed hard and said, 'That would be great, Dad. Thanks.' Then she put her knife and fork down and got to her feet. 'I'm afraid I haven't got much of an appetite. I think I'll go upstairs for a bit of a lie-down,' she said quietly. 'Thanks for dinner, Mum.'

She could hear her parents' concerned whispering as she left the kitchen and headed up the stairs to her cramped little room.

Her father had said that he was going to bring her things 'home'. He had meant nothing by it. Home was just the farm, where he had lived all his life. A safe haven, a port in a storm, the centre of his world. But for Pip the word was spring-loaded like a mouse trap. She had spent years ensuring that she could leave, working hard to earn her ticket out. And now, now they were going to suck her back to the very place she'd been trying to escape. It was like the pull of a whirlpool, and swim as hard as she could, she couldn't seem to get out of it and back to safety. And not only that – they saw it as a good thing, that they were doing her a favour by bringing her 'home'.

If Pip could have cried, then she would have done.

17

Pip retrieved the 1983 diary from its hiding place between a couple of other books on her shelves, sat back on her bed and began to read.

Evelyn seemed to live a quiet life, not dissimilar to hers in fact, although where Pip's days had been curtailed by the accident and what had happened since, it seemed that Evelyn's world had been shrunk by the presence of her child. It felt a little as if Evelyn was too big for the space she was occupying, as if there were more of her than there was room for in the house with Joan. And yet Pip had the impression that her spirit was being slowly crushed with each day that passed.

The diary seemed to have three themes – how much Evelyn loved Scarlet, how much she hated Joan and how unfair her life's events had been, although Pip was struggling to work out exactly what had happened. It was something to do with why she'd left London and the fact that she was an unmarried mother. There was very little mention of her former life as an actress, but Pip could feel Evelyn's sense of claustrophobia, her urgency to get herself and her daughter back to where she felt they belonged, together with her frustration at not being able to do so. There was also a sense, though, of making the most of the situation. Yes, Evelyn Mountcastle was unhappy at being trapped in the house with her sister, but she was still managing to find joy in little moments spent with her daughter.

The contrast with how Pip was adapting to the changes in her own life made her feel ashamed. Until now, she had spent most of her time either drilling down deep inside herself to examine her own misery, or worrying about how much longer she would have to stay where she was.

Now, though, she thought she might be starting to reconnect with her surroundings. Just that morning, she had heard a cuckoo calling from the copse behind the farm. It had been years since she had heard a cuckoo, and its distinctive cry had cut through the noise in her head so that she'd stopped what she was doing and just listened. Was it the very first time it had called that spring, she wondered, or was it merely the first time she had heard it? Either way, it felt like a step forward.

Evelyn seemed much more aware of the simple pleasures in life, and it was the tiny moments of happiness that Pip enjoyed reading about the most. The diary was full of notes about the things Scarlet had said and done, and Evelyn's obvious delight in them. They made life seem so straightforward in a way that Pip had forgotten was possible. She wasn't sure her own life had ever been as simple as that, although it surely must have been once.

Thursday 31st March

Today S and I went puddle-jumping. She wore the darling little wellington boots and I gave her my umbrella to carry, although it was far too big for her and she couldn't get the hang of holding it upright at all. I suggested that we might want to float it upside down and ride in it like Winnie-the-Pooh did, but S just stared at me as if I was

*the stupidest person on the planet. She planted her little
wellingtoned feet in the puddle, put her hands on her hips
and looked up at me, shaking her head.*

*'You are silly, Mummy. The umbrella is far too weak to
hold us. We'd sink.'*

*It was all I could do not to laugh at her sweetness. But
I didn't. I kept a straight face and told her that she was
very wise and I was indeed very silly. Bless her. I could
just eat her up.*

It couldn't have been easy to be a single mother in 1983. Pip
hadn't even been born until 1989, but she instinctively felt that
the stigma Evelyn faced, particularly in a small, conservative
town, would have been challenging. There was something about
the way Evelyn described their days that made it sound like it
was her and Scarlet against the world. What was also crystal clear
was that Evelyn's sister Joan didn't approve of the situation, or of
anything about Evelyn's life. There were rarely any kind words for
her in the diary.

Wednesday May 11th

*I sometimes wonder what J is thinking. I know she's sup-
porting S and me for now, and I'm grateful for that, but
has she forgotten that this house belongs to all three of us?
She's got no more right to it than Peter and me, and just
because I left and she chose to stay doesn't mean that she
suddenly gained any extra entitlement. But she manages
to make me feel beholden to her every day. It's like she sees*

me as a second-class citizen who she only tolerates in the house because of her own magnanimity and not because we are flesh and blood. S is her niece, for God's sake, but there's no affection for her, no kindness for either of us, in fact.

And she holds the purse strings so tightly it's like she actually wants me to suffer. Yesterday I asked her for some money so that I could buy some sandals for S. She can hardly wear her wellingtons all summer and anyway, she is growing so fast that I doubt they will still fit her by the autumn. But the fuss Joan made. You'd have thought I'd asked her for the Crown Jewels and not a few pounds to buy my child some shoes. She made me feel like I had to beg. My own sister. Sometimes I hate her.

But there's nothing to be gained from making life more difficult than it already is, so I bit my tongue and in the end she gave me the money, all deep sighs and eye-rolling, mind you, just so I knew how grateful I was supposed to be. So S and I went to the shoe shop. I let her choose for herself and she picked out the dearest little pair in red with tiny flowers punched out of the leather. If they'd done them in bigger sizes, I'd have bought some, too – not that I had the money, of course. And then on the way home we went for an ice cream with raspberry sauce, which we ate as we walked on the prom, and we chased seagulls, and then we ran into the sea and got our dresses wet. The water was perishing and our legs went blue, but we didn't care. I want to make the most

of the sea whilst we're here. When we go back to London
it won't be so easy.

But they had never made it to London. Audrey had told Pip that Evelyn was still here. For all her talk of moving back with Scarlet and picking up her acting career again, she seemed to have become trapped in Southwold. Scarlet would be nearly forty by now. Pip hoped that she, at least, had spread her wings.

18

Having decided that she'd like to chat to Jez, Pip managed to catch him after breakfast the next day.

'Hi there,' she began. It felt a bit forced, but she had to start somewhere.

'Hi,' he replied. His tone wasn't unfriendly, but neither was it warm.

'Look, I'm really sorry I've not spoken to you since I've been back,' Pip said. 'It's been a bit . . . Well, you know. But I am sorry. I should have made a bigger effort.'

Jez's expression said, 'You're only just working this out now?' but his lips remained sealed. It seemed he wasn't going to make it easy for her.

'Anyway,' she continued, 'I was wondering if you fancied going out for a drink, for old times' sake. A bit of a catch-up. You know . . .'

In the face of no response, Pip tailed off a little. Had she misjudged things? Maybe his girlfriend was the possessive kind who wouldn't take kindly to him going out for a drink with an old flame, even if their relationship had been almost a lifetime ago. Or perhaps, more worryingly, there had been too much water under the bridge since they were teenagers, and he wasn't interested in spending any time with the person she had become in the intervening years. Pip really hoped it wasn't that.

He looked up, his eyes finding hers and transporting her straight back to her childhood in an instant. He hadn't changed a bit, she thought, whereas she had done nothing but change.

Then he grinned at her. 'Go on then,' he said, 'seeing as you asked so nicely. For old times' sake, was that it? And also so I can tell you everything I know about old Miss Mountcastle.' He raised an eyebrow as he spoke, and she knew he'd seen straight through her – of course he had. He knew her, or at least had known her, far too well for her to get away with a trick like that.

Pip felt her cheeks glow and she rolled her eyes. 'You got me,' she replied, giving him half a smile. 'But it would be nice to have a catch-up too. Where do people drink these days?'

'How about the Nag's Head? Seven thirty suit?'

Pip nodded gratefully. 'That'd be great,' she said.

◆ ◆ ◆

Pip spent most of the day daydreaming about what she should wear. It most definitely wasn't a date with Jez – he had a girlfriend, and there was the whole thing with Dominic, still so new and raw – but she still wanted to look nice. Her lacklustre appearance had been pretty much the last thing on her mind recently and she had hidden herself away in jeans and baggy jumpers, but at the thought of seeing Jez it felt like a switch was flicked in her. She wasn't sure she knew quite what she was feeling, feelings of any kind being so rare, but she wondered if it might be pride that made her want to look her best for him, or maybe something else more essential, a part of herself that she had lost sight of but was perhaps now flickering back into life.

But set against that was the idea that she didn't deserve to look nice or enjoy herself, considering what she had done. How could she contemplate getting dressed up when the mother of the boy she had killed would probably never care about her appearance again?

In the end, she settled for jeans and a crisp white shirt. It was a neutral choice, neither particularly stylish nor broadcasting that she was making an effort, and in any event, it was unlikely that Jez would even notice.

Not wanting to draw her parents' attention to her movements, she had intended to sneak out, leaving a note on the kitchen table as to her whereabouts but, with an unsurprising second sense, her mother appeared in the kitchen just as she was putting on her jacket.

'Going out, love?' she asked, her expression a mixture of curiosity and delight.

'Just for a quick drink,' replied Pip, hoping against hope that this would be an end to the questions but knowing that it wouldn't be.

'That's nice. Who with?'

It was like going two rounds with the Gestapo sometimes. Pip knew it was perfectly reasonable for her mother to wonder where she was going, particularly when she had so rarely left the farm in the evening since her arrival, but constantly having to account for her movements made her feel claustrophobic and she resented the intrusion. She was tempted to lie, but that would only backfire on her. Better to be honest and ignore the raised eyebrows.

'Just Jez,' she said without meeting her mother's enquiring gaze.

'Oh,' replied her mother simply, but Pip could hear the pleasure oozing from the single syllable. Her parents had always thought she'd have been better marrying a nice local boy instead of running off to London, and to be fair, it was starting to look like they might have been right.

'Not sure what time I'll be back,' she added. 'Don't wait up.'

It was a deliberatively provocative parting comment. She knew she'd be home long before they went to bed, but she was irritated by her mother's trespassing into her privacy. She strode out of the kitchen without looking back, letting the door bang behind her.

'How will you get home?' she heard her mother call after her.

Damn. She hadn't thought about that. In the past, she would just have hopped in her car, but obviously that wasn't an option. The car had sat in the yard untouched since her father had recovered it from the police. Even if she were up to driving it, the battery would probably be flat by now.

'I can get your dad to run you down,' her mother continued. 'And pick you up.'

It was like being a child. No privacy, and now no independence, either.

'No, thanks. I'll go on my bike,' Pip shouted back, though every part of her wanted to accept a lift.

'Well, be careful on those roads,' her mother added quite unnecessarily, as if Pip could be anything else these days.

The pub was quiet. The tourist season hadn't quite got underway and the clientele looked local. Jez was already there, chatting to the barman, pint in hand. As she walked in, they both looked over in her direction. Jez winked at her and Pip felt sixteen again.

'You remember Pip, don't you, Will?'

Will nodded. 'Hi,' he said.

There were no questions about what she was doing back or how she had been, and Pip had the feeling that she had been the subject of discussion before her arrival. She smiled a hello, ordered a drink and gestured to a table far away from the bar where Will wouldn't be able to overhear their conversation. It wasn't that she had anything to hide, but she objected to having her business discussed any more than it already was. In London nobody gave you a second glance. Here it was almost impossible to pass unnoticed.

'So,' said Jez when they were sitting at the table opposite one another. 'Long time no contact. Of any sort.'

He placed a heavy emphasis on his barbed words, but his tone seemed jocular enough. Pip searched his face for clues as to how his mind was working. It was true that she had barely said more than a handful of words to him since she'd left for university. She could have replied that they had just gone in different directions, but she knew it had been more of a concerted effort on her own part to separate them. Jez, like so many other things in her old life, just hadn't fitted with her new environment, didn't slot neatly into the amended version of herself. Did he know that? Looking at him now, Pip was horribly sure that he did.

'I know. I'm sorry,' she said, deciding in that moment to go for raw honesty. 'I have no excuse. I went to London, got ideas above my station, came a cropper, and now I'm back with my tail between my legs.'

It felt so incredibly wrong to dismiss what she had done in these terms, but making light of it was generally the best way to prevent the conversation going in a direction that she wasn't ready for.

Jez, however, appeared to be having none of her diversionary tactics. 'I'm sorry about the accident,' he said. 'It's crap and I have no idea how you're coping with it. It must be hell.'

That was the closest anyone had come to summing up how things really were.

'Thanks,' she said.

'And what's it like being back?' he asked.

'Honestly?' she asked. 'It's shit.'

He raised an eyebrow as if to say, 'Thanks very much,' and so she added, 'No offence. Mum and Dad don't know what to do, so they have decided to treat me as if I'm five. My hard-won stellar career is disintegrating with every week that goes by, and now the love of my life has decided that I'm not worth waiting for. And that's on top of . . .' She took a deep breath. 'Well, that's all on top of everything else I'm dealing with. So yes, it's all pretty bad.'

There was a pause whilst Jez allowed what she had just said to settle on the table between them like dust from an explosion.

'Could be worse,' he said. 'You could be dead.'

She might have replied that that would be preferable, but she knew he wouldn't stand for any self-pity on her part, so instead she just nodded weakly.

'So, what are you going to do?' he asked her. 'How are you going to fix it?'

The baldness of his question surprised her. In the whole time since the accident nobody, not even Dominic, had spoken to her so directly. Everyone else had pussyfooted around, talking in euphemisms and half-finished sentences as if, by not actually discussing the facts, they would somehow evaporate of their own accord. But Jez had known her forever. They had shared their first cigarette, their first stolen can of cider, their first kiss, and other firsts that she held close to her heart. And with that level of intimacy came the privilege of being able to cut out all the white noise and go straight to the pure ringing note at the situation's heart.

'I haven't got a clue,' she replied. 'I have to get the flashbacks and the panics under control first. Then I can go home and get back to work, but I don't know how long that will take. Plus, just to put a cherry on the top of the whole stinking pie, I'm now officially homeless because my ex-boyfriend has kicked me out of my flat. Technically his flat, to be fair, but still.'

Pip was surprised at how refreshing it was to express out loud what she was really thinking, instead of having to sugar-coat everything. When she spoke to her parents, she gilded every word. They were worried enough as it was, without her adding to their concerns by being overly candid.

'Are they bad, the panics?' Jez asked. He was looking directly at her, as if he were trying to judge the truth of her answer by what her eyes told him.

'Bad enough,' she said. 'It's the unpredictability that makes it so hard. I can go days and days without anything and then, bam, I'm right back where I started.'

Jez nodded as if he understood exactly. 'My mate was in Iraq. He's the same. It doesn't matter what we say to him, about how it was a war, and that he was there to do a job, that shit happens. He just can't deal with the guilt. They say it just takes time. Not sure how helpful that is, though.'

She shrugged, but then suddenly she didn't want to think about herself and her problems any more.

'Less of my doom and gloom,' she said, trying to raise her face into a smile. 'How about you? What have you been up to?'

'Not nearly as much as you!' he replied wryly. 'I'm working on the farm, obviously. I love it, working outside. I thought for a bit that I should have gone to uni like everyone else, but I don't think that now. And I'm as good as hitched.'

Waves of something that might have been jealousy washed over Pip. She didn't want Jez or the life that he could offer, but the thought that he didn't want her either snapped at her heart like a terrier.

'Do I know her?' she asked, although she really hoped that she didn't.

Jez shook his head. 'Teresa? I don't think so. She manages one of the big hotels in town. She's from Ipswich originally.'

'And have you set a date?' Pip asked lightly, hoping that her expression wasn't giving away her odd sense of disappointment.

'No. We keep putting it off. We can't agree on what we want. She wants a huge do. Top hats and all that. I'd rather something a bit less flash. Your dad said we could have a marquee at the farm, which was decent of him, but Teresa wants a hotel.' He shrugged. 'I'm sure we'll get there in the end.'

'I'm sure you will,' Pip replied, closing the subject down. She didn't want to hear about Jez and his happiness any more than she had to. 'So, tell me everything you know about the Mountcastles,' she said.

Jez narrowed his eyes, scrutinising her steadily. 'Are you going to tell me why you want to know?'

'Nope,' she said.

He tutted. 'You always did like to be mysterious,' he said. 'Well, I don't know much more than I told you the other day. There were two of them, sisters. They lived together in a house on the prom. Mum used to clean for them. Then one of them died, took a fall apparently. I'm not sure which one, but the rumour was that one of them had pushed the other down the stairs. Then the one that wasn't dead sacked Mum. Accused her of nicking something when she hadn't. Or maybe that happened the other way around. I'm not sure. It was years ago, long before we were even born, but Mum's still going on about it now. She said that even though everyone knew that she'd never steal, it still left a stain on her reputation. Every time we went past the house, she'd start up again about how unfair it all was.'

'Can you remember which house?' Pip asked hopefully.

'Of course I can. I still can't walk past without spitting on the door.' Pip's jaw dropped, but Jez's face cracked into a grin again. 'Not literally. But Jack and I did used to spit at the house when we were lads. We made sure no one saw, though. We reckoned if the woman was a murderer, then we'd better not let her catch us.' Pip began laughing at him and Jez, playing to his audience, continued. 'We used to make up stories about her being a witch. Stupid really. I'm sure the woman did no wrong. I mean, if she really had killed her sister, then the police would have arrested her and she'd have gone down for it.'

'And you don't know which one died?' Pip asked.

Jez shook his head.

'But the other one is still there, in the house?'

'As far as I know. The place doesn't look any different.'

Something was ringing a bell in the very depths of Pip's memory. 'I think I remember something about a witch,' she said vaguely. 'God, kids can be horrible. It's just like Boo Radley.'

Jez looked at her blankly.

'You know. In *To Kill a Mocking Bird*? We did it at school? Oh, never mind.'

'Did you hear that Jack's a trader in the City now?' he said. 'Worth a fortune.'

'I always liked Jack,' Pip mused, a little smile playing on her lips.

'No, you didn't,' snapped Jez. 'He might be my brother, but he's always been a dick.'

Pip shrugged. 'Yes, okay,' she said. 'I'll give you that.'

As Pip cleaned her teeth later that night she thought about Jez. She'd forgotten what easy company he was. For the first time in as long as she could remember she had felt like herself, had almost forgotten everything, just for an hour or two. And he was getting married. That was another opportunity missed, another boat sailed off into the sunset without her. Even though it wasn't going anywhere that she wanted to go, she couldn't help but wonder.

19

1979

Evelyn lay in the bath. The water was getting cold now and the last of the bubbles had long since fizzed and burst. It was so quiet without Brenda in the flat. Even though they hadn't spent that much time together, Evelyn liked hearing someone else moving around the place. The landlord had said she could continue to pay only her share for the time being and she had assumed that he would fill the vacant room, but so far, she had been left very much alone.

She really needed someone to talk to. She had almost come clean to Ted the day before, but something had pulled her up short. Even though he had been such a good friend to her and she could make a fair guess at how he would react, she didn't know for sure, and she couldn't risk losing him. Ted was about the only person she had left, apart from Julian, and she definitely wasn't going to tell him. Not until she had decided what to do.

Evelyn ran her fingers over her stomach. She thought she could feel it changing shape already, a small dome forming where there had been none before; it was rounder, fecund. The clothes at her costume call today had felt tighter than they ought to have done. Of course, no one had noticed. No one knew her and so they wouldn't have spotted a couple of extra pounds that hadn't been there when she auditioned.

She could fix it, go back to the way things were before with a simple appointment. It wasn't illegal any more. She wouldn't have to seek out some dirty backstreet clinic. This was the 1970s. It was her right as a woman to choose what she did with her own body. Evelyn contemplated the irony of this, considering how she had got into this mess in the first place.

She assumed that her situation would work in her favour when it came to persuading a doctor she was in need of help. She was unmarried, without a boyfriend or even any relationship with the father of her child, and no steady income. Anyone could see that she wasn't best placed to bring a child into the world. She could just take herself off, get it sorted, and no one need ever know.

But she would know. She would know, and that knowledge would eat away at her for the rest of her life. Children had always been in her future. There had never been a time when she hadn't assumed she would have some one day, and she couldn't imagine herself growing old without children around her. And somewhere deep inside her, she knew she would make a wonderful mother – she had learned enough about how to be a terrible one from her own.

The trouble was, she hadn't imagined it would happen just yet. She had no husband, wasn't even close to getting married, and more importantly, she had just landed the job of her dreams, which would open up a whole world of possibilities. Evelyn Mountcastle was on the cusp of everything she had ever wanted for her career. Surely, that ought to make her decision an easy one. And yet . . .

She stood up and shivered as she reached for a towel. The bump was more obvious when she was upright. She looked down and marvelled at it, the way it proclaimed the existence of new life, impossible to ignore.

But her timing couldn't have been worse. This was precisely the wrong moment to be pregnant. Julian would kill her for a start, his big fat agent's fee going up in smoke when they had to recast her role. There was no way the production company would wait for her to have the baby, and in the meantime her dream job would be gone. But if she hung on to the part, then she would lose the baby. She was no spring chicken – thirty already. In fact, this might be it. The egg that was busy dividing inside her right now could be her only chance to be a mother.

As she got dressed, she thought it through for the hundredth time: the logistics of how she could make it work. She would have to go back to Suffolk. With no job and no savings behind her, she couldn't afford to live on her own in London. She'd need to speak to Joan and demand her share of their parents' inheritance. Until now she had shown no interest in it. She'd been so determined to be independent and make her own way in the world that to make Joan sell the house and release her share would have looked like a failure, and there had been no way she would give her sister the satisfaction of that.

But a baby would change everything. She couldn't afford to be independent when there weren't just her own needs to consider. Puritanical Joan would be horrified, but she wouldn't kick her out on the street, and even if she wanted to, Peter wouldn't let her. She would make Evelyn's life hell, though. There would be all the snide comments about having to come home – and come home in disgrace to boot. There was no way Joan wouldn't make the very most of any opportunity to make Evelyn look small and cheap, but that was just the price she would have to pay if she decided to keep the baby.

It wouldn't be forever, though. When the child started school, Evelyn would be able to go back to work. That was what modern women did, wasn't it? Women like Detective Constable Karen

Walker. Evelyn would only lose four years of her career, five at the most, and she would emerge at the end of that time with a beautiful child and a whole host of new life experiences on which to draw for her acting. Sacrificing the role in *Into the Blue* would be a very, very great shame, but it would be worth it in the long run.

As she brushed her hair, Evelyn realised she had made her decision. It wasn't a surprise. If she was honest with herself, she had known all along that she wouldn't be able to let the baby go. She would never tell a living soul who the father was, though. She had her reputation to think of, and she definitely didn't want him to find out. Her baby was nothing to do with him. She had been so very naive, but she had learned her lesson and she would never let anything like that happen again. If there was ever a next time, she would walk into it with her eyes wide open.

So now all she had to do was . . . Evelyn felt sick at the thought of it. Julian, Joan, Ted. She would have to tell them all that she, Evelyn Mountcastle, was going to have a baby on her own.

20

'You want to do what?!'

Julian whisked his stockinged feet off his desk, sat forward in his chair and stared at her open-mouthed.

Evelyn swallowed and then repeated what she had just said. 'I want to resign from *Into the Blue*. Well, it's not that I want to, but I'm going to have to do it all the same. I'm very sorry.'

She dropped her eyes, trying to look contrite, but Julian was having none of it.

'You can't just "resign",' he snapped, his voice harsh, spiked, as his delicate fingers made quotes in the air around the word. 'That is not how it works, Evelyn. You signed the contract. We all signed the contract. You can't just change your mind.'

Evelyn raised her gaze to look at him and he met her eyes and then softened a little, falling back against his chair and sighing deeply.

'What is going on here, Evie?' he asked her, his tone now exasperated more than angry. 'Is there something you're not telling me?'

Evie nodded and swallowed hard. This would be the first time she'd say the words out loud, and once she did there was no going back. It would no longer be her secret.

'I'm pregnant,' she said in a voice so quiet she feared he wouldn't have heard, but she could tell from his reaction that he had.

He dropped his head into his hands, knotting his fingers through his thinning hair. 'Oh, my dear God,' he said. 'Of all the stupid . . .' But then he sat up straight again, his eyes shining. 'Well, that's not the end of the world, Evie,' he said. 'There's no need to panic or do anything knee-jerk. We can fix this. I know people. Obviously, this isn't the first time I've had this happen and it's easy enough to sort. I'll just make a few phone calls and . . .'

He reached to pick up the phone receiver, but Evelyn shot her hand out to stay his.

'No, Julian,' she said quietly. 'I've decided I want to keep the baby.'

Julian shook his head in disbelief. 'But Evelyn. You are at the peak of your career. If you walk out now, there's no guarantee that anyone will want you when you come back.'

Evelyn shrugged. The baby was more important to her than what she might be giving up, and was growing in importance with each passing day. If what he was saying was true, then she would just have to deal with that when she reached that point.

Julian's head hit the desk and he moaned to himself.

'I'm sorry, Julian,' she said gently. 'I didn't mean for any of this to happen and I really didn't want to mess things up for you. But it did, and now I have to live with it.'

Julian looked up, and now Evelyn could see something else in his eyes; concern perhaps, or maybe pity.

'I didn't even know you had a boyfriend,' he said.

Evelyn shrugged again. 'I don't,' she replied.

The corners of Julian's mouth turned down as he considered the other possibilities. 'I didn't have you down as a one-night-stand kind of girl,' he said, his brow furrowed in confusion.

'I'm not. This was . . .'

What was it? How was she supposed to describe what had happened to her? It wasn't rape exactly. Whilst she hadn't gone into the

123

hotel room expecting what she got, she hadn't run away, either. She was no ingenue. She knew these things happened to actresses all the time. She had just never imagined it would happen to her. It wasn't right, what Rory MacMillan had done, but it was the way things were, and if having sex with him was what it took to secure the job in his show, then it appeared that was a price she'd been prepared to pay. That she'd got pregnant was just damned bad luck.

But something stopped her from telling all this to Julian. She had thought that maybe it was to protect her own reputation, or perhaps even MacMillan's, but now she realised that her silence was tinged with something she hadn't noticed before – shame.

'This was . . .' she continued. 'Well, it doesn't really matter what it was. The fact is I am pregnant and I want to keep the baby, so I can't take the part. I'm sorry, but there you have it. My hands are tied.'

Julian sighed deeply. 'All right,' he said. 'If you're sure your mind is made up then I'll make the calls.'

'Thank you, Julian,' she said, getting to her feet. 'I'm sorry.'

She held out her hand, but Julian had already turned away and so she left him to his phone calls.

As she left the agency and headed out to the street, Evelyn knew it would be the last time she ever went there. Julian would take her off his books as she wasn't available for work, and when she came back it was unlikely he would see her. She would need to find herself new representation. But for now, that wasn't important. Now she had to pack up her stuff and get herself back to Southwold, back to Joan and the life she had fought so hard to escape.

21

Evelyn took a long, lingering look around her little room before she left it for the last time. The flat had never been much to write home about. It was cramped, cold in the winter and stifling in the summer, with shabby fixtures and fittings and a creeping damp issue, but it had been her world for the last five years and she had loved it. For all its failings, which were many and varied, it was what it represented that was important. The flat spoke of independence, a determination to succeed; dreams, if not quite fulfilled, then at least works in progress. Evelyn had left the safety of a world she knew behind and had pushed out on her own to make her fortune in a city where the pavements sparkled in the spotlights. She hadn't exactly made a fortune, but she had managed to support herself without ever once asking for help, and that had made her proud.

But now she was going back, back to Suffolk, to the family house, to her sister. It felt like a retrograde step, a move in the wrong direction that discredited everything she had achieved so far. And not only that, she was taking with her the scent of scandal. She was pregnant, with no sign of a wedding band on her finger or a father for her unborn child. Such a situation might have been fairly commonplace and even acceptable in London, but where she was going it would shroud her in disgrace. Tongues would wag from one end of the town to the other. Ironically, Evelyn thought, she would be the most exciting thing to happen to the place in years.

In fact, if the whole situation weren't so overloaded with complication, Evelyn would have been quite proud of the bomb she was about to drop on her former hometown. In other circumstances, she would relish the expressions on the faces of people from her past as they saw her expanding form and realised why she was suddenly back living with Joan in their parents' house. Evelyn would have enjoyed flaunting both her bump and her status as a singleton.

But life wasn't as straightforward as that. She was going to have to throw herself on the mercy of her sister, and so she would need to toe the line. It was clear that Joan was keen to add a gloss of respectability to her story. In one telephone conversation, she had suggested that Evelyn come up with some lie about her 'husband' dying unexpectedly.

'It would be better all round, Evelyn, if we just pretended that you were a decent woman who had fallen on hard times,' Joan had said.

Evelyn had ignored the obvious slur and chipped back with her objections to the plan. 'But that would mean lying every day to everyone. I happen to think that it's important to be honest at all times. And anyway, I would probably get into a terrible pickle trying to remember what I was supposed to say. I'd be bound to trip myself up, and that would be worse than just telling the truth from the start.'

Joan had harrumphed down the telephone line.

'In any event, I don't suppose anyone will be interested,' Evelyn continued disingenuously, 'but if they are, I will just tell them that I'm having a baby on my own and I'm back at home to get some support from my loving family.'

She could feel the frost radiating from her sister even though she was a hundred miles away. It was crystal clear that Joan was only taking Evelyn in out of a sense of duty, but Evelyn hoped that if she made herself useful and was good company then perhaps she could win her sister round. She was prepared to try, at least, which was more than could be said for Joan currently. Maybe when the baby arrived, her sister would soften a little. It would be difficult to stay so angry with her nephew or niece smiling and cooing and kicking their little legs in the air, or whatever it was babies did. And there wasn't much either of them could do about the inevitable gossip around the town. They were just going to have to ride that storm out.

'All set?'

Evelyn turned and saw Ted behind her, a cardboard box in his arms.

She nodded a little forlornly. 'I suppose so,' she said. 'If we must.'

'Don't be like that,' Ted said, putting down the box and wrapping his arms around her shoulders. 'It's only a flat. Bricks and mortar, that's all. It's the memories that are the important part.' He picked the box back up and headed towards the stairs. 'Come on. If we set off now, then we'll miss the worst of the traffic. It's a nice little run out to Suffolk and I'm looking forward to getting a bit of sea air in my lungs, get rid of some of this city smog.'

God bless Ted. He had borrowed a van from somewhere and had offered to drive her and her belongings up to the house. If he hadn't, then she would probably have had to take out a loan to pay a removal firm, money that she had no prospect of repaying any time soon. The arrangement was that she would contribute to his fuel costs and keep him entertained on the way. Well, she could manage that, at least.

Evelyn chattered as they left London and headed up the A12, regaling him with stories of her childhood that made him laugh, roll his eyes and look horrified in equal measure.

'Your family sound like a right bunch of horrors,' he said.

'It was always me in bother,' laughed Evelyn. 'I was the one that got caught and had to be punished. I think Joan used to snitch on me, but I could never prove it. I knew, though. She always looked so pleased with herself when I got into trouble.'

'I'm not sure I'm going to like Joan much,' he said.

As they drew close to the town, however, Evelyn's chatter slowed until the only words she uttered were the directions to the house. She'd hadn't been quite sure how she'd feel when they got there – whether there would be nerves, disappointment or even anger, but as the van pulled up in front of the house she had grown up in, the house from which she had fled, Evelyn was surprised to discover that her overwhelming emotional response was sadness. She was delighted to be having this baby, of course she was, and if she hadn't, what would have been the point of all this disruption? But now that she stood on the doorstep of her former home, she knew being here marked the end of the life she had worked so hard to achieve.

'Do you want me to come in?' asked Ted. 'I can just turn round and head back home if you'd rather.'

'You'll do no such thing,' Evelyn replied. 'You have kindly driven me all the way here. The least we can do is offer you some lunch. Come on. We'll unpack later.'

Evelyn still had a front door key – it was her house too, after all – so she slipped it into the lock and turned. The door swung open and immediately the aroma of the place hit her. It didn't seem to have changed at all. Furniture polish, bleach and coal tar soap – all clean smells, but ones she associated not with a welcoming home but with strict order and regime. The hallway was shadowy because all the doors leading off it were firmly closed to keep the transference of dust to a minimum, just as they had been in her parents' day. As a child, Evelyn had longed to fling them all open and wander around willy-nilly, sitting on plumped cushions and leaving finger marks on polished wood. She never had, of course, being too worried about the consequences of such impetuous actions. She had once dropped a candlestick on the hearth and broken a tile. She had been forced to stay in her room for a month, coming out only for school and meals. But things would be different for her and her child. She wasn't going to let Joan treat the baby as she herself had been treated.

The place was very quiet, with no signs of life anywhere. No radio played, no dog barked; there was no sound at all. Even the air felt silent.

'She does know you're arriving today?' asked Ted. 'I thought she'd be here to welcome you home.'

'Oh, she's here all right,' replied Evelyn darkly. 'She misses nothing.'

Evelyn stepped into the hall and walked down the gloomy corridor to the kitchen. Her sister Joan was sitting in a chair by the range, a newspaper folded open at the crossword in her hand. She didn't look up when Evelyn walked in.

'Hello, Joan,' she began. 'I'm back.'

'So I see,' said Joan.

'And this is my friend Ted. He's been kind enough to drive me and my things up from London.'

'How do you do,' said Ted, and held out a hand.

Joan regarded Ted with disdain and made no attempt to take his outstretched hand. 'Is he the one, then?' she asked, cocking her head in Ted's direction but without making eye contact with him.

'No,' replied Evelyn, unable to keep the irritation from her voice. 'I said. He's my friend.'

'Funny kind of life you lead, having friends who are men,' replied Joan stiffly.

Evelyn rolled her eyes at Ted and sighed, as if to say this was what she was going to have to put up with from now on.

'I have a perfectly normal kind of life,' she said. 'And now I'm going to make him a cup of tea. Would you like one? Sit down, Ted,' she added.

Ted picked a chair as far away from Joan as possible and muttered his thanks.

Evelyn refused to let Joan's rudeness fluster her, and she got on with making the tea, opening cupboards to retrieve teapot, cups and tea leaves, all still exactly where they had been when she left.

'Nice place you've got here,' said Ted.

Joan didn't reply.

'I've always fancied living by the coast myself. I had an aunt who lived in Margate. Used to visit when I was a nipper.'

Joan's stony silence continued, and so Evelyn stepped in to help Ted.

'You never told me that,' she said brightly. 'Is she still there?'

'She passed over,' said Ted, dropping his head and crossing himself, even though he was no more a Catholic than she was. 'God rest her gentle soul. They gave her flat to the Cat's Protection League in the end. Shocking waste.'

He was messing about now. Evelyn knew his humour and could spot it at twenty paces. He had obviously cut Joan as much slack as he was prepared to and was now wanting to have some fun. Normally, Evelyn would have played along, asking him questions so he could embellish the answers, but it would do her no good to upset Joan before she had even brought her things in from the van.

When she turned around, pot of tea in hand, she could see Joan's eyes trained on her stomach, her lip slightly curled.

'There's not much to see yet,' she commented scornfully. 'That's a blessing, at least. Heaven only knows what the neighbours will say when they realise the shame that you've brought on this house.'

Evelyn put the teapot down on the table with enough force that a little splash of tea bounced out of the spout and on to the Formica mat.

'Oh, for goodness' sake, Joan,' she snapped. 'It's 1979, not 1929. Who cares what the neighbours think? I haven't done anything illegal. I am having a baby. Millions of women do it all the time.'

'When you can afford your own house, then you can disregard what your neighbours think, but whilst you're living under my roof then you'll show due respect.'

Ted bristled. 'I thought the house belonged to all three of . . .'

Evelyn shook her head at him to silence him. He was right, of course, but no good would come of picking fights. Evelyn really wanted this to work out and she would do what she needed to to win her sister round.

'Listen, Joan,' she tried more gently, 'I know this is a lot to take in and believe me, it's not what I wanted to happen . . .'

'You should have thought of that before you opened your legs,' muttered Joan.

Evelyn sucked in a breath and ignored her. 'But we are where we are, so why don't we all just try to get along, shall we? There's no point us fighting all the time. Let's just make the most of it. And you might even like having the patter of tiny feet running about the place when the time comes.'

As the words left her lips, Evelyn thought of the glass cabinets filled with china ornaments, the precious books that her father had never let them touch, let alone read. From the little she had seen of the house so far, it looked as if Joan hadn't changed a thing. It was still the least child-friendly place you could imagine.

Still, she was here now. In time, she could change things herself, introduce a new way of living in the space. She had no money, but perhaps she could persuade Joan to make a few improvements, bring the house up to date. It might even be fun.

'You respect my way of doing things,' Joan said, 'and keep out of sight, and everything will work just fine.' And then she went back to her crossword.

Evelyn caught Ted's eye and rolled hers heavenwards, and he gave an almost imperceptible shake of his head to show that he understood; but he couldn't, not really. Evelyn had hoped Joan might be different, that somehow the two of them would muddle along until they were able to form a relationship that kind-of worked. But now she was here, it was clear that had been a pipe dream. Joan was exactly the same as she always had been, and there was nothing Evelyn could do to make her any warmer or more empathetic. She was just going to have to try and find a level that worked for them both.

Ted was glaring at Joan, as if he was ready to leap in and defend Evelyn at any moment, and she felt grateful for his moral support. At least she wasn't entirely on her own.

'So, shall we start bringing my things in?' she asked him. 'Am I still in my old room, Joan?' she said, although she knew the answer.

Joan tutted. 'I don't know where else you think you'd sleep,' she snapped.

'Fine,' replied Evelyn as evenly as she could manage.

She was back at home, and it was as if the last ten years had never happened.

22

2019

Pip stood on the opposite pavement and surveyed the Mountcastles' house. Behind her the waves crashed on to the shore and the seagulls called, their plaintive cries whisked away by the breeze. The place hadn't been hard to find. Jez had described the outside in enough detail that Pip could identify it pretty confidently. Now that she saw it, the house did ring a few distant bells. She probably had scurried past as a child, picturing all kinds of terrible truths about the women who lived inside, her imagination no doubt fuelled by Jez's ghoulish stories.

These days the house looked shabby and unloved. Paint was peeling away from the window frames and the glass didn't look as if it had seen a chamois leather for years. In fact, it was so dilapidated that it might have been empty but for a light burning in an upstairs window. Someone was there. But who?

Jez hadn't been sure which sister had died in the accident, but Pip really hoped it was Joan. Wishing one sister dead over the other was an unworthy thought, but Pip's affection for the chirpy, positive Evelyn grew with every diary post she read. Looking at the state of the house now, however, it was hard to believe it was the Evelyn of the diary who lived inside.

Pip wondered what could have happened to her to bring her so low. Maybe she had just had her spirit crushed by being trapped here and not being able to get back to her former life. There was a lesson in that, Pip thought, but she didn't want to go there. Her situation was entirely different, she told herself. She wasn't trapped like Evelyn had been. She had money and a job that she loved to go back to whenever she was well enough. Her stay in Southwold was temporary, just whilst she got herself together. Evelyn might still be here all these decades later, but that definitely didn't mean she, Pip, would be. She was starting to sound desperate, even to herself.

She pushed the idea of getting stuck out of her head. It made for uncomfortable thinking, and instead she pulled her thoughts back to the house over the road and the reason she had come. There was only one way to find out if Evelyn Mountcastle was still living there and discover what had become of her. She was going to have to knock on the door and introduce herself.

Pip felt an unfamiliar flutter of something approaching excitement at the thought. She was almost halfway through the diary now, and was certain that she would like Evelyn Mountcastle if she met her. It wasn't just the parallels she could see between their lives. There was something else about her: a drive, a thirst that Pip recognised in herself. If she knocked on the door and got her into conversation, she felt sure they would get along rather well.

But that would be an adventure for another day. It wasn't even nine in the morning, and so far too early to call, and anyway, Pip wanted to get to the end of the diary before she relinquished it. She would come back when she had read the whole thing, explain who she was and then hand it over. Perhaps she could gather a little more information about Evelyn Mountcastle the actress in the meantime, see if she couldn't get the old lady to invite her inside the house by employing a bit of flattery.

Judging by the state of the house, though, it didn't look as if Evelyn had many visitors. That might be because visitors weren't welcome, or just that there was no one to visit her. Pip wondered where Scarlet was now. Maybe she no longer lived locally. She indulged herself with a little fantasy that Evelyn's daughter had also become an actress and picked up where Evelyn had left off. There would be a kind of neatness to that which appealed to Pip. It might also explain why the house looked so down at heel. Scarlet could be living in London or maybe she had moved abroad. Perhaps she had a job on a cruise ship entertaining the passengers. Pip smiled to herself as she invented a whole life for the little girl. Of course, she would be in her mid-thirties by now, which felt odd, as the little Scarlet who came dancing into Pip's bedroom each night was still a child, not yet even old enough to be at school.

Pip had reached August 1983 in the diary now. She had been reading the entries after dinner, letting herself become absorbed in Evelyn and Scarlet's simple lives. According to the diary, they led a quiet existence with very little happening to them on a daily basis, but, as well as complaints about how badly Joan treated them, the handwritten pages were also filled with Evelyn's daily thoughts, some of which Pip didn't properly understand.

Sometimes, when S is having her nap and I'm doing my household chores, I let my imagination roam back to how things might have been if she had never come along. Into the Blue is about to start its second season. It's been a great success, just as I knew it would be. Julian must still be furious at all that lost commission! I think it's so popular because the storylines aren't just all car chases and drinking. They're about real women and how they juggle their jobs with being wives and mothers. Ironic, really, seeing as that's exactly what I can't seem to do.

And I have to admit that the girl playing my part has made a decent job of it, even if I would have been better. I can't think about that for too long, though, because it makes me cross. It's so unfair. The only thing I did wrong was to be naive. Yet I'm the one who was punished and is still being punished to this day. He doesn't even know that he has a daughter – not that I would ever tell him – but in my head, if I ever saw him again, I would make sure he knew how badly I've been treated.

I won't ever tell S about him. She doesn't need to know anything. She has asked me about her father once or twice, but she's so little and it's easy just to distract her. Obviously, I shan't get away with that forever, though. One day she will want something more.

This had been the first comment she had come across about Scarlet's father, and Pip had scoured the entry for any clues as to his identity, but there weren't any. She assumed it was just the usual old story – boy meets girl, girl gets into trouble, boy runs for the hills, and Evelyn clearly didn't want him to have any part in Scarlet's life, despite how hard her own life appeared to be as a result. Evelyn was very bitter, though, which didn't seem to square with that story. Pip couldn't really work it out.

Her sister Joan continued to be hellish to her as well, and Pip often found herself seething with outrage and indignation at the way she treated Evelyn. She seemed to be little more than a skivvy in the house and Joan had her doing all the domestic tasks as if she were her maid and not her sister. It reminded Pip of Cinderella and her ugly stepsisters, but Evelyn seemed to accept her treatment, a few waspish diary entries aside.

Pip felt forced to draw comparisons between Evelyn's situation and the way her own mother sometimes asked, very nicely, if she could perform a particular task for her, only for Pip to fail to do it. The thought made Pip ashamed and her insides squirmed at the contrast between her own behaviour and Evelyn's. She would try harder, she decided as she read on. Her life was challenging and she was finding it hard to cope, but that was no excuse for snapping at her poor mother or stropping around the farm like a teenager.

Pip turned to leave, but as she did so she looked up at the house one more time. A pale face appeared in the lit window. It was hard to make out any details through the dirt, but it looked like a woman, white hair caught up in a bun on top of her head. Even though Pip couldn't see her features clearly, it felt as if their eyes locked, just for a moment, and Pip found that she couldn't pull her gaze away.

Was it Evelyn?

For a wild moment, it crossed Pip's mind that the other woman knew she had read her diary, was party to her innermost thoughts, but of course that was ridiculous. How could she possibly know?

And yet, as the two women stared at each other across the street, it felt to Pip as if there were some connection that she couldn't quite fathom.

Then the woman stepped away from the window and was gone, leaving Pip alone on the street.

23

Pip was just unlocking her bike ready to ride home when she heard someone calling her name. She turned and saw Jez in her father's van on the opposite side of the road.

'So this is what you get up to all day?' he said, cocking his head towards Have a Heart and grinning at her as if it were a sex shop.

Pip left her bike where it was and, taking care to check for oncoming cars, crossed the road to talk to him.

'I know. The glamour, eh?' she said. 'If my friends could see me now.'

'Oi!' replied Jez. 'I'm your friend, don't forget, and you look pretty good from where I'm sitting.'

Pip smiled, despite her best endeavours not to. 'Flattery will get you precisely everywhere,' she said.

'Is that a promise?'

Electricity crackled between them for a moment and then dissipated into the evening air.

'Listen, I've got half an hour,' said Jez. 'Fancy a quick drink? Then I can chuck the bike in the back of the van and give you a lift back up to the farm.'

'Great. Why not?'

They went to a different pub this time. Pip wondered whether maybe Jez didn't want to be seen out with her too often.

He bought her half a cider, her favourite tipple when they were teenagers, and a pint for himself, and they sat on a bench underneath the window. A silence rested between them, but it wasn't awkward. They both sat, contentedly looking out at the other customers and enjoying their drinks.

'Do you still see anything of the others?' she asked after a while.

She had dropped her school friends almost as soon as she'd left for university, but that didn't mean she wasn't interested in what had become of them all. Jez rattled off a list of who was still in the town, who was married and divorced and other choice bits of scandal from the intervening ten years, and Pip listened and made appropriate sounds when the news merited it. Jez seemed to relish telling the stories as if he, like her, had no one to tell them to. She assumed that his fiancée Teresa would have little interest in stories about people from his past and so he was probably enjoying having a new audience for them. One or two of the names he mentioned meant nothing to her.

'God, you must remember Robbo,' he said, eyes wide. 'The one with the twin sisters in the year below us. They were tiny and they had white-blonde hair. Looked like little ghosts wandering round the corridors?'

Even this description did nothing to bring Robbo, whoever he might be, back to her mind, and Jez shook his head in exasperation, as if she were defective in some way.

'Well, I suppose when you left you just forgot us.'

His tone was jokey but Pip thought she could detect a tinge of sadness in his voice, or possibly bitterness. She couldn't be sure which. She shrugged an apology.

'Tell me about Teresa,' she said, and immediately regretted it. She didn't want to hear about her, about how his life had moved on whereas hers was stuck in the doldrums and going nowhere. But it was the polite thing to do, so, at the very least, she could smile and show interest.

Jez sat up a little. 'She's hot!' he said with a grin.

Pip rolled her eyes. 'Is that it? No other reason why you're marrying her?'

Jez smiled fondly. 'Nope!' he said.

There it was again, that rakish sense of humour that she used to love so much.

'Seriously, though,' he continued. 'She's great. That perfect combination of beauty and brains. She manages one of the big hotels in town. In fact, she pretty much runs the whole chain. Her boss is crap. She covers for him all the time. And she's the youngest out of all of them.'

He looked so proud as he spoke and, even though the slightly peculiar twinge of jealousy was still hovering at the back of her mind, Pip was pleased for him. Unlike her, he deserved to have some happiness.

'Have you got any photos?' she asked.

Jez fished his phone out of his coat pocket, typed in his password and then scrolled through his photographs, rejecting one or two until he came to one he seemed to think would do.

'There you go. My beautiful girl,' he said, looking fondly at his phone before handing it over.

Pip looked down at the screen. Teresa was attractive but not really beautiful, and Pip felt a sense of relief. Having established that her 'rival' wasn't a supermodel, she allowed herself to consider her more carefully and concluded that she looked like a nice enough woman, although something about the way she held her head suggested that she, too, had some of that inner confidence Pip had come across at bar school. Well, that was fine. At the end of the day, Teresa was a hotel manager in a small English town, and she was a leading human rights barrister at one of the best chambers in London. Not that it was a competition, of course.

And then again, could she really make that claim for herself any more? She was no longer sure of who she was, and she certainly didn't have the right to look down on Teresa, who appeared to have far more things going in her favour than Pip could currently lay claim to.

She handed the phone back to Jez. 'She looks lovely,' she said quietly. 'I know you'll both be very happy.'

Suddenly she couldn't bear it for a minute more, the maintenance of the facade that she'd built up around herself. She needed to be on her own.

Looking at her watch, she feigned surprise. 'Goodness, is that the time?' she said. 'I promised Mum I'd help with supper. Could I have that lift now, please?'

Jez finished his drink in one swift gulp and they headed back to the van, chatting about the things that had changed on Southwold High Street since they were children and the things that had remained resolutely the same. This felt like much safer territory to Pip. The past. Even though she had spent so long running from it, it suddenly felt a much more secure place to be than the present.

24

Pip needed a stamp for a birthday card. This in itself was surprising. She had no idea how many of her friends' birthdays had rolled by whilst she had been at the farm. Birthdays had been the last thing on her mind as she struggled to hold herself together. But then, out of the blue, she had remembered that in a couple of days it would be a friend's thirtieth and she had bought a card in her lunch hour. This felt like a normal thing to do, the kind of little chore that she would have sorted without thinking before the accident. And now, here she was doing it again. Was this progress?

She had fished in her purse for a stamp and found one of Dominic's business cards. He had written the phone number of a restaurant he'd wanted to try on the back. She had been going to book them a table and had slipped the card in her purse to deal with later. But there had been no later.

Seeing his name pulled her up short. It was a shock, and she hadn't been prepared for it. In the few days since his visit, she had tried not to think about him, worried that it would make her feel sad or, more likely, that she would realise she didn't feel anything at all. She wasn't sure which of the two options would be worse, so she had just avoided thinking. Avoiding thought was a skill she had perfected over recent months – keeping busy so nothing unwelcome could creep into her head.

Now, though, as she stood there holding something Dominic had once touched, she couldn't help but bring him to mind. It wasn't that she missed him, exactly – she probably wouldn't have spoken to him since his visit anyway as their contact had dwindled to almost nothing recently – but there was a sadness there that he was gone, that that part of her life was over. But it was like she was in a theatre watching someone playing her life out on the stage in front of her, rather than living through it herself. Objectively, it was a very great shame that her relationship with a man she thought she loved had broken down and come to nothing, but it felt as if it was happening to someone else. She could see that it was upsetting and that she should feel dejected and disconsolate, but actually she didn't feel anything. The wiring inside her just wasn't joined up properly any more. Maybe it never would be again.

She had extracted a stamp and stuck it firmly in the corner of the envelope. Then she dropped the business card in the bin.

Later, she and her mother were working side by side in the kitchen preparing the evening meal. As a teenager, Pip had prompted many an argument by complaining about the gender-stereotypical way her parents ran the farm. Now, though, she could see that even though her father did labour in the fields whilst her mother tended to hearth and home, this arrangement actually served them very well. They were a team. Her father could not work as well as he did on the farm without her mother providing him with hearty meals, clean clothes and a safe, warm home to come back to, and without the money her father earned, her mother would have to look for work elsewhere, which would prevent her from running the house. On top of that, each of them was happy with their allocated tasks and wouldn't have wanted to do either what the other did, or, indeed, anything else. Gender-defining though the arrangement was, their lives were symbiotic, each one vital to the well-being of the other. It was a true partnership.

Being happy with your lot, Pip thought, now there was a concept she had struggled with over the years, but she was starting to see that perhaps there was more to it than she had given her parents credit for. Before the accident she had been dismissive of what she had seen as their narrow vision of the world. Their apparent lack of ambition had always frustrated her, but now she wondered whether what she had always seen as a weakness could actually be more of a strength.

'Did you have a nice drink with Jez?' her mother asked as she scrubbed mud from the carrots, passing them to Pip to peel and chop for the pot. 'That's twice you've been out now, isn't it?'

The question was innocently asked, Pip knew, but she baulked at it. Her default setting as a teenager had always been to guard any information about her life preciously, but what harm could it possibly do to share her thoughts with her mother now – or even then, for that matter?

'Yes, although tonight's was a bit spur of the moment,' she said. 'It was lovely to chat, though. He hasn't changed a bit. I'm not sure why I left it so long to talk to him, to be honest.'

'You've had a lot to deal with,' her mother said simply.

'And he's getting married?' Pip continued, anxious to make light of the news before her mother mentioned it. 'You never said.'

'Didn't I?' replied her mother casually. 'I must have forgotten.'

Pip could see straight through her mother's attempts at insouciance.

'I was never going to marry Jez, Mum,' she laughed, although a tiny part of her was still smarting at his announcement.

'You could have done a lot worse,' her mother replied. 'He's a good man.'

Pip thought of the trouble she and Jez sought out when they were young, something her mother had either forgotten or had never known of in the first place. Or perhaps she was just choosing to overlook that, now Pip was very firmly on the shelf and Jez was about to tie the knot.

'Jez and I would never have worked,' she said. 'In fact, we'd have been disastrous together.' She had been aiming for confident, but her voice sounded closer to wistful. 'What's she like, anyway, the fiancée? Have you met her?'

'Teresa? Oh yes. She's very . . .' Her mother paused, and Pip knew that she was searching for a way to express her doubts without being critical. 'Very . . . confident.'

Pip smiled to herself. Pushy, then.

'I think there's money there,' her mother added, in that way that she talked about people she considered socially superior to her and that Pip had always hated. 'Jez has never said, but there's something about the way she holds herself. You can tell. And her clothes. I think she's quite posh.'

Pip could read her mother's code as clearly as if it were written in the Queen's English. Too posh for Jez. But not as posh as me, Pip wanted to say. Not as posh as Rose Appleby, at least. Her mother wouldn't understand, though, and anyway, what was the point? What did it matter how you behaved or spoke or dressed? There were so many more important things to life, not least being alive.

'I gather she's got a good job,' Pip continued.

'Yes. She's the manager of that big hotel on the front. I forget the name.'

She hadn't forgotten the name, Pip thought. Her mother really didn't like Jez's fiancée.

There was a pause in which Pip knew her mother was girding her loins to ask a difficult question. She braced herself.

'And did you manage to talk to Jez?'

She pressed the word 'talk' so that her meaning would be crystal clear without her having to spell it out. She had Pip's best interests at heart and just wanted her to recover, Pip knew, so she curbed her irritation.

'A bit,' she replied, and could almost feel her mother's relief pass between them like a current.

'That's good,' said her mother, and Pip was relieved that she seemed content to leave it at that.

◆ ◆ ◆

After dinner, Pip excused herself as usual and retreated to her room and the diary for her nightly foray into Evelyn's life. She settled herself on her bed and opened up where she had left off the night before.

Tuesday 16th August

Such a perfect day today. I took Scarlet crabbing off the end of the pier. We dug Peter's old line out of the garage and I stole a couple of rashers of bacon from the fridge as bait. High tide was madly early – no problem for us, of course – so it wasn't too busy, and we got a great spot. S wasn't very patient about the waiting part, and I kept telling her it might take a while, but then, lo and behold, we struck gold within ten minutes! He was a whopper, too, and we managed to get him all the way up and into our bucket without dropping him. Scarlet was so excited (and a little bit scared), but I showed her how to hold him so he didn't pinch her, and she gave him a bit of a stroke on his shell. Then we put him back and went to get hot chocolate and a bun in the café. S didn't finish hers – I think she might be coming down with something – but I polished it off for her. Then we built her favourite

sandcastle – the one with a moat and bridge – and wan-
dered back home for her nap just as the beach was filling
up. It was perfect.

Pip had only vague memories of going crabbing herself. Her parents had always been too busy to take time away from the farm for activities like that, and by the time she was old enough to go alone she was too caught up with her studies to be interested. It did sound like the perfect day for Evelyn and Scarlet, though. She could picture them, Evelyn dressed like someone from Dexys Midnight Runners, her hair held out of her eyes with a polka-dot scarf and Scarlet in a little sundress, walking hand in hand along the beach with their bucket and line. It was such a happy, carefree image that it made Pip smile.

She flicked over the page, eager for the next day's entry, but it was blank. That was unusual. Some days Evelyn didn't manage to fill the entire space, but she always wrote something. Pip turned the pages over, and over again. Nothing. There was no entry for ten days. Perhaps they had gone on holiday, but surely Evelyn would have taken the diary with her, and there had been no build-up to a holiday in the diary entries.

Finally, on Tuesday 30th August the entries started up again, although the words seemed to have been formed with no care, as if Evelyn had been writing with the wrong hand or been half asleep when she wrote them.

> *We buried her today. Ted came. I couldn't have got*
> *through the day without him. Peter was there, too, with*
> *his wife. Joan was not. She said she had a cold, but I*
> *know it was just an excuse. I was glad she didn't go. I'm*
> *too angry with her just now. I wouldn't have been able*
> *to hold it in.*

147

I don't know what to do without her. I don't know how
I'll live without her. My life is over. I have nothing left.

Pip reread the words and then reread them again and again. What was it that Evelyn was saying? Was there another way of interpreting her entry other than the most obvious? But really, Pip knew.

Scarlet. Lovely little Scarlet, not yet at school. Scarlet, the light in Evelyn's life, the centre of her universe. Scarlet was gone.

Tears pricked at Pip's eyes and then, before she could control them, came streaming down her face. Poor Evelyn. Pip knew that to lose a child was the worst that could ever happen to a parent, causing the most unbearable, unhealable pain. She knew because she had been haunted night and day by how much it must hurt.

Nausea rose fast in her throat and she ran from her bedroom to the bathroom on the landing, only just getting there in time. She vomited noisily into the toilet bowl.

To lose a child. To kill a child. They were two sides of the same coin. Evelyn had lost Scarlet. She had killed the boy.

But it wasn't the same pain. Evelyn had lived through the hell that the boy's mother must be enduring now. Pip's hell was different. She had been the cause of pain. Without her, it would never have been there.

Pip sat on the bathroom floor, shivering with cold until the shock had passed.

When she finally felt in control enough to move, it was dark outside. The low murmur of the television drifted up the stairs to her. She thought she heard the ten o'clock news theme tune. Her parents would be coming to bed shortly, and she knew they mustn't find her collapsed on the bathroom floor.

Laboriously Pip got to her feet, her head still spinning. Her stomach ached, her skin felt cold and clammy and she had the slightly out-of-body feeling that often followed an attack, as if she wasn't quite in control of her own actions.

Back in her room, the diary had slipped to the floor when she'd raced to get to the bathroom. Gingerly, she picked it up. She went back to the entry she had read, hoping that somehow she had been mistaken, but there it still was. On one unremarkable day in August 1983 Evelyn Mountcastle's world had been changed irrevocably, just as hers had been on an unremarkable day the previous October.

Pip curled up small on her bed and wept as if she might never stop. It felt like all the tears of the previous months, the ones she had been unable to cry, were falling now. A switch had been flicked in her head, a voice giving her the previously withheld permission. 'You may now cry,' it said. 'Please commence forthwith.'

By the time her mother tapped lightly on her bedroom door to wish her goodnight, Pip had no tears left.

25

Morning came. Pip could hear movement in the rest of the house, her father getting ready to go out, her mother preparing the breakfast. It was an ordinary day, just like any other. And yet something had changed.

She could tell from how tight her eyes felt, their skin stretched so thin over swollen lids that she knew she must look terrible. Her mother would know at once that she had spent the greater part of the night crying, but for once Pip didn't care. Let them see. What harm would it do? What was the point of pretending?

In the bathroom, she threw cold water over her face and made little cold compresses out of damp toilet paper which she pressed into her eye sockets, but it made little difference. Nothing but time was going to erase the evidence of her tears.

However, even though she looked so dreadful, Pip felt different. She wasn't well, or anything that came close to feeling like she had done before the accident, but she definitely felt less hollow than she had the day before. This was good, she thought. Maybe she was finally making some progress. She didn't want to shrug off all the pain she was carrying – that was her burden, and it was only right she should bear at least part of it until her dying day – but allowing a little of its weight to slip from her shoulders? Surely no harm could come of that.

The second her mother caught sight of her it was obvious she could see the change, too. Pip saw her take in the pinched and swollen eyes, and then saw the relief crossing her face as she began to understand what had happened. How often had she urged Pip to cry over the previous months, assuring her that it would be cathartic to let some of the hurt and pain out? Now it was obvious Pip had done exactly that, she must have been a little reassured.

But she said nothing.

'Are you going into the shop today?' she asked instead.

Pip nodded as she poured herself a bowl of cornflakes and then buried them with three spoonfuls of sugar. Her mother didn't even tut.

'Mum?' said Pip when the bowl was empty.

'Yes, love,' her mother replied. Pip noticed that she stopped what she was doing so she could give Pip her full attention, understanding instinctively that this was an important moment. 'Thank you. You know, for having me back here. I'm sure it's not been, well . . . I just wanted you to know that I am grateful.'

Her mother gave a tight little smile, and Pip could tell that she was fighting to hold her own emotions back.

'You can always come home,' she said softly.

After a pause, during which each of them clearly wanted to move on but didn't know quite which way to go, her mother tapped her forehead and said, 'Oh, I forgot. I asked some people about Evelyn Mountcastle. There's quite a story there. Remind me, why were you interested in her?'

There seemed little point in hiding the fact that she had taken the diary. It was more important to find out as much as she could about Evelyn.

'An old diary turned up at the shop,' Pip explained.

Her mother raised an eyebrow.

'It was in a box of things to throw away,' Pip replied defensively. 'So. Who is she?'

'Well,' her mother continued. She was emptying the tumble dryer; her mother was never still. She smoothed wrinkles from a checked flannel shirt, folded it and put in in a wicker basket, ready to be ironed. 'She lived with her sister and a little girl, her daughter, I think. Anyway, the child died in an accident and then not long after that the sister fell down the stairs. Broke her neck, or so they say.' Her mother shook her head at the tragedy of it all and began to pair thick working socks, pulling one inside the other to form soft woollen balls. 'She's been in that house ever since. Never really goes out. Lives there by herself. Apparently there's a nephew who keeps an eye on her, but I don't think he lives in town.'

So it was Joan and not Evelyn who had died. Pip felt almost giddy with relief. 'I gather she was an actress,' she said, hoping that a simple prompt would elicit more information, but her mother turned the corners of her mouth down.

'Was she?' she replied vaguely. 'I didn't hear that. All I was told were the tragedies. Poor, poor woman. Losing a child. You never really get ov—' Her mother stopped, a blush flying across her cheeks like a wildfire. 'Oh, Pip. I'm so sorry. I didn't mean . . .'

But Pip just waved her comment away with her hand. 'Don't worry, Mum. It's true. You never do.'

They gave the thought the respect it deserved for a moment or two before moving the conversation on, beyond the death of children.

'So, what do you think I should do with the diary?' Pip asked. 'I can't believe she meant for it to go to the shop.'

'Yes,' her mother agreed. 'It is odd. From what I've heard, the house is a real mess. It doesn't feel right that she'd suddenly decide to start clearing things out after all this time. Unless she's died, of course.'

No, thought Pip. She couldn't be dead. She had only just had it confirmed that it was Joan who had fallen down the stairs. Evelyn couldn't be snatched away again so soon. Pip wanted to know what had happened to her career, where Scarlet's father was, why Joan was so horrible to her and how Scarlet died. Then she remembered the woman at the window.

'I think I saw her,' she said, 'looking out at the street.'

Her mother pulled a face at her, making it clear that she didn't feel standing outside people's houses and peering in was quite the done thing, but she didn't say anything.

'So, what do you think I should do?' Pip asked again. 'Shall I take the diary back to her? I think it must be part of a set. It would be a shame if one year got lost.'

Her mother picked up the laundry basket. 'You should do what you think's best,' she said. 'But if I were you, I'd leave well alone. People don't thank you for nosing about in their lives, especially not when they've kept themselves so private.'

This wasn't the answer that Pip was expecting or wanted to hear, but she smiled at her mother. 'Okay. Thanks, Mum.'

Her mother's eyes lingered on her face a second longer. 'And you're all right?' she asked quietly, a wealth of questions hidden in just one.

'Yes, Mum,' Pip replied. 'I'm okay. Actually, I feel a bit better today. Maybe things are finally starting to change.'

'Good,' said her mother.

And then she bustled away.

Were they? Pip wondered. Were they really starting to change? She hardly dare believe it, and yet she had just said it out loud. She had finally cried, which had to be a good thing, and she had felt something when she had gone out with Jez. Granted, feelings like that weren't that helpful, but at least she had some. She had been numb for so long that she had forgotten what it was like to have an emotional response. And reading Evelyn's diary every night had given her an interest beyond her own grief and guilt. Each indicator of change was only small on its own, but they were all pointing in the same direction. Pip was finally moving forward.

26

2019

When Evelyn woke, the sky outside was a milky pink. It would rain, she thought. Not that it mattered, as she wouldn't be going outside. She never went outside any more. Slowly she shifted her position, every inch of her back and hips crying out in pain. She felt so very old these days. It was as if simply moving was a luxury granted only to younger people, whilst she was expected to bear the agony of stiff and frozen joints until she died. She had to remind herself that she was only seventy. That was no age, she knew, and yet she felt every single month of it.

Nicholas told her endlessly that if she insisted on sleeping in her chair then she only had herself to blame, but really, what was the point of shuffling from chair to bed? At least she could get up from her chair when she needed to. If she took to her bed, there was no guarantee that she'd ever bother to raise herself out of it again. They would find her, if they came looking, flat on her back, her body rigid and unmoving even as her heart still pumped blood around her veins.

Reaching for her spectacles, Evelyn placed them on her nose and peered out at the street beyond her window. In truth, it was becoming increasingly difficult to see out. The salt together with the grime from the street below and decades of dirty rain had combined to coat the glass in a smeary film. Maybe she should ask Nicholas to clean this one pane. She didn't care about the other windows, but she missed having a clear line of sight to the street and the sea beyond. Almost nothing ever happened directly outside the house, but it would be a shame to miss what little there was to see because she couldn't make it out through the murk.

That girl yesterday, for example. She had stood in the street and stared up at the house for five minutes straight. The staring wasn't that unusual. People often stared – children, mainly, and those who had nothing better to do than waste their time wondering about what went on behind her front door. But they didn't often stand and stare quite so blatantly, or for quite as long. Evelyn hadn't recognised her either, although that meant nothing. She knew no one in the town any more. Nobody visited other than Nicholas, and that suited her just fine.

On a side table next to her chair sat a mobile phone and a diary with a pen tucked into its spine. She didn't keep a diary these days, not like she had done. She had stopped all that when she'd realised there was nothing in her life worth recording, but she did like to keep a track of the days as they passed. Otherwise they all ran into one another with no way of telling them apart.

Today was a Friday. Friday was the day her groceries were delivered. She had set the online shopping order up herself. Nicholas had shown her how to do it, and she had taken to it like a duck to water, although there were some aspects of managing it that still bamboozled her. Sometimes she played a game with herself. She would imagine she was organising an enormous party, like the ones she had gone to back in London, and she'd fill her little basket with everything that she needed. Smoked salmon and blinis, jars of caviar and all kinds of canapés that you could buy ready-made nowadays. And champagne – bottles and bottles of champagne. It was surprising how quickly it all added up. Throwing a party was an extremely expensive business.

And then, once she had amassed everything she would need to host the kind of affair people would be talking about for months, she took every item out of her basket, the total spend dropping click by click until she was left with the bare remains of her needs for the week – a paltry selection, as she lived a very simple life.

So if it was Friday it must be her morning for a bath. She liked to look (and smell) at her best to greet the delivery man. It was always a man, she'd noticed. In all the years her groceries had been delivered, it had never once been a woman who brought them. Was that because women weren't allowed to do the job? Evelyn had been cut off from the ways of the world for a long time, but she felt sure that couldn't be right. There couldn't still be one set of rules for men and another for women. Surely, things had moved on.

It was far more likely that women didn't want to do the job, she concluded. It couldn't be much fun, shifting crates all day and having other women give you orders about where to put everything.

Evelyn was very clear about her own delivery requirements. The man emptied the plastic bags out of the crates and left them on her doorstep, and then she brought them into the house herself. One Friday, an over-officious driver, no doubt in an attempt to be helpful, had ignored her increasingly loud protestations and pushed past her into the house.

'Through here, are we, love?' he'd asked as he made his way past the piles of newspapers down to the kitchen.

She could tell from his face that he had found her living standards questionable. There had been a wrinkling of the nose and a shaking of the head.

'You need some help here, my love,' he'd said, his eyes roaming round the mess that had once been the kitchen. 'Do you have anyone you can call?'

Evelyn had made it clear in no uncertain terms that she had everything she needed, and was in no need of any kind of assistance. The delivery man had tutted, shaken his head again and looked as though he was about to protest, but then he had seen something in her expression and changed his mind.

'Whatever you say, my love. There's people what'll help, you know, though. You just have to ask.'

After he'd gone, Evelyn had cast her eyes over her environment, trying to see it as a stranger might, but then she had pushed the man to the back of her mind, and now she kept the inner porch door firmly closed when she took delivery of her groceries to deter any further intrusions.

If she was being really honest with herself, she had allowed the place to get into a bit of a state. It was difficult, being on her own. Some days she just couldn't muster the energy to clear up as she went along, which was perfectly understandable at her age. But then the next day there was more to be cleared up and consequently more energy that required mustering, and that was how things had got a little out of hand. Every so often she would set to with a bin bag, but it very quickly became apparent that it was going to take a lot more than a bin bag, and so she gave up.

Nicholas tried sometimes, too. He had arrived with cardboard packing boxes just last week.

'Please let me clear some of this stuff, Auntie Evelyn,' he had said, brandishing the box like a weapon. She could hear him moving around on the landing outside her room.

'What are you doing out there?' she shouted. 'Those are my things. Stop touching everything. You'll mess it all up. I'll never find anything.'

He had stuck his head round her door at that point, a wry smile on his lips.

'You may well mock,' she'd said, 'but I know exactly where everything is, and I'll thank you not to go muddling it all up.'

A few minutes later he had appeared in her room, his hands raised in surrender. 'Okay, okay. I give up. I don't have time to sort it all out anyway. It would take me all year. But honestly, Auntie Evelyn, please let's get someone in. It can't be good for you, having so much clutter around the place.'

Evelyn had given him one of her hardest stares, the kind reserved for when people were particularly irritating. She had copied the look from Joan back when she was still in the business of collecting facial expressions, fully expecting to have to use them in front of a camera in the future. Somehow, her impression of her sister's stare had never been quite as withering as the original, but it seemed to work quite well on Nicholas, who shrank a little under its blast.

'I'll thank you not to go interfering with my life,' she snapped. 'How I choose to live is my own business and nothing to do with you.'

Nicholas had shrugged and muttered something about just wanting to help, and had left shortly thereafter. When he had gone, Evelyn regretted her waspish words. What harm would it do just to sort things out a little? But then again, what would be the point? She was just waiting in her house to die. She had been waiting there for over thirty years. No one would ever see how she lived except Nicholas, and she didn't care about such matters. Why would she want to change things when the only change she had ever wanted was totally beyond her power, beyond anyone's power?

Slowly, with stick-thin arms, she pushed herself up out of her chair, her back crying out at being forced to alter its curvature. Then, step by painful step, she shuffled her way to the bathroom to perform her weekly ablutions.

27

It wasn't until later that Evelyn noticed that something was missing. The food order had arrived, and she had taken delivery of it without anyone trying to infiltrate her private enclave. It had been more than she could face to put it away, however, and so, other than the few chilled items that she had stowed in the fridge, she had left the groceries sitting on her kitchen table to be dealt with later.

Then she had taken herself back up to the first floor and into the little room that Joan had used as an office. She didn't go in there often, mainly because she couldn't remember whether it was still relatively accessible or if the quantity of books stacked behind the door were a barrier to entry. But she was pretty sure this was where Nicholas had been moving things around earlier, and she just wanted to check.

As she climbed the stairs, slowly pulling herself up using the bannister step by step, she thought about her nephew's visit, noticing a tightness in her chest as she did so. She shouldn't have snapped at him like that. He'd only been trying to help, and he didn't deserve the tongue-lashing she'd given him.

In fact, it was a miracle he kept coming back. Anyone else would have been driven away by her unfriendliness and her temper long ago. And where would she be without him? Entirely alone, that was where. Then she could snap and snarl to her heart's content with precisely no one to hear her. If she wasn't very careful, she would turn into Joan, and wouldn't that be ironic?

Perhaps that had already happened? It had been so long since she had spent any time in company that she had no idea whether she was still capable of it, although, going by the time she spent with Nicholas, she feared she had quite lost the knack. In fact, she quite enjoyed presenting herself as grumpy and difficult. It was a role she could play easily, barely having to delve into her actress's box of tricks at all, and it served to keep people in general at bay, which suited her mood these days. But Nicholas was family, and she should be kinder to him.

Finally, she reached the landing. She pushed against the door to the office, but it resisted her, no doubt prevented from opening fully by a pile of something or other on the other side. Evelyn shouldered the door as firmly as she dared – broken bones were to be avoided at all costs. It gave a little, but she had to turn herself sideways to slink her way in.

Once she was in, the room didn't look nearly as bad as she had feared. In fact, she wasn't sure what Nicholas had been making such a fuss about. Yes, there were books piled on every surface, but she could still see the fading red medallions on the Persian rug.

It was clear someone had been in there relatively recently, however. There were gaps in the dust where items had been picked up and put down elsewhere. It looked a little like a stage set, which pleased her in a perverse kind of way.

Then she turned and took in the shelves that lined the wall behind the door, and her heart stopped beating. Where were the books? She stood, mouth gaping, and stared at the newly created space on the shelf. A run of about three feet was completely bare;

not a single book was left. Evelyn swayed slightly, then pushed her way through to the shelf, not caring what she knocked over in her rush to get there.

She had no idea which books were missing, but that was of no importance. Books could be replaced if necessary. It was what else had been sitting safe and sound next to them that was crucial.

Her heart was thumping so hard in her chest now that she could hear it in her ears. She stumbled to the shelf, hardly daring to look for fear of what she might see, but when she did, there they all were, lined up neatly in date order. Her diaries. Evelyn had been an inveterate diary-keeper since childhood. Growing up in a house where she didn't fit in with the other occupants, her diary had provided a welcome escape from the torments of day-to-day life. Back then, she had kept them safely hidden away from her family, never quite trusting any of them not to read what she wrote and then mock her for it.

Of course, there had been no need to hide the diaries in recent years, and so she had decided to place them on the shelf. Even though she didn't read them often, their mere presence reminded her of the life she had had before. And there they had sat, untouched, for over a decade. It had been too unbearably painful to open their covers and read the most intimate thoughts of the person she had been before, and yet it was impossible to throw them away. There was too much of herself woven into her words. Each diary recorded a part of her life before – growing up in this very house, then her escape to London and the wonderful years she spent there, and finally the miracle of living with her beautiful baby girl. Before . . . Evelyn had left them all untouched on the shelf.

But then gradually, as the years ticked by, she had begun to feel that she might be ready to open these little snapshots into her life and peek in. She had started tentatively with her own childhood and the years spent growing up with Peter and Joan. Her words reminded her of how little she had had in common with her family. She had always been different to them, and consequently, in her own mind at least, a little bit special, from the moment she was old enough to develop a sense of self.

Feeling emboldened, she had continued working through them. The London years had been fun to revisit. She had enjoyed rereading the tales of life in the shabby little flat on Kentish Town Road, and Brenda, and then dear Ted.

And then finally, she had turned to the volumes that catalogued her life with Scarlet. There were so few of those in comparison to the rest, and she had cherished every entry, lingering over them as you might a fine wine, savouring every sentence and the memories each one evoked. By the end, she had even been able to reread the last one. There had been no more diaries after 1983. What would have been the point?

But where was it? Evelyn could see at once that it wasn't in its place. The 1983 volume was different to the others and so easy to spot. Rather than the plain business diaries she had favoured before, it had daisies on the cover because Scarlet had been with her when she'd bought it, and she had let her choose. But now it was nowhere to be seen. Her eyes flicked backward and forward as she became more and more desperate, but she couldn't see it.

The space on the shelf that Nicholas must have cleared was to the right of her diaries. Surely, he wouldn't have swept up the final one as he removed the old paperbacks? But it appeared he had. In a panic now, Evelyn hunted the floor for the box he might have used to pack the books into. It could still be here. He had said he would take them to the charity shop, but perhaps he hadn't yet got round to it.

But there was no box. The box, the books and the missing diary were nowhere to be seen.

Evelyn felt sick. Of all the diaries, that one was the most precious to her. It couldn't be gone. And yet it appeared that it was.

Evelyn threw herself out of the office and into her bedroom to retrieve her mobile phone. She had to ring Nicholas. Wherever he had taken that box to, he had to get it back.

28

Pip pushed open the heavy wooden door, stepped into the library and was immediately transported back in time. She hadn't been aware that the library had a smell, but now it hit her so hard she wondered how she'd not noticed it before, given how much time she had spent in there as a girl. There was that familiar scent of old papers, but there were other smells as well – decades of beeswax rubbed into the shelves, the musty dampness that sea salt added to old buildings and a slightly unsavoury odour of unwashed humans. The combination flew Pip back to her childhood as fast as any chart hit of the time might have done.

She was delighted to see the old place didn't look any different. There were a couple of extra tables in the centre of the room that now bore computers rather than the daily newspapers, but other than that it could still have been the 1990s.

Pip stood on the threshold and took in what she saw, feeling strangely nostalgic. She had been in far grander seats of learning than this one over the years, and yet there was something intangibly special about here. A lump formed in her throat, but she swallowed it back down. After the previous evening's experience, she didn't dare start crying again – who knew when she might stop?

She squared her shoulders and headed towards the wooden desk where the books had been stamped back in her day. Now it would all be done by the swipe of a smart card, but that would be less magical. There was nothing quite like the sound of that stamp.

A man was standing at the desk and for a moment Pip thought it might be Mr Lancaster, who had been the librarian when she was a girl, but when he looked up his face was unfamiliar.

'Can I help you?' he asked kindly.

'Do you still keep microfiches of the *Southwold Gazette* here?' she asked.

'We do indeed,' he said with a smile that suggested that not many people asked him for such items and it would be a librarian's pleasure to dig them out for her. 'Do you know which year you're interested in?'

'1983, please,' she replied quickly. 'From August to December.'

'I imagine that's before you were born,' the librarian commented, and then immediately looked a little awkward, as if this were too personal a statement to have made, but Pip smiled broadly back at him and nodded.

'Just give me one moment and I'll locate them for you,' he said, and disappeared towards the stairs.

Pip entertained herself by flicking through the tourist information leaflets that were sitting in a rack on the table. There were so many interesting-looking things to do nearby. It was funny, when you lived in a place, how few of them you ever thought about visiting. She checked herself. She didn't live here. She was just passing through. She would be back in London before she knew it.

'It's Philippa, isn't it?' a voice said at her back. 'Philippa Appleby. Please tell me that I'm right or I'm going to feel awfully foolish.'

Pip knew the voice at once. 'Mr Lancaster!' she said, spinning round to look at him.

The librarian had seemed ancient to her when she had been a girl, although she supposed he hadn't been much over forty. He looked unchanged now except that his thick dark hair was grey. Even his glasses were the same: unflattering gold frames in a retro shape.

'Well I never,' he said, holding out a hand for her to shake. 'How very lovely to see you. And you must call me Keith. You're not a schoolgirl any more, you know.'

Pip thought there was more chance of hell freezing over than of her addressing Mr Lancaster by his first name, but she grinned at him.

'How are you?' she asked. 'Are you still working here? I did wonder when I came in, but I thought that . . .'

'I'd be far too decrepit to still be holding down a job?' he finished for her.

'No! Of course not,' protested Pip, although that was precisely what she had thought. She felt her cheeks betray her.

'I'm very well, thank you, my dear. And I just work part-time these days. Things are done differently but I try to keep up. Don't want to be accused of being an old fuddy-duddy.'

He smiled, and Pip saw that his teeth were almost the same beige as his jumper. Then his expression changed, and he put a hand out to touch her gently on her arm.

'And I was so sorry to hear of your trouble,' he said.

It was all Pip could do not to roll her eyes. Was there anybody in this whole town who didn't know about 'her trouble'? The evidence suggested not, but they all meant well, and their wishes were kindly given.

'Thank you,' she replied.

She was saved from having to say anything else by the arrival of the first man carrying a cardboard storage box with '*Southwold Gazette* – 1983' written on its side in black marker pen.

'Here you are,' he said as he approached.

'Now then, Ian, this young lady has been coming to this library since she was knee-high to a grasshopper. I could barely keep up with her. She was always in here, changing her books and ordering things in from Ipswich. But it didn't go to waste, because she went on to be a barrister in London. That's right, isn't it, Philippa?' He looked to her for confirmation, looking almost as proud as if he had fathered her himself.

'That's right,' said Pip as she reached for the box of microfiches, anxious not to get into a discussion about her more recent history. 'Are the readers still in the back room?' she asked, cocking her head in that direction.

'Oh yes,' laughed Mr Lancaster. 'We don't like change for change's sake around here.'

Pip saw him eyeing the box curiously, but she wanted to talk about what she was looking for even less than she wanted to discuss the accident.

'Thanks for your help,' she said dismissively. 'And lovely to see you again, Mr Lancaster.'

She could feel his eyes boring into the back of her head as she walked away.

In the back room, she picked the machine in the corner that faced outwards so that she could see people approaching, and set the box down on the desk. Then she sat down, flicked the light on and took the first tape out. The label read June 1983. That was too early. She put it back, skipped past July and pulled August out. Then she fitted it into the machine and began to scroll through the pages.

According to the diary, Scarlet must have died on Wednesday the seventeenth, or at least that was the first day when Evelyn hadn't written anything. It didn't take long to locate the story. As Pip had assumed, it was front-page news.

Child dies in drowning tragedy

A local family is in mourning after a devastating accident last Wednesday. Three-year-old Scarlet Mountcastle wandered away from her family home and was found drowned in a shallow pond in a neighbouring garden a short time afterwards. The child's mother, Evelyn Mountcastle, an actress, was born and bred in the town. Miss Mountcastle, who lives with her sister Joan in the family home, is said to be too distraught to speak to our reporters but we understand that she has been helping the police with their enquiries into the death of the child. Miss Mountcastle appeared in minor roles in several television series in the 1970s before settling back in the town with her daughter. A neighbour told our reporter, 'Scarlet was a delightful child, always smiling. She was never on her own and her mother totally doted on her. It's hard to see how this could have happened.' When asking about Scarlet's father, our reporter was told that 'there was no sign of him on the scene. The Mountcastles always kept themselves to themselves.' A private service for family only will be held at St Edmund's.

Pip realised that she had been holding her breath as she read, and let it out in a long sigh. Even though she knew Scarlet had died, it was still difficult to see it written there in black and white. And the story confused her. It seemed to make no sense. The Evelyn she knew from reading the diaries would never have let Scarlet out

169

of her sight, let alone leave her to wander around alone for long enough to drown. There had to be more to it than that. Scarlet was only three. Pip knew parents were more relaxed with their children in the eighties than they were nowadays, giving them a greater freedom to roam and find their own fun, but surely basic concerns for a child's safety were the same. Three was far too little to be wandering about unaccompanied.

Pip ran her eyes over the story for a second time, but nothing new sprang out at her. She sat back in her chair and contemplated the ceiling. It didn't appear to have seen any paint for many a year and was now more of a cream colour than the white it no doubt had been originally. A water leak at some time had caused a series of brown spots in one corner that looked a little like a map of the UK.

Then a thought crossed her mind. Scarlet's was not the only death in the Mountcastle family. Joan had died, too, and in the same year, if what Jez had told her was correct. Pip began to scroll again, more slowly this time as she didn't know the exact date of death. The paper came out once a week so it didn't take too long for her to flick across the headlines and obituaries in each edition, but there was nothing about Joan.

Then, in the last edition in November, something caught her eye. She stopped scrolling and read the article more carefully.

Tragedy hits family a second time

Tragedy has hit a local family for the second time in three months. Joan Mountcastle, local resident and sister of television actress Evelyn Mountcastle, has fallen to her death in the family home. Miss Mountcastle, thirty-seven, was found by her sister at the bottom of the stairs. She suffered catastrophic injuries and we understand that death would have been instantaneous. In August this year Miss Joan Mountcastle's niece Scarlet, three, was found drowned. The police have confirmed that the death was an accident, Miss Mountcastle having lost her footing at the top of the stairs, and the coroner is expected to return a verdict of accidental death.

Pip shook her head at the screen. Poor Evelyn. To face two deaths in three months must have been devastating for her, particularly when she didn't seem to have anyone else in her life – although, Pip thought, wasn't there a brother? She was pretty sure there had been mention of him in the diary, and her mother had talked of a nephew, which suggested that Evelyn had another sibling. She reread the story again, but the brother wasn't referred to.

Even though Pip knew nothing about Evelyn other than the flashes of insight that her diary had given, her heart ached for her. She thought of the pale face she had seen staring down at her from the first-floor window. Evelyn had seemed so vivacious in her diary, so full of life. It was hard to reconcile the two.

And then Pip remembered something else Jez had said. The rumour had been that one sister had killed the other, but there seemed to be no truth in that, if the newspaper article was to be believed. It was probably nothing more than local tittle-tattle, stories invented by schoolboys to scare one another. But still, it was an interesting idea.

'Did you find what you were looking for?' said a voice, making Pip start. Instinctively, she flicked the light off on the machine so the page she had been reading disappeared.

She looked up and saw Mr Lancaster, his benevolent smile present on his face as it always used to be. Pip had no reason to hide what she was doing, but something made her guarded. This was her story and she wanted to protect it, at least for now.

'Yes, thank you,' she said, removing the cartridge from the machine and slotting it back into the box.

'Excellent,' replied Mr Lancaster, but he made no further attempt to pry into what she had been reading. 'Well, I hope we see you in here again soon. Are you staying with your parents for a while?'

Pip bristled, but she kept her smile fixed and said, 'I'm not sure, but I imagine I'll be heading back to London in the not-too-distant future.'

He nodded, as if this was good news, and then retreated back to the shelves. Pip shouldered her bag and picked up the box, carrying it carefully back to the desk. Was she going back to London soon? She had no idea, but she realised that for now, at least, she wanted to stay where she was. She had things she needed to do here in Southwold.

29

That night Pip read to the end of the diary. It was heartbreaking. With no Scarlet to light up her days, Evelyn's life seemed to have become even more insular than it had been before. Gone were the bubbly anecdotes of activities undertaken with her daughter, the painstaking recording of funny things Scarlet said or did. It was as if someone had turned Evelyn's world down from vivid technicolour to black and white, and she was merely going through the motions of her life rather than living it. Her pain seeped out from every word.

Friday 2nd September

I don't know how I can go on. Just taking a breath is sometimes more than I can manage. I wonder whether there is any point in even trying. What would it matter if I just stopped? What does anything matter now that my beautiful baby girl is gone? I didn't know it was possible to hurt this much. People always talk about their heart breaking, but I thought that was just a figure of speech. Now I understand. It is a physical pain. It stabs me in the chest and feels as real as if someone has actually plunged a dagger between my ribs. Every part of me aches. I can't sleep because when I close my eyes all I see is the tiny coffin. I can't eat – even the thought of food makes me nauseous. If I do drop off, then I wake up and for just one instant everything seems normal, like I will just go into her room and find her giggling in her bed. And then I remember.

As Pip read Evelyn's words, her cheeks were slick with tears. Since the diary had opened her emotions back up, it seemed as if there would be no closing them again. She wept without pausing, months and months' worth of stopped-up tears. She wasn't only crying for Scarlet and Evelyn. She was also, finally, crying for herself.

The parallels between herself and Evelyn were undeniable. Both had had their lives snatched from under them in one cruel, ill-fated second. They had both been merrily going about their business with no inkling of what was about to happen when an outside force had struck them and changed everything irreparably.

Now, though, Pip was starting to see that there were some differences in the two situations. The boy had died under the wheels of her car – that was undeniable – but, despite the guilt that tortured her night and day, she knew that objectively she was not at fault. The witness, the police and the coroner had all agreed. It had been a terrible accident. No one could have prevented what had happened, except the child himself.

But after her trip to the library, Pip now had a slightly different view about Scarlet's death. The child had been left on her own long enough to find her way out of the house and to the neighbour's pond. She was only three, and so surely some blame had to attach to that lack of supervision. Yes, it was a terrible accident, but it had been preventable simply by discharging a normal parental duty of care, and Pip found it hard not to place that at Evelyn's door. She had been the child's mother and her sole carer. Some of what happened surely had to be her fault.

Yet again Pip thought that that kind of slapdash parenting just didn't tally with the view of Evelyn she had built up through her reading. There was no way the Evelyn of the diary would leave her child unattended at all, let alone in a place where she might be in such mortal peril; and yet, according to the news report, that was exactly what she had done. If that were true, Pip couldn't help but judge Evelyn and find her lacking.

The diary, however, seemed to tell another story.

Wednesday 14th September

I can't believe how Joan is just carrying on as if nothing has happened. I caught her hanging out her washing and whistling this morning. Whistling! Like she didn't have a care in the world. Whilst my baby lies cold in the ground. I screamed at her. I told her she should show some respect. I said that this was all her fault and if it hadn't been for her then Scarlet would still be here, but she said she didn't see how that could be true because Scarlet was my child. How could she be to blame when S was my responsibility? But it was her fault. I know it and she knows it. I don't know exactly how, but I know she hasn't told me the truth.

I can no longer be in the same room as her. Just seeing her face turns my stomach. She cooks extra for me when she makes her own food and leaves it on a plate in the oven, but when she's left the kitchen, I go in there and throw it all away. I cannot eat anything that she's prepared. I would rather starve.

It was clear Evelyn blamed Joan, but Pip couldn't work out why. She scoured her words for some clue, but found nothing. The relationship between the two women had been strained before Scarlet's death, but afterwards animosity had turned to hatred, and it showed no sign of abating as time went on. Pip began to wonder whether it was actually a symptom of Evelyn's grief. Perhaps she was transferring guilt from herself to her sister to make the pain easier to bear. That made sense. Blame and denial were two of the recognised stages of grief.

Or could it be that there was more to Scarlet's death than met the eye? Despite the tragedy of the story, Pip couldn't help but be a little intrigued, and this was also the point where the parallel paths between herself and Evelyn diverged. Pip was crippled by guilt for what she had done. It haunted her day and night, and had destroyed everything she had built. And yet there was no such remorse in Evelyn's thoughts. It was grief that had blighted her life, not guilt.

Pip read on, becoming increasingly frustrated that she was getting such a limited snapshot of the situation, but at the same time feeling Evelyn's grief as if it were her own child who had been killed. Tears continued to pour down her cheeks as she absorbed Evelyn's pain.

Thursday 27th October

Two months and ten days. The days keep ticking by, but I stay still, frozen in time, like my baby. Each morning I wake and know I have to live another day without her. Actually, I'm not really living. I breathe, yes, and go about the bare necessities to stay alive, but that is not the same. This is no way to exist. If I could, I would go to S in a

*heartbeat. But I can't, because if I take my own life then
I will have won, and I cannot accept that. So I trudge
on, making my way through each day in the best way I
can. I am broken beyond repair. I can't imagine a time
when I will be anything but entirely destroyed. There is
no purpose to my life without my darling Scarlet.*

Pip heard her parents going to bed and then the house fell silent, the only sounds the ticking of the cooling pipes and the owls hooting in the trees outside. She read on, still wiping away her tears, until she reached November.

Wednesday 30th November

Joan is dead and I am glad. It serves her right, the bitch.

The stark sentences pulled her up short. She remembered what Jez had told her – 'The rumour was that one of them had pushed the other down the stairs.' Could that really be what happened? But the diary entries from that point told her nothing else. They became more and more sporadic, sometimes just a list of seemingly unconnected words. It was as if Evelyn was unravelling, and then finally, halfway through December, the entries stopped entirely.

The story was irritatingly incomplete. She had no idea why Scarlet had been out on her own, why Evelyn seemed to feel so little guilt nor whether she had actually killed Joan. She would have to find out the truth, though, or she was going to drive herself mad with speculation.

For a moment she considered talking to Jez about what she suspected, but then dismissed the idea almost at once. If the entry for 30th November was a confession of sorts, then it wasn't her secret to tell, and anyway, she might just have got the wrong end of the stick. That was most likely to be the case, she told herself, but at the same time something about the abruptness of the entry made the hairs on the back of her neck stand to attention.

One thing was certain, however. There had to be more to all this. What she had gleaned from the diary and her investigations at the library told her part of a story, certainly, but not all of it. She needed to find the missing pieces.

30

The next day Pip was in the back room of the shop sorting through a pile of children's clothes to be put out for sale when she heard raised voices. There was some sort of rumpus going on at the till between Audrey and a man Pip didn't recognise. Even though she couldn't make out the words from where she was, their body language made it clear this wasn't a friendly discussion. Audrey had raised herself up to full, but slightly short, height, her chin jutting defiantly, whilst the man pointed an accusing finger.

As nothing ever happened in the shop generally, a confrontation like this constituted entertainment. Pip raised an eyebrow and edged closer to the doorway to try to hear what was going on.

'That's bloody ridiculous,' snapped the man. 'Don't you have any systems at all?'

'I can assure you that we do have systems and this shop is run entirely in accordance with them,' Audrey replied archly.

'Then you should be able to locate one simple item,' the man said.

'Sir,' Audrey said, clearly struggling to maintain her temper, 'this is a charitable donation establishment. Generally, people bring us the things they no longer want. We put the items out for sale. Items are sold. It is as simple as that.'

The man's shoulders slumped a little. 'That's just it,' he said with a sigh, the fire going out of him. 'This wasn't an item that was no longer wanted. It came to your shop in error and it is of the utmost importance I get it back.'

Whilst it wasn't as common as one might think, Pip knew people did occasionally come to retrieve items they had given away, and it was just chance whether the shop still had them or not.

Audrey pursed her lips into a tight little line. 'Perhaps if you could give me some indication of what it is you have lost, then we might be able to help.' She emphasised the 'you', just to make it absolutely clear who was at fault.

Pip felt her stomach knot. It was going to be the diary, she just knew it. It had been clear from the very beginning that it didn't belong in the box of books she had opened.

'It's a book,' the man said. 'A diary, in fact. It's about this big.' He indicated the size with his hands. 'And it has flowers on the cover. Daisies, I think. It was accidentally swept up with some other books I brought in, but that was a mistake. It should never have been in the box in the first place. I really need it back.'

He looked totally forlorn now and Audrey, seeing that she was holding all the cards, seemed to soften her stance a little.

'And when did you bring the box in?' she asked him.

'I left it on the doorstep about a week ago,' he said.

Audrey sprang back up. 'You see, that's why we have rules,' she said, pointing at the sign on the wall. 'Had you brought the box to us in working hours, we would have checked the contents with you and this would never have happened.'

She gave a triumphant little smile, and the man sighed and ran his hand through his hair.

'Yes,' he said. 'But I was in a hurry, and it isn't always easy to park . . .'

'During the day,' Audrey finished for him. 'Yes. I know. But we are where we are.'

'So?' he asked a little impatiently. 'Do you remember the box?'

Audrey cocked her head to one side and made a play of trying to remember, but then she conceded that no, she didn't remember the box in question.

The knot in Pip's stomach twisted tighter still. She knew exactly which box he was talking about and knew the precise location of the diary he was so desperate to recover – in her chest of drawers, hidden underneath her knickers. But if she admitted it then she would have to confess to having taken the diary herself (which was entirely against Audrey's rules) and then keeping it, which would make it obvious that she had read it. The voice of her conscience was screaming at her to speak out, but she ignored it. She didn't have the energy to be in trouble with Audrey and anyway, she didn't know this man from Adam. He might have no more entitlement to the diary than she did, although she had to admit that was unlikely.

'What would have happened to the box?' asked the man. 'In the ordinary course of events, I mean.'

'Well, assuming it wasn't stolen from the doorstep . . .' replied Audrey, taking an exaggerated look at the sign, 'then it would have been emptied the next time we were open, prepared for sale and then added to the shelves.'

'But surely not the diary,' the man said. He sounded truly desperate.

Audrey gave a little shrug in acknowledgement. 'We wouldn't usually put a diary out for sale unless it was of particular significance,' she conceded.

The man seemed to brighten. 'So where might it have gone? If it wasn't put out for sale, I mean.'

'Well, as I am the manager of the shop, any such items would be brought to me. And it wasn't. I'm terribly sorry, Mr . . .' She paused.

'Mountcastle,' he muttered.

Audrey seemed to do a little double take, but the gesture was so small that Pip might have been mistaken.

'I'm terribly sorry, Mr Mountcastle, but I don't seem to be able to help you.'

The man gave a huge sigh, and Pip felt sick. She should just tell them what she'd done. What did it matter if she had broken Audrey's rules? Who cared about them except Audrey anyway? Then again, if she gave the diary up now, she might never get a chance to speak to Evelyn and then she would never find out the answers to all her questions. The diary was her way into that house. Even more so now she knew Evelyn clearly wanted it back.

'Well, if it turns up, could you contact me?' the man said, fishing a wallet out of his jacket pocket and extracting a business card, which he placed on the counter in front of Audrey.

Then he turned and left the shop.

As soon as he had gone, Pip breezed out of the back room, a pile of clothes in her arms.

'What was that all about?' she asked casually, as if she had no interest in the reply but was just making conversation.

'Things given away in error,' said Audrey. 'People are so careless with the items they profess to hold dear to their hearts.'

'He seemed terribly upset,' said Pip. 'Poor chap.'

Audrey just harrumphed and bustled off to put the kettle on.

Pip picked up the business card from the countertop and slipped it into her jeans pocket. Now she faced a quandary. The obvious thing to do was ring the man – Nicholas Mountcastle, according to his business card – and tell him she had the diary. But if she did that, then he would just take the diary from her and she would lose her opportunity to meet Evelyn.

Alternatively, she could turn up on Evelyn's doorstep and say she had heard that this Nicholas chap was looking for the diary. The trouble with that plan was that it raised the question as to why she hadn't just given it back to him. Also, Evelyn might not even be aware her diary was missing, so that would get Nicholas into all kinds of trouble. She didn't actually care about that, but she liked that it supported her third, and preferred, option: she should ignore the fact that she now knew they were looking for the diary and just turn up at the house with it, as she had already planned to do. That way she would get to see Evelyn, hopefully, and could pretend she wasn't aware of Nicholas's visit to the shop.

She would go after she'd finished work, she decided, and then realised she didn't have the diary with her. It would have to be the following day, Saturday – not a day she generally went to the shop. She could go in the morning and try to blag her way into the house, using the diary as bait. It wouldn't be her finest hour, preying on defenceless old ladies, but needs must, and anyway, she wasn't intending any harm to Evelyn. She just wanted the chance to talk to her. Old women liked to talk; she knew this. So hopefully Evelyn would welcome the opportunity. She would have to pretend she hadn't actually read the diary, though, which would make questioning her difficult. Pip shook her head. She was a barrister, for goodness' sake. What she didn't know about getting information out of witnesses wasn't worth knowing. How hard could it be to get a lonely old lady to engage in a touch of nostalgic chat?

Pip busied herself amongst the racks of clothes so she wouldn't trigger Audrey's idleness radar. Since getting over her feelings of revulsion at handling the cast-off clothes of strangers, she was able to find a kind of affection for these pre-owned, pre-loved things. Sometimes, to pass the time, she even imagined little backstories for the garments, trying to picture the people who had bought them, worn them for something special and then passed them on to be worn and loved by someone else. She didn't want to buy the clothes herself but perhaps she could understand the process a little more. It was as if her sharp edges were being gradually smoothed, just as the perpetual rush of the sea smooths a jagged rock face.

Pip tried to visualise Nicholas Mountcastle. He had been quite tall and rangy, although most people would look rangy when standing next to Audrey. His hair was the colour of gingerbread and long enough to reveal curls. He'd worn it pushed away from his forehead, which made his face look very long, too, and his nose matched. In fact, that was Pip's overall impression of him – long. Did he look like Evelyn, she wondered? It was hard to say what the woman in the window had looked like at all, let alone whether there was a family resemblance.

He'd been quite desperate to get the diary back, she thought, which either meant he felt bad at losing it or Evelyn was formidable and he was scared of her. From the way he had spoken to Audrey, Pip had the impression that it might be the latter, but this didn't quite chime with her own impression of Evelyn. Maybe she'd hardened in the years since Scarlet's death, though. Perhaps she had grown into a bitter spinster, surrounding herself with cats and rebuffing any offers of help or compassion.

Pip smiled to herself and let out a little huff of laughter. What on earth was she doing, wasting all this time thinking about a complete stranger? It was madness, even bordering on obsession. Ever since she had found the diary, its contents and Evelyn herself had occupied Pip's mind almost constantly. It wasn't normal, she knew, but then again not much had been normal since the accident. It probably wasn't healthy, either. She knew what she was doing, focusing on the diary so she could avoid thinking about Dominic, although each time she did allow thoughts of him to creep into her mind she felt a little less sad. The longer she was at home, the further she felt from Rose. She was fading in her memory, like the scent of her namesake flowers kept overlong in a vase. Dominic had loved Rose – or at least the idea of her; Pip wasn't sure which. But when Rose had started to wither, so had Dominic's interest in her, and he had shown no interest at all in Pip. Pip was beginning to think that spoke volumes. Didn't these things generally work out for the best? Maybe that was the case here. When she got back to London, she would see Dominic almost every day at work, but that thought didn't worry her at all. That must mean something, surely?

For the first time, a new idea appeared in her head: cautious, like a snail stretching out its horns as it checked for signs of danger. Maybe she could start looking for a new flat. After all, she couldn't spend the rest of her life hiding out up here in the sticks. She was going to have to get back to work sooner or later, and she would have to live somewhere. She could simply transport her things from one place to another, rather than bring everything to the farm. There was something very final about bringing her possessions back to Suffolk. It would feel like a failure to her, and she was certain there were others in the town who would think the same. She would be the girl who flew too close to the sun, and everyone knew what happened to her. A new flat would avoid all that, she thought.

But then, out of nowhere, came the memory of her sliding to the floor in the Grand Hall of the Supreme Court. How could she contemplate returning to London when she had no idea when she might have a panic attack like that one? Just thinking about it made her heart beat harder. She gripped the clothes rail tightly and breathed slowly in and out, as she had been taught. It took a good ten minutes before she felt in control again, and every part of her was exhausted by the strain of trying to hold herself together. Despair crept into her heart yet again. She might be improving, but clearly she was a long way off being better.

31

Every morning, Evelyn had a bowl of cornflakes for her breakfast. She didn't even like cornflakes that much, but when she had first set up her online food shop, cornflakes had been the only cereal she could think of. And so they had ended up in her basket, and there they had stayed. She knew it couldn't be that hard to switch the order to something else, but somehow she never seemed to have the energy to think about it. It was much easier to keep reordering the same things week after week: bread, milk, Granny Smith apples, tinned pilchards, Philadelphia cream cheese, Jacob's cream crackers and cornflakes. It made for a very dull diet, but it hadn't killed her yet. Each week she promised herself she would shake things up a little, and yet the same food kept arriving.

She had just finished that morning's bowl when she heard a knock at the front door. Evelyn started. She wasn't expecting anyone. Nicholas generally called on a Sunday, and the food delivery had arrived yesterday. No one else ever knocked.

It couldn't be important, she thought as she dropped her bowl into the sink, already filled with crockery from previous meals that she hadn't got round to washing up. She would ignore the knocking. The kitchen was at the back of the house so no one could see she was there. She picked up the plastic carton of milk and went to replace it in the fridge.

The knocking came again and this time there was another sound as well. Evelyn stood stock still and strained to listen. It was a woman's voice.

'Miss Mountcastle?' it said. 'Are you there? I really need to talk to you.'

Evelyn shuffled to the door and peered into the hallway just as the flap of the letterbox slammed shut. The cheek of it. Whoever it was had shouted through her door without so much as a by your leave, Evelyn thought indignantly, and they had invaded her privacy to boot. There were rules about that kind of thing, she knew.

But a part of her was curious. Who was so eager to talk to her that they would prostrate themselves before her front door in full view of passers-by just to attract her attention? And what could be so important to require that?

Against her better judgement, Evelyn felt herself being pulled towards the front door just as whoever it was knocked again, harder this time. Then the letter box opened for a second time. From where she was standing at the end of the corridor, Evelyn fancied she could just make out a pair of eyes and possibly a nose.

'Miss Mountcastle,' the disembodied head called out. 'Are you in there?'

'I'm coming,' barked Evelyn. 'Give me a chance, for goodness' sake.'

The letter box snapped shut and the knocking stopped. Approaching the door, Evelyn reached her hand out to slide the bolt across, but then she stopped. She had no idea who this person was. Yes, the woman had referred to her by name, but how hard could it be to discover that? The Mountcastles had lived in this house for over eighty years. All the person had to do was ask a couple of questions and she could have found out enough details to blag her way in like a long-lost friend. Nicholas was always warning her about scammers. Who was to say this wasn't one of those? Evelyn stayed her hand.

'What do you want?' she asked through the door.

'I just wanted a quick word,' came the voice.

'About what?' asked Evelyn, her suspicions growing by the minute.

'I think I have something of yours,' the woman said.

Evelyn had to concede that the woman didn't sound like a scammer, although she had only the shakiest notion of how such a person might speak. This woman's voice was clear and distinct and she was well spoken, with only a hint of a local accent. Evelyn was still sceptical, though. She had barely left the house in years and it seemed highly unlikely that the woman really did have something of hers, but now she wanted to know for sure – exactly as the woman, if she were a scammer, no doubt hoped. Evelyn decided to proceed with caution.

'Oh yes?' she replied in what she hoped was a disinterested tone.

'Yes,' the woman continued. 'A diary. From 1983.'

Her words made Evelyn sway a little, and she had to hold on to the doorjamb to steady herself.

'I work in the Have a Heart charity shop,' the voice continued.

Evelyn didn't need to hear any more. She slid the bolt across, turned the latch and opened the door. Standing on the doorstep, but at a respectful distance, was the young woman from the other day, the one she had caught staring up at the house. She looked around thirty, Evelyn thought, but was somehow more careworn than she should have been for her age. Fine lines radiated out from her dark eyes and narrow mouth, and her cheekbones protruded severely, although something about her face suggested it was used to being a little more filled out. Her dark hair was cut into a neat, shoulder-length bob that she kept touching as if fearful it would fall out of place. She might have been pretty had she not looked so drawn.

'Do you have the diary?' Evelyn said without introduction.

The woman looked a little taken aback at the lack of social niceties, but she nodded obediently, her bottom lip caught between her front teeth. Evelyn assumed the book must be in the cloth bag slung over her shoulder, but her visitor made no effort to remove it and hand it over.

'Can I come in, please?' the woman asked. 'I would love to talk to you for a moment.'

'What about?' asked Evelyn, her hand still outstretched to receive the diary.

The woman tucked a piece of flyaway hair behind her ear and shuffled from one foot to the other. 'Are you Evelyn Mountcastle, the actress?' she asked.

For a second, something in Evelyn's heart soared. Evelyn Mountcastle, the actress. The mere words evoked in her a nostalgia so strong that the corners of her mouth turned up a little. She fought to push them back down.

'I am,' she replied grandly.

The woman smiled then, her entire face lighting up so that instantly she looked younger and less ravaged.

'My mother told me you were,' she said. 'I gather you were quite famous.'

Evelyn shrugged. 'I had my moment,' she replied. 'Although that's all in the past now. I don't act any more.'

'Why not?' asked the woman.

It was such a direct question that Evelyn was at first taken aback by it and then intrigued by the questioner. 'The opportunities just never presented themselves,' she said.

The woman nodded as if considering this, but still made no effort to hand over the diary. She was bold, Evelyn would give her that. Well, two could play at that game.

'And you? You work in a charity shop, you say.'

The woman nodded, but the accompanying expression in her eyes suggested something that Evelyn couldn't quite put her finger on. Was it a disappointment that that was what her life amounted to – not that Evelyn could see anything inherently wrong with the job herself – or sadness? Or loss? Yes, that was it. Evelyn could see loss in the woman's face. It was something she recognised because she saw it reflected in her own features every time she caught sight of herself in a mirror.

'But there's more to it than that,' Evelyn continued thoughtfully, as if she were a stage medium. 'That's not your job of choice, is it?'

The woman gave a brief shake of her head. 'I'm a barrister,' she said, her eyes no longer meeting Evelyn's and focusing on the wall of the house instead. 'But I'm not currently practising.'

She didn't say any more, but there was more to be said, Evelyn could tell. Perhaps she should let her in? She could try to get to the bottom of this story as well as getting the diary back. She didn't seem like a scammer or an axe-murderer, and Evelyn realised suddenly how much she ached to have a conversation with another human being, someone who did not feel obliged to be there and talk to her.

She opened the door a little wider and invited the stranger in.

32

Pip followed Evelyn inside. The door closed behind her, the sound heavy in the silence of the house, and suddenly the hum of the street outside was gone.

She found herself in a dark corridor, the air cloying and thick with the smell of dust. Evelyn led the way, and after a moment's hesitation opened a door on her right into what Pip imagined would be the sitting room. There was no daylight in there either, but Evelyn stepped sure-footedly and opened the window blinds to let the sun in. The dust, so recently disturbed, floated around her, catching in the rays of light that now sliced through the space. There was a musty, neglected feel to the room, and Pip wondered how long it had been since the door had last been opened. She longed to fling wide the windows and let fresh air circulate, but instead she instructed her lungs to accept the poor-quality oxygen without complaint.

'Please, sit down,' said Evelyn, indicating the high-backed chairs that sat on either side of the tiled fireplace.

A thick layer of sticky dust caked the chairs as well, so it was almost impossible to discern the colour of the tweed upholstery. Somewhere between green and brown, Pip guessed, and definitely from the early part of the twentieth century. Somebody somewhere would part with a fortune for this retro look, but here it just had an air of being forgotten and unloved.

She chose the seat with its back to the window and managed to resist her natural urge to brush away the dust before sitting down. Aside from a general lack of use, the room retained the formality it must have had when it was used for best. There was no television, for a start, and none of the day-to day-clutter that family life usually generates. Through the murky glass of a Victorian display cabinet, Pip could see several pieces of china in the distinctive pale blue and white of Wedgwood jasperware, together with various other ornaments that looked like expensive collectors' pieces rather than tacky souvenirs. Her sharp eye also spotted a coffee service that she thought might be an original Clarice Cliff. There had clearly been money here at one time, Pip could see.

Pip could sense Evelyn sizing her up and hoped that she wasn't found to be lacking. The old woman's pale eyes were staring at her intensely, unwaveringly, like those of a bird of prey. Pip had the impression that they missed nothing, but she was determined not to feel intimidated. She had withstood far deeper scrutiny than this in the court room. If Evelyn was hoping to frighten her, then she was going to be disappointed.

So far, things seemed to be going according to plan. Pip had managed to get into the house, at least, even if Evelyn didn't quite know what to make of her. It felt to Pip as if the pair of them were playing a tactical game of cat and mouse, each waiting for the other to reveal themselves first. It made a change to find herself pitched against a worthy adversary, and she realised that she was enjoying herself, even though the pleasure was tinged with a bloom of anxiety that she might not be able to get what she wanted from the encounter. At work she had learned to use silence to her advantage, and so she fixed a gentle smile on her lips and waited.

'Well, then,' said Evelyn after a second or two. She was clearly less comfortable with silence than Pip. 'You say you have my diary.'

'Yes,' replied Pip. 'It came into the shop in a box of books. I thought it was probably there by mistake, so I retrieved it and then did a little detective work to find out where it had come from.'

'I saw you outside the other day,' Evelyn said.

'Was that you? At the window?' Pip asked disingenuously. 'I thought I saw someone.'

'And may I have my property back?' Evelyn asked. Her tone was bordering on sharp, and Pip, noting this, decided to change tactics. She didn't want to be dismissed before she had managed to start a real conversation.

'Of course,' she said, reaching into her bag and bringing out the flowery diary.

Evelyn drew in her breath when she saw it, then reached for it with a wavering hand. She held it for a moment before dropping it into her lap. A strange sense of loss came over Pip as she relinquished it. She had no rights over the diary, but she was reluctant to give it up, much like Bilbo Baggins with the precious ring.

'Would you tell me about your acting?' Pip asked, to break the tension.

Now that the diary had been returned, her hold over Evelyn was all but gone – unless she let it be known that she had read it, of course, but she was reluctant to do that at this point. She smiled as she spoke and tried to look charming, hoping that the joint temptation of a conversation and the opportunity to share something of her past would be enough to tempt Evelyn to open up a little. She could see that Evelyn was weighing up the pros and cons of allowing her to stay now that the diary had been returned. After a moment's hesitation, she appeared to choose conversation, and the tension ebbed a little from her narrow shoulders.

She took a breath and returned Pip's smile with one that didn't quite reach her eyes.

'I worked mainly in London in the 1970s,' she said, 'which will have been before you were even born. I did a little stage work and some things for television. There were only three channels back then, of course, so you tended to be recognised in the street a little, but most actors weren't thought of as being famous at all. The Queen was famous, and The Beatles, but not television actors.'

'How refreshing,' Pip replied. 'It isn't healthy the way we treat celebrities these days. Not for them or us.'

Evelyn didn't agree or even react to the comment, and Pip wasn't sure she had understood her meaning, but then she supposed that if Evelyn had been living here as a virtual recluse, she would have no idea what the tabloids had made into their bread and butter.

'Anyway, I had ten years living that life,' Evelyn continued, 'and then . . .' She paused. She appeared to be considering what to say next, how much information to share. Did she assume, Pip wondered, that she hadn't read the diary? She felt her stomach squirm. 'And then things changed,' Evelyn continued neutrally. 'I moved back up here, and this is where I've been ever since.'

As a story it was unsatisfactory, Pip thought, for without including the real reason why she had left London, it was bland and unremarkable, but it appeared to be all she was prepared to give her for now.

Evelyn shifted a little in her seat, causing a bloom of dust to appear before it resettled itself. She lifted a hand to her ear, running the pads of her fingers across her earlobe. In court, such a movement might be used as a tension creator, a tiny pause in the pace designed to pull the judge up and think a moment about what was happening. Nobody would generally notice it, but Pip was trained to see these things. Then again, she might be overthinking it. It was probably just an unconscious gesture made without thought, as such movements generally were.

But Pip could play games, too. She was more than a match for Evelyn when it came to body language. She paused for a moment and cleared her throat, the sound a verbal tic to signal to her brain that she was ready to move on with her argument.

'My mum tells me that you came back to have a baby,' she said.

Evelyn's demeanour changed instantly. Her sharp eyes narrowed and she pulled a little further back into her seat to increase the distance between them. Pip worried that she had overplayed her hand, gone in too far and too fast. She could kick herself. It wasn't like her to make a tactical error like that. She was clearly out of practice in reading people. She gave her widest and most open smile to try to convey her harmlessness, but Evelyn still eyed her warily and the hint of warmth that had been kindled between them was gone.

'Before we go any further,' Evelyn said sharply, 'I think you should tell me your name. Here you are in my house and you haven't even introduced yourself.'

Blood rushed to Pip's cheeks, and the carefully poised interrogator of the moment before deserted her.

'Oh God, I'm so sorry,' she said. 'I'm . . .' She hesitated.

Evelyn raised a suspicious eyebrow. Pip couldn't blame her. What kind of person hesitated over their own name? She saw Evelyn's fingers tighten around the diary in her lap.

'It's very complicated,' Pip continued, although she could see Evelyn wondering how this could be true. Your name was generally your name, wasn't it? Unless you had a stage name, or a pen name. Or you were lying.

Ignoring Evelyn's apparently growing animosity, Pip began to explain. 'Until recently I called myself Rose,' she began. She could feel a sheen of tears glossing over her eyes and she blinked them away. This was not the time to cry, but she thought she saw Evelyn soften a little; something around the mouth, maybe, a certain curiosity in her gaze. 'But my first name is Philippa, Pip. Pip Appleby.'

'And why don't you call yourself Rose any longer?' Evelyn asked.

Pip took a deep breath and then let it out very slowly.

'It's a long story,' she said.

'I have all day,' replied Evelyn.

33

This was not going at all as Pip had imagined her first meeting with Evelyn. She wanted to listen to Evelyn talk, not the other way around, and yet somehow the tables had been turned. Was this a game of tit for tat, Pip wondered – I'll tell you my dubious and dark backstory, but only if you tell me yours first? Maybe opening herself up to Evelyn was the price she was going to have to pay.

Quickly, Pip ran through her options. She could refuse to answer, and subtly shift the conversation on to safer ground. Or she could lie, either making something up or telling a more palatable version of her story. But if she did that and watered down her own history to something bland and safe, then how could she expect Evelyn to be open and honest in return?

She should just tell her the truth, even though her reasons for changing her Christian name were starting to make her uncomfortable. Before the accident, when she had been totally caught up in her London life with her rich friends, she had never given it a second's thought. It was only now, now that she was back at home and had time to consider her actions, that she could see the impact of what she had done. And it made her feel ashamed. But if she wanted to learn anything about Evelyn, then she was clearly going to have to give her something to start the ball rolling.

'I grew up on a farm just outside the town,' she began. 'My parents are lovely, but their aspirations were limited to making a living on the land. So when I said I wanted to go to university and be a barrister they were pleased as punch, but they didn't really understand why I wanted something so different to them. They tried to support me, but it was always on their terms. If I wanted to go up to London to see an exhibition that might help with my studies, they'd complain about the cost or worry that I wouldn't be at the farm to do my share of the chores. They didn't make my life difficult as such. They just didn't get it.'

Pip searched Evelyn's face for any clue that she understood. Hadn't it been the same for Evelyn growing up in this house, wanting to break free from her family's expectations? She thought she saw a glimmer of comprehension in Evelyn's eyes, but she couldn't be certain. Evelyn was hard to read, far harder than Pip had anticipated. She pressed on.

'Anyway, I worked hard at school, got the grades I needed and then left home. It was only when I got to university that I realised how sheltered my life here had been. All at once, I was surrounded by new people and new points of view. Things that I had never even considered suddenly seemed to be hugely important to everyone else. Politics, art, philosophy; there was so much to learn, so much I needed to know. And I needed to do it quickly, before anyone noticed how unsophisticated I was.'

Pip rolled her eyes, mocking herself, but Evelyn just sat still in her chair and didn't react. It was really disconcerting, this lack of response, but Pip had started now, so she might as well just keep talking.

'When I got to bar school it was even worse,' she continued. 'Most of the other students had been to private school. They had this air about them, this inner confidence. I understand now that it comes from being told you're the best and can do anything you want from a very young age, but at the time I just thought they were better than me. So that made me even more determined to get myself on a par with them.'

Pip felt her cheeks start to pinken. It sounded so shallow when she said it out loud, but it had been so important to her younger self. Fitting into her surroundings had been vital in order to thrive.

'At home they'd always called me Pip. I didn't mind. In fact, I never even thought about it. It was just my name, you know. But in London, where I was surrounded by Louisas and Tamsins, Pip suddenly sounded very childish. Rose is my middle name so about three weeks into the course I decided to switch. It felt more polished, more suited to the person I was trying to be . . .'

Pip paused, and looked towards Evelyn sheepishly. 'It sounds so silly now,' she confessed. 'Superficial and . . . Well, anyway, at the time it felt very important.'

Evelyn's expression altered minutely, and Pip had the impression that she was with her, that she understood.

'You were reinventing yourself,' Evelyn said, and Pip nodded urgently. That was exactly it. Evelyn had hit the nail on the head.

'Don't we all do that,' Evelyn continued, 'to a greater or lesser extent? Not everyone goes as far as to change their name to shed their old skin, though many do, but trying to become something new is a human affliction.'

Evelyn stroked her hand over the diary as she spoke, as if she were gaining an inner strength from touching it. Perhaps she understood, Pip thought. She had also fled her home to begin something new, but she hadn't tried to hide where she came from, as far as Pip knew. Evelyn seemed to have an integrity that Pip's name-changing story showed she lacked.

'Well, my parents weren't that impressed with my decision,' Pip continued. 'My mum thought I'd changed my name because I was ashamed of them.'

'But you were, weren't you?' asked Evelyn, her pale eyes focused so exactly on Pip's that she had to look away for a moment. 'Isn't that precisely why you did it?'

Pip's insides twisted, but then she wrinkled her nose and sighed. 'Yes. I suppose so.'

'And now you've gone back to Pip?'

Pip hesitated. Had she? Had she metamorphosed into a butterfly only to find herself slipping back to being a caterpillar once again?

She shrugged. 'It's easier to be Pip at home. Mum and Dad can't get the hang of Rose and, well, Mum seems to think it means she's got her daughter back.'

'And when you go back to London?' asked Evelyn. Pip noticed that she showed no doubt that would happen.

'My professional name is Rose,' she replied simply.

'And what should I call you?' Evelyn asked, her head cocked to one side.

Did this mean, Pip wondered, that there would be further conversations? She felt a giddy rush of excitement at the prospect.

'You must choose,' she replied, and Evelyn raised an eyebrow.

'I asked for that, I suppose,' she said with a smile, and Pip relaxed.

Now it was Evelyn's turn to tell her a truth. Pip sat back, mentally if not physically, and waited for what was to come next.

'I must get on now,' Evelyn said, getting laboriously to her feet. 'I have matters that I need to attend to.'

Pip's heart sank. No, she wanted to say; we've only just begun, and you haven't told me anything at all about you and your story! And on top of that, she had handed over the diary, so she had no bargaining chip left.

'But I would like it very much if you would call on me again, Philippa Rose. I feel that we have still a lot of story to be told.'

Pip grinned, unable to keep her delight from her face. 'I'd love that,' she said. 'I meant it when I said I was interested in your acting career.'

'Shall we say Wednesday?' Evelyn asked.

'I could come in the afternoon,' replied Pip, her mind already working out what she would tell Audrey. She was only a volunteer in the shop, but she didn't want to let anyone down.

'How about two o'clock?' Evelyn suggested, and Pip nodded.

'That would be perfect,' she said.

34

Evelyn closed the front door and then stood with her back against it, her head resting on the flaking paintwork. She could hear the muffled tones of a siren somewhere outside and it sent a shudder through her whole body, as it always did, even now. Her hand was still clutching the diary and she raised it to her lips and kissed the daisy cover lightly. Then she held it to her heart as she considered what had just happened.

A visitor was not what she had been expecting today, and certainly not one as interesting as Philippa Rose Appleby. Evelyn had liked her. Even though she had clearly come with an agenda, the nature of which was still a little unclear, she had been prepared to talk honestly. It can't have been easy for her, confessing to being – well, there was no other way of putting it – to being a snob. She hadn't believed her name was posh enough and so had simply ditched it in order to fit in.

Evelyn wasn't surprised her parents had been put out. She tried to imagine how she would have felt if Scarlet had done the same thing to her, but it was a thought she couldn't process. Scarlet had still been largely unformed when her little life had come to a halt. Picturing what she might or might not have thought about her origins was nigh-on impossible. Evelyn couldn't conceive of her daughter not wanting to be known as Scarlet; it was such a fabulous name, particularly back in 1979. But then what was wrong with being called Philippa? Or Pip, for that matter? Absolutely nothing. Whatever had been going on for Philippa Rose when she left her sleepy Suffolk town for the bright lights of London, it had nothing to do with having the wrong name.

Evelyn made her way into the kitchen to make herself a cup of tea. There was another reason why she had been so taken with her visitor, she thought as she sat at the table, her hands wrapped around the steaming mug. Philippa Rose had wanted something different from what was expected of her. Her clear vocation hadn't matched her parents' ideas of what her life should be, and that had caused ructions within her family home.

It all had such a familiar ring to it. Peter and Joan had been happy to stand inside the box their parents had built for them, but Evelyn had not. For her, a dull office job felt like a prison sentence. Keeping her in Southwold had been like trapping a tiger in a camper van and then parking it on the drive where it could see the road to freedom. Every time she had switched on the television, she saw actresses doing precisely what she wanted to do, but in order to have this for herself she'd had to defy her parents and flee. In this regard Evelyn supposed that she and her visitor were very much alike.

That wasn't everything, though, Evelyn was sure. There was something more than just a need to break away and follow their own path that the two women had in common. Even if she hadn't managed to identify exactly what the connection was, she had definitely felt it. There was something in Philippa Rose's past that didn't sit straight with what she had told her so far, something shadowy and unspoken. There had to be, or else what was she doing living here and working in a charity shop, rather than being a barrister in London? Something must have dragged her back. She had mentioned both her parents so it was unlikely to be a recent bereavement, but nonetheless she seemed to be carrying a melancholic burden deep inside her. Evelyn would be prepared to put money on there being something heavy in her heart. She could see it in Pip's eyes. It was something Evelyn saw in her own eyes every time she looked in the mirror.

That was why she'd invited the girl back. She wanted to get to the bottom of her story, and she felt, given the right encouragement, that Philippa Rose would open up to her. Evelyn might even be able to help.

It was a risky strategy, though. It was crystal clear that she had read the diary. Why else would she manufacture all that guff about wanting to hear about Evelyn's acting past? No. Our Philippa Rose was trying to find out what had happened here. She was fishing.

Evelyn opened the diary and flicked the pages over until she came to the relevant entry. Wednesday 30th November. There had always been a risk in writing it down, but the risk had always felt infinitesimally small. After all, who was going to read her diary? There had been no chance that it would be opened by anyone but her; not until she died, at least, and by then it wouldn't matter.

But that had been before Nicholas had done his mucking out of his Aunt Evelyn. Evelyn rolled her eyes and sighed. The boy had meant well, but really, he could have no idea of the potential damage he had done. And of course, sod's law dictated it had to be that diary he sent to the shop. If it had been any of the others . . . Well, the 1979 one might have caused some eyes to stretch, but the dangers of the casting couch were hardly shocking news. Hers was just another story in a very long chapter. Reading about what had befallen her might have prompted a few lines in the local paper, nothing more. But the 1983 diary? That was a horse of a different colour altogether.

Maybe Evelyn would be better leaving well alone. She had the diary back now. She could destroy it and there would be no evidence against her, assuming that Philippa Rose hadn't made a copy. She might have done, given her legal background, but Evelyn doubted it. She hadn't come to dig the dirt; Evelyn was sure of it. She was just curious, as Evelyn was about her.

Still, she told herself that she would do well to proceed with caution. She'd focus on whatever it was that had brought Philippa Rose back to Southwold and leave her own story out of it for the time being. And once she had heard the bones of the other woman's history, then she would be in a better position to judge whether she was at risk.

And she would call her Pip, Evelyn decided. She felt far more like a Pip than a Rose.

35

When Pip got back to the farm, she found Jez sitting at the kitchen table, his head in his hands. Her mother was standing over him, her hand not quite on his back but hovering just above it. There was an awkwardness to the gesture. Even though her mother had known Jez since he was a boy, she seemed uncomfortable with their close proximity now that he was a man.

As Pip entered the room Jez didn't move, but her mother looked up and, seeing her, seemed to sag a little with relief.

'Oh look, here's Pip,' she said over-brightly. 'Jez has had a bit of bad news so he's just taking a few minutes.' She pulled a face over the top of Jez's crumpled form and shook her head. Pip frowned, and her mother pointed first to the ring finger of her left hand and then made a slashing gesture across her throat. It was so unlike her that it was all Pip could do not to giggle, but she restrained herself. If she had this right, then Jez's engagement to the confident Teresa was off.

Pip raised her eyebrows, and her mother pulled another face and shrugged. Pip pulled out a chair and sat down next to Jez. Her mother might feel awkward quizzing him, but Pip had no such qualms.

She laid a hand on her friend's forearm and squeezed lightly. 'How are you doing, mate?' she asked, her voice gentle.

Jez made no reply, but he sighed deeply, his shoulders rising and falling heavily. Pip looked up at her mother and cocked her head towards the door. Her mother nodded, grateful to be excused, and disappeared.

It was the just the two of them now. Behind them, the Aga hummed away to itself and there was the sound of a tractor engine in the distance.

Pip waited. There was no point in rushing him. He would tell her in his own good time. Or maybe not at all; either was fine. It just felt very important that he knew she was there for him, no matter what had happened.

She felt him draw in another huge breath and let it out again as a deep sigh, as if he was expelling something from his body. Then he raised his head and ran his hands through his hair.

'Shit,' he said.

'Want to tell me?' asked Pip.

He let out another big breath, blowing it through his lips.

'Not much to tell,' he said. 'I've been dumped.'

Instinctively, Pip reached over, put her arms round his neck and pulled her into him in a tight squeeze. Totally compliant, he dropped his head on to her shoulder and let her hold him. They hadn't been so close for over ten years, but the shape of him was immediately familiar. She knew exactly where his head would fit, where her hands should rest. Even the scent of him was the same, and for a second it tossed her back in time to a place that felt easy, comfortable, safe. It had been a while since Pip had experienced that feeling and she relished it, even as she knew that she should be trying to comfort Jez. This was about his pain, not hers. She continued to hold him tightly and hoped it was helping him as much as it was her.

After a couple of minutes, he drew away from her, his eyes focused on the yard beyond the kitchen window.

'It's my own stupid fault,' he said.

'How do you make that out?' Pip asked. She might not know the details, but she wasn't about to let Jez shoulder any of the blame.

'Just look at me. I am a farmhand, son of a farmhand. I'm never going to add up to much else. I didn't make it to uni, I settled for this life instead, and now I'm thirty and all I've done so far is work on the land less than five miles from where I was born.'

Pip was confused. She couldn't see what this had to do with Teresa calling off their engagement, if that was indeed what had happened.

'Well, there's nothing wrong with that,' she said cautiously, unsure of the right thing to say.

'No. I know that,' Jez replied. 'And don't get me wrong. I love what I do. Your dad's great to work for and the job suits me.'

'So where's the problem?' Pip asked.

He pulled his gaze from the window and focused on her instead. 'I've been punching above my weight with Teresa. She's way out of my league. Always has been. Her dad works in futures, whatever that is, and her mum's a consultant at Colchester Hospital. They're hardly like you and me.'

Pip could feel herself bristle a little at being lumped in with Jez, but she checked herself. She had to accept that they were fundamentally the same, despite all her efforts to differentiate herself.

'And Teresa's got a degree and an amazing job. She's flying high. Pretty soon it was going to dawn on her that Jez Walker, lowly farmhand from Hicksville, didn't fit into the picture. To be honest with you, I can't believe I got away with it for as long as I did.'

'That's crap,' said Pip, angry now on his behalf. 'She was marrying you for you, not your job description. The rest of it shouldn't matter if she really loves you.'

Jez peered at her through his lashes. 'Says the girl who changed her name to something posher the minute she moved away,' he said, and there was something bitter in his tone that made her feel ill at ease. Was that really what he thought, what they all thought? Then again, that was exactly what she had done; she just hadn't realised it was so very transparent.

Jez seemed to understand that he might have hit a nerve, and he lowered his eyes again to defuse the tension.

'Anyway, none of that matters,' he said, 'because Teresa's called the whole thing off. Returned the ring. The works.'

He pulled a black velvet box out of his jeans pocket and flicked it open with his thumb. Inside was a very pretty ring with a diamond solitaire. Pip knew it was probably only around a quarter of a carat and immediately hated herself for both knowing that and thinking it.

Jez snapped the box shut and slammed it on the table.

'So that's that. I'm a single man once more. No big country wedding for me. Shit, the grapevine will be having a field day.'

'Ignore them,' Pip snapped. 'It's none of their bloody business. You just need to talk to Teresa. She'll change her mind. It's probably just pre-wedding nerves.'

'Nah,' he said, shaking his head. 'That bird's flown. We've been talking round it all week. Her mind's made up. She's very sorry and all that, but I'm history.'

He dropped his head again and rested it on his forearms. There was nothing else Pip could say or do except let him know she was there for him if he needed her. She gave his rounded shoulders a little squeeze then left him to his misery.

As she climbed the stairs to her room, it occurred to her that for the first time in almost as long as she could remember, she was the one offering help rather than having it offered to her, and it felt good.

36

Pip spent the following few days thinking about her forthcoming meeting with Evelyn, and each time she did her insides fluttered. She thought it was nerves at first, the feeling, any feeling in fact, being so unfamiliar. It wasn't that Evelyn was at all scary, but she did seem to have a way of seeing straight to the heart of Pip in a way that others hadn't done. Pip was used to being more guarded, to keeping her own counsel, and yet all that had gone out of the window the moment Evelyn had begun to probe. Pip couldn't decide if it was because Evelyn was particularly perceptive, or because she was ready to open up, and in the end she settled on it being a little of both.

But it wasn't nerves, Pip recognised now – it was excitement. She couldn't remember the last time she had felt excited about something, and she liked it. She thought about what they would talk about, imagined the two of them finding numerous points of connection as each spread out their lives before the other in ever-increasing detail. There was definitely a certain something between them, a mutual understanding, a bond. Pip could feel it even if she wasn't quite sure how it was going to pan out yet.

Audrey had sniffed a little when she told her that she wouldn't be in the shop on Wednesday, but there wasn't much she could do about it, and until now Pip had never missed a shift so she didn't really have that much to complain about.

When Wednesday finally rolled round, Pip was ready and standing on Evelyn's doorstep at exactly two o'clock. She could feel her heart beating a little faster than usual, but it wasn't warning her of an impending panic attack. This was more about the pleasurable anticipation of what was to come.

She knocked on the door, and this time heard the bolt being pulled back almost at once, as if Evelyn had been waiting on the other side for her to arrive.

Inside, the house was still dark, but Pip thought it smelled a little less fusty than it had done the previous week. Perhaps Evelyn had prepared a little for her visit. Pip liked this idea because it suggested that Evelyn was as enthusiastic about their meeting as she was and had also been looking forward to it. Maybe she wanted to make a favourable impression on Pip, too. The idea made Pip feel a little bit special, like she mattered to Evelyn, and that gave her a warm feeling in her stomach along with the butterflies.

Evelyn ushered her into the same room as before, though, before Pip could see any other part of the house. There had been slight improvements in there as well. The curtains were already open, and the carpet and upholstery had been hoovered after a fashion, although it hadn't made a huge impact on the overall feeling of neglect that still hung around the room. Still, Pip thought, it must show something.

Evelyn herself, however, seemed much the same as she had been before. Whilst she was considerably less suspicious than she had been at their first meeting, she was still guarded, and her smiles were cautious and short-lived. In fact, if it hadn't been for the obvious attempts to clean the house for her visit, Pip might have thought she wasn't welcome, but she tried not to feel too disheartened by this. Just because Evelyn didn't share her excitement didn't mean she wasn't pleased to see her, and the most important thing was that she had been invited back when there was no real need, the diary having already been returned. Pip would just have to make the most of the visit and ingratiate herself with Evelyn as much as she could so she would come to trust her, over time.

When Pip was settled in the same slightly sticky seat she had taken previously, Evelyn said, 'Would you like a cup of tea? It was very remiss of me not to offer last time, but you did rather catch me on the hop.'

It was a small step, no more than a gesture really, but Pip was delighted.

'That would be lovely,' she said. 'Thank you. Can I help?'

Evelyn put up a blocking hand, signalling clearly that help would not be required. 'No, no,' she said firmly. 'I may be older than you, but I'm perfectly capable of boiling a kettle and carrying a tray.'

Something in her tone sounded a little offended, but Pip ignored it. An offer of help was just that, and if Evelyn chose to give it more significance then that was her issue. Pip was beginning to wonder if Evelyn wasn't quite as old as she had looked on her last visit.

She went out to make the tea, leaving Pip on her own. Now that she was here as an invited guest, it felt more appropriate to have a good look around and take in her surroundings. She stood up and took a little tour about the room. As well as the two armchairs, a matching uninviting couch and the china display cabinet, there was also a mahogany bookshelf. It contained an ancient *Encyclopaedia Britannica*, and leather- and gilt-bound copies of what looked like the complete works of Dickens and Shakespeare. The leather, which might once have been crimson, had faded to a dull ox-blood colour and was stiff and brittle. Pip pulled *Great Expectations* off the shelf and opened it carefully. The pages were tissue-paper thin and the font so tiny it was hard to imagine anyone could ever read it, but the book had a well-handled feel to it. Someone had loved it once. She slipped it back into its space.

The fireplace was squat and ugly, tiled in buttercream-coloured tiles and with a large hearth tiled in the same. One of the tiles had cracked, spoiling the whole; something heavy had been dropped on it, and Pip thought she could imagine the fuss that would have been made at such carelessness. This didn't feel like the kind of house where cracked tiles would be acceptable, and yet it hadn't been replaced. If the china in the cabinet was anything to go by, it wouldn't have been through a lack of funds, so maybe the broken tile had been left on purpose as a constant reminder of someone's mistake. Evelyn's, perhaps?

On top of the display cabinet were two black-and-white photographs, each in austere black frames. The first was of a couple on their wedding day, or at least she assumed it was their wedding day. The woman was carrying a bunch of roses, but her dress was neither long nor white and not at all what Pip would think of as a wedding dress, and neither she nor the assumed groom were smiling. The second was of three children, a boy with blond curls in a smart sailor sweater and two little girls in pinafores. Pip looked more closely. The smallest one must be Evelyn, Pip thought, scanning for any feature that looked familiar, but finding nothing. The little girl beamed out at the camera, her head tipped coquettishly to one side. She looked like a proper character, much as Evelyn had described Scarlet. Then she turned her focus to the older girl – Joan, maybe? Pip searched her face for the cruelty that Evelyn's diary had hinted at, but could see no sign of it. She looked like a perfectly ordinary child, if a little solemn in comparison to her sister.

Just then there was a loud crash, and the bell-like sound of something smashing on a hard floor rang through the house. Pip jumped, and her heart immediately began to pound. She still

213

couldn't deal with loud, sudden noises. Maybe she would always struggle with them.

She took a deep breath to steady herself then called out into the silence. 'Is everything okay?' When there was no reply, she rushed from the room to try and trace the sound, running through various disaster scenarios in her head as she went.

The kitchen appeared to be at the end of the corridor and Pip headed in that direction, calling out again. This time she got a reply.

'I'm fine, I'm fine. No need to panic,' snapped Evelyn as Pip entered the kitchen. Pip was relieved to see she was on her feet, but she was standing in a puddle of tea, the teapot lying in pieces around her. 'Damn,' Evelyn tutted. 'How careless of me. What a mess I've made.'

However, as Pip approached, she saw that the broken teapot was almost insignificant next to the catastrophe that was the rest of kitchen. Every surface was piled high with stuff. Pip couldn't really be more specific about what it was. Most of it was unidentifiable clutter. It didn't smell any worse than the rest of the house, so it probably wasn't stale food, although there seemed to be a lot of cartons. In one spot, a pile of cornflakes boxes was stacked almost to the ceiling. There was a similar pyramid of toilet rolls and another of teabags.

Instantly Pip formed a pretty clear idea about how they had appeared.

'Do you do online shopping?' she asked with a grin.

Evelyn looked peevish, but then her pinched expression widened into something softer.

'I don't know how to stop it,' she admitted. 'Nicholas said he'd help, but I said I was fine. Pride, I suppose. Now I think I could eat cornflakes every meal for the rest of my life and not get to the end of them.'

'I do . . . did the same,' confessed Pip. 'The same things keep arriving week after week, and before you know it, you're inundated. Once, I ordered what I thought was four bars of soap, but it turned out that each packet had six bars in it. The flat I shared with my boyfriend was quite small and there definitely wasn't room for twenty-four bars of soap. He wasn't best pleased.'

'That's funny,' Evelyn said, and started to laugh, a light tinkling sound, almost a giggle. 'I'm so glad it's not just me. And what's even funnier is I don't even like cornflakes that much.'

She rolled her eyes at her own foolishness. When she smiled, she looked ten years younger, and Pip thought she could see something of the Evelyn she had come to know through the diary.

'I can help you change your order if you like,' she offered.

Evelyn dropped her gaze towards the tea lake. 'That would be most helpful,' she said. 'I don't know how things got into such a pickle. I used to keep on top of the house, but then I sort of lost interest in it, and the messier it got the harder it became to tidy up. Nicholas despairs of me. He's always at me to let him help, but I can't bear the thought of him rooting through my things, even if it is mainly rubbish. That's how the diary ended up in the charity shop, by Nicholas trying to be useful, although I wish he'd told me what he was doing. I have no idea what else was in that box, what other treasures he might have seen fit to give away.'

'It was just old paperbacks,' replied Pip helpfully. 'I don't want to make assumptions, but I don't think there was anything precious in there – except the diary, of course.'

There was a heartbeat's pause. Evelyn opened her mouth to speak and Pip felt certain she was about to ask her if she had read the diary, but then she seemed to change her mind.

Instead she said, 'I'd better get this lot cleaned up. Such a nuisance. So silly of me. And that was my favourite teapot as well.'

Pip dropped to her hands and knees and began to pick up the bits of pottery, nestling them in the largest piece whilst Evelyn tip-toed out of the tea and went to find a mop. When she returned, Pip got Evelyn to sit down whilst she set to clearing the mess, putting the kettle on to boil for a second time and locating another teapot in a cupboard, all under Evelyn's direction.

Soon everything was sorted, and a fresh pot of tea sat brewing in a tiny space that Evelyn had cleared on the table.

'You can get help with all this, you know,' said Pip gently.

'I know,' said Evelyn. 'But the mess isn't really the problem. If I cleared it all away it would just come back. I need to sort out in here first . . .' She tapped the side of her head with her hand. 'Or there'll be no point.'

Pip nodded. She knew exactly what Evelyn meant.

37

They drank their tea surrounded by the teetering piles of groceries. Now that Pip had seen the state of the kitchen for herself, Evelyn couldn't see any point in shielding her from it any longer. There was a kind of relief in allowing another person to see how she lived, not having to keep it as a guilty secret any more. She had felt so ashamed of her mess, but Pip hadn't batted an eye at it; she seemed to have seen it as perfectly normal. Evelyn had been surprised at how quickly Pip had guessed how things had got so out of control. Immediately Evelyn had felt better and less inadequate.

Pip had moved seamlessly into clearing up a bit.

'So, you grew up here?' she asked as she rinsed their cups out. The sink was full of Evelyn's washing up, but Pip had run a bowl of hot soapy water and set to work, quietly and without drawing attention to what she was doing.

'I did,' replied Evelyn to Pip's back. 'Then I left. And then circumstances pulled me back again.'

'Yes, that's kind of what happened to me, too,' replied Pip.

She had hinted as much at their previous meeting and Evelyn was desperate to ask her to explain, but something stayed her tongue. It felt too soon to delve around in Pip's past, unless Pip raised it of her own volition. Perhaps if Evelyn shared something of her own story then Pip would reciprocate. Evelyn considered the implications of this. Until now, her game plan had been to extract as much information from Pip whilst at the same time giving away as little as she possibly could, but now that felt petty. Did she think her story was too precious to be told to a stranger? Of course, she couldn't expect Pip to open up to her if she wasn't prepared to reciprocate. And she did want Pip to open up. What had started as curiosity about the name business had grown into a real desire to get to know her better. The young woman had been sensitive enough to realise that the diary was important and had returned it, and now she was here, quietly cleaning her kitchen for her. Evelyn could search a long time for someone as thoughtful.

So instead of asking Pip to explain why she had ended up back in Southwold, she began with her own tale.

'The truth was, I couldn't get away from here fast enough,' she said. 'I was desperate to be an actress, but my family, particularly my mother, thought that was frivolous. They discouraged me at every turn, which of course just made me more determined, and as soon as I could, I left here and went to London to seek my fortune.'

'And what brought you back?' Pip asked.

It was an innocent enough question, the obvious one, in fact, but part of Evelyn still baulked at having to answer it, although she wasn't entirely sure why. How could it possibly matter now?

'I got pregnant,' she replied as boldly as she could. This was the twenty-first century and no one seemed to hide behind euphemisms as they once had. I got into trouble, I was in the family way; such expressions were quaint and antiquated in this new age of forthright and direct speech, an age that Evelyn suddenly felt the need to embrace. After all, she had thought herself progressive in the 1970s, so why not now?

Pip didn't comment, and nothing about her facial expression suggested that she was in any way shocked. Either she didn't understand the ramifications of the words, or she didn't consider them to be anything other than a statement of fact. Evelyn wasn't sure which it was, but surely it would be the latter.

Encouraged, she pressed on. 'It was a bit of a scandal at the time. I wasn't married or even in a relationship with the father. I'd also just been cast in a huge role in a television drama series that would have sealed my career, and I gave it all up. There was no support for single mothers back then, so I had to make a choice. The baby or the job. I chose the baby, but I couldn't support myself and so I had no option but to slink back up here. My parents were dead by then, but my sister Joan took a very dim view of it all.'

'Is that her in the picture in the other room?' Pip asked. 'The miserable-looking one?' She turned around and winked at Evelyn, but then immediately looked unsure of herself, as if she feared she had been too familiar, stepped over some invisible line.

'Yes. That's her,' Evelyn replied, and rolled her eyes to show that no offence had been taken. 'Joan was miserable as a child and she never grew out of it,' she said. 'Once I got up here, she made my life as wretched as she could.'

Evelyn saw Pip nod as if she already knew that and was entirely sympathetic.

'I had no money, so she had to keep me, and boy, did she let me know how much she disapproved of the whole situation. It was ridiculous really. She was living here on the money our parents left us. I had just as much entitlement to it as she did. But she held the cheque book. She made me feel bad about myself every single day.'

Pip had finished washing up now and began searching for a tea towel. Evelyn flinched as she pulled open drawer after drawer, all stuffed to the gunwales with rubbish, and was relieved when she eventually abandoned her quest, leaving the dishes to air dry. She wiped her hands on her jeans and came to sit down next to Evelyn at the piled-high table.

'After Scarlet was born Joan continued to be scandalised. I thought that when the baby was here she'd mellow a little, but she never did. It was almost as if she wasn't prepared to allow herself to love her niece. And she was so very loveable . . .'

There was a pause.

'She died, didn't she?' asked Pip gently. 'My mum told me.'

Evelyn nodded. Just thinking about Scarlet sent a stabbing pain straight to her heart, and she put a futile hand to her chest, as if that could ease it.

'She was only three,' she said. 'Just a baby, and with her whole life ahead of her.'

'That's such a tragedy,' Pip said.

'Yes. You never get over the loss of your child,' Evelyn added. 'It haunts you forever.'

Evelyn watched as Pip ran her hand through her hair then closed her eyes, breathing slowly through her nose. She seemed to be struggling with some unspoken emotional response to what she had just heard. Had she lost a child, too? Was that what had brought her back from London? Evelyn was curious, but this was her story and so she kept going.

'And then Joan died,' she continued in as matter-of-fact a tone as she could manage so that she didn't draw any attention to that part of the story. 'And I just stayed here. I did mean to go back to London, to start working again, but somehow, I could never quite get myself together enough to go. And the years ticked by.'

It was such a long time since Evelyn had thought about her life in these terms, about how she had lost so many years. Now that she did, it felt like such a waste. She had only been thirty-four when Scarlet died. There had still been plenty of her life left, but she had let things get away from her. And then the years rolled by and picked up speed and nothing changed. And now it was all too late.

'There's only me and Nicholas left now. He's my nephew, my brother Peter's boy. Peter's dead too, of course. A heart attack in his fifties. And soon I'll die, and then the house will be sold, and no one will remember that the Mountcastles were ever here.'

'I think you'd be surprised,' said Pip. 'I asked a few people about you when I was trying to find out where to return the diary to, and they all knew who you were.'

There was a warmth to her smile that spoke to the part of Evelyn that needed to be acknowledged, to be talked about. She hadn't realised she still had that, but here it was. It must be the actress in her, she thought, that made her enjoy being the centre of attention. Fancy it still being inside her after all this time.

'It's just the gossip that makes people remember,' she replied modestly. 'There were two tragic deaths in this house in almost as many months. It's a small town and people have long memories. They don't forget things like that.'

Pip shrugged in a way that suggested she wasn't convinced. 'And do you ever go out?' she asked casually, as if not going out was the most normal thing in the world.

Evelyn thought about this question. In her heart, she wasn't the kind of person who allowed herself to be confined to a house, but actually she could barely remember the last time she had left it. Why was that? she wondered.

'Not often,' she replied. 'There doesn't seem much to go out for.'

'Don't you even walk along the beach, watch the waves?' Pip sounded incredulous. 'I mean, with it being just there, just across the street.'

When had she stopped doing that? Evelyn couldn't remember. It hadn't been a conscious decision; it had simply happened over time. And once she became stuck indoors she had lost the habit of going out. And then a winter had arrived, the wind coming off the sea cutting through her clothes and eating into her bones, so it had been easier to stay in. And then . . .

These were just excuses, of course, and although she didn't feel like a recluse, she supposed she might be one, or at least appear that way.

'No,' she said to Pip. 'Not any more. I used to, but then . . .'

'And would you like to go out?' Pip asked.

Evelyn paused. Would she? Did she feel that her life would be better if she ventured beyond her own front door again?

She was considering her answer when Pip added, 'Because I could take you. I mean, we could go together. If you like.'

Again, Pip blushed, as if she thought she might have gone further than was appropriate. She was such a lovely girl, Evelyn thought. This afternoon had shown her that. She could tell she was caring and considerate simply by the way she had helped in the kitchen, quietly and with no fuss. Even knowing barely anything about her, Evelyn believed she had got Pip pegged.

'Yes,' she said shortly, her decisiveness surprising her. 'I rather think I would. It's not good for one, being cooped up all the time. Nicholas has offered, too,' she added quickly. She didn't want Pip to think she had been abandoned by the only bit of family she had left. 'But he's always in such a rush. And he doesn't have that much conversation for an old woman like me.'

Pip smiled as if she understood completely. Yes, Evelyn thought to herself, this had the makings of quite an interesting relationship.

'So, Pip,' she said. 'You haven't told me why you're back in Southwold.'

She smiled warmly as she spoke. She had had her turn, opened up and shared a little of her life, and now she could sit back and relax whilst someone else took the spotlight.

Pip turned her head and looked directly at Evelyn, dark eyes seeking out pale ones. She drew in a breath before she spoke and it caught a little in her throat.

'I killed a child,' she said simply.

38

Pip felt the atmosphere in the room darken. She could have kicked herself. Why had she said that? They had been having such a lovely time, the two of them, and now she had spoiled it all.

She hadn't even intended to tell Evelyn, not yet at least, and certainly not by blurting it out so baldly. The truth of what she had done wasn't something she had ever had to voice aloud before. Everyone in her world already knew, and they had been trying to help her by steering clear of the subject. But somehow, despite all her years of training at the bar, all those sentences spoken in court, constructed so very carefully in order to achieve the precise result she needed, when she was asked a direct question, she had replied in the most direct terms possible.

Part of her wanted to pull the words back now, to snatch them from the air between her and Evelyn and bury them deep where neither of them would ever hear them again. What she had done needed to be tempered with softer language, built up to, crept up upon like a sleeping dragon, and not faced head on with all its fiery breath and jagged teeth on display.

Yet the words had been spoken and now it was too late. There was nothing she could do to change that. She resisted the urge to look away and hide her face, and instead kept her eyes trained on Evelyn, waiting for a reaction. It was bound to be bad. Evelyn herself had lost her daughter. She knew exactly what that felt like, how unbearable the pain that accompanied the death of a child was. She had been living it for thirty-five years, making Pip's last few horrible months a mere drop in the ocean of her tears.

Pip saw a variety of emotions register on Evelyn's face in the aftermath of her confession. First shock, then anger, then repulsion followed by a dark curiosity, and now something that Pip hoped might be pity.

Neither woman spoke, each apparently considering what could possibly be said, and then Evelyn swallowed. She appeared to be measuring her response. She'll throw me out now, thought Pip. This embryonic relationship we were delighting in just moments ago is going to evaporate into thin air. It was a fair reaction. How could Evelyn be expected to tolerate her, given what she'd done, particularly when you put it into the context of Evelyn's own life?

Pip began to push herself to her feet. She would leave now, before Evelyn had a chance to ask her to go. That would be best for both of them. She had returned the diary, which was the most important thing. Now the two of them could go back to the way things had been before and forget they had ever spent a pleasant couple of hours in each other's company.

'Did you do it on purpose?' Evelyn asked calmly.

Pip, who had been caught up in her own thought process, was thrown for a moment. When she didn't reply, Evelyn repeated herself.

'Did you do it on purpose, kill the child on purpose?' she said, louder this time.

Pip was horrified. Her cheeks burned and she could feel her throat close up as tears filled her eyes. 'No!' she said, her voice small, childlike. 'No! Of course not! It was an accident. A horrible, terrible accident. He ran under the wheels of my car. It wasn't my fault.

The police, the coroner, they all said that I wasn't to blame . . . But I killed him. If it hadn't been for me, he would still be alive.'

Pip waited for the wave to engulf her, but nothing happened. Neither of them moved. Pip knew she was hollow inside – the last few months had shown her that – but so, it appeared, was Evelyn. She sat still, staring first at Pip and then, when that appeared to become too uncomfortable, at the mountain of cornflake boxes. The tap dripped steadily, the droplets of water thrumming on the stainless steel like the ticking of a clock as the moments passed. It was such an insistent noise that Pip couldn't believe she hadn't heard it before, even though it must have been there, punctuating their conversation.

Then Evelyn stood up. This is it, thought Pip. She's going to ask me to leave now. She braced herself ready to receive the dismissal, but instead Evelyn said, 'Come with me. I want to show you something.'

She walked stiffly but with purpose across the kitchen to the door. When Pip failed to follow, she stopped and beckoned her to go with her.

She led them into the corridor and towards the stairs, Pip following cautiously in her wake. Where were they going? For the briefest of moments, Pip worried for her own safety, but what could Evelyn do to her? She was so frail, and Pip was young and fit, and anyway, why would she want to hurt her? What Pip had done was awful, but it didn't impact on Evelyn.

Evelyn started up the stairs. She had to pick her way through the debris that was waiting on either side of the treads, things that must have been left there to be carried upstairs and then ignored and added to until the path through became narrow and treacherous.

Upstairs Pip saw the door to the room that Evelyn must have been in when she had seen her at the window, but Evelyn didn't take them in there, choosing instead the door to a room at the back of the house.

Evelyn paused slightly before putting her hand out and pushing the handle down. The door swung open, and Pip's heart fell still in her chest. The room was painted in a delicate pink. In the centre was a bed with posts attached to each corner, also painted pink, and over which white organza had been draped. A multitude of teddy bears and other unlikely creatures were resting on the pillow, each carefully placed as if they were having a conversation amongst themselves.

On the floor between the bed and the window was a single sock, white with the little embroidered pattern running up it that Pip remembered from her own childhood. It lay where it had been dropped decades before, slightly balled and without its partner. Pip didn't think she had ever seen anything so poignant.

'This is Scarlet's room,' said Evelyn, although the explanation was not required. 'This is how she left it the day she died. It's not a shrine to her memory, not like I imagine some people keep for their dead children. I leave it like this because it's the last place on earth where a part of her still lives. When I come in here, I can feel her with me. Does that sound peculiar?'

Pip shook her head. She didn't trust her voice not to let her down if she spoke.

'My sister wanted to clear everything away after Scarlet died,' Evelyn continued. 'She said it was unhealthy to keep it all like this, to dwell on what was passed, but I wouldn't let her. I'm so glad now that I held firm and stood my ground on that.'

Evelyn crossed the room and looked out at the gardens beyond.

'You see that rose bed?' She nodded to a circular flower bed in the garden next door. 'That's where it happened. That is where my child drowned. They filled it in, the pond, but I still see it every day, the place where my baby died.'

Tears welled in Pip's eyes and trickled down her cheeks. She put a hand to her face to wipe them away. This was not her grief – she had no right to cry, just like she had no right to cry for the lost life of the boy. Yet the tears still came.

'The damage done by sudden death is devastating and irreversible,' Evelyn continued, her voice low and very calm as if she were preaching or delivering a sentence. 'Attaching blame can only take you so far. Believe me, I know. Just because everyone says it wasn't your fault doesn't mean that you can move on. But you do owe it to yourself to try. You're young, Pip, with your whole life ahead of you. You mustn't let that one terrible moment blight your entire future. Yes, you'll feel guilt. That's only to be expected. It's misplaced, but it's unavoidable. But you can't let it define who you are for the rest of your life. I let that happen to me. At the time, I couldn't find any other way through the pain, but now I see that it might have been a mistake. I urge you to look at things differently and not to do what I did.'

Evelyn's words confused Pip. Was she saying that she had felt some guilt for her part in Scarlet's death, despite how it had come across in the diary? If so, then maybe the two of them had more in common than she'd thought. Their bond was not merely because neither of them had fitted into the place they had been allocated in life. There was this other, much bigger and more painful connection binding them.

But then again, Evelyn's child had drowned under her care. Pip had knocked the boy down, but she had no responsibility for his being there in the middle of the road. Did that somehow make her guilt different to Evelyn's? Was there a way to rank levels of guilt? Pip didn't know what to think, but something about Evelyn's calm yet intense grief superseded all that. It was this powerful sense of loss the two of them shared. Loss and pain. And at this moment, it made the connection Pip felt towards Evelyn stronger than anything she had felt with any other person since the accident. Even though she was as good as a stranger, Pip wanted to reach out and hold her, comfort her, and in doing so, be comforted herself. But she held herself back.

Instead, the two women stood shoulder to shoulder at the window and watched as a tortoiseshell cat prowled across the rose bed in search of easy prey.

39

'So, tell me again who this woman is,' said Nicholas as Evelyn stood in her hallway dusting down her coat.

Evelyn didn't like his tone. It was laced with suspicions that she knew were entirely misplaced and that she should dispel for Pip's sake, but at the same time she resented having to explain herself to her nephew. She was perfectly capable of forming her own judgements about people, and she definitely didn't need them tainted by his dark imaginings.

'Her name is Pip and she works in the charity shop. The one, might I add, where you abandoned my precious possessions without having first asked my permission to remove them from my house,' she replied pointedly.

Evelyn was glad to see him squirm a little at this. He should squirm as well, causing all that heartache over the diary, but at least something good had come out of his interference. If he hadn't taken the box to the charity shop then she wouldn't have met Pip, and for that at least she owed him something. Not that she was about to tell him so.

She was grateful, though, that in his cack-handed way he had brought Pip into her life. In their two brief meetings, Evelyn had grown fond of her. She recognised something of herself in Pip's self-contained confidence, which was, although a little battered and bruised, still there, shining from her like a flare. Her quiet determination to follow her own path despite all the obstacles placed in her way spoke to Evelyn, the old Evelyn at any rate, the one who had taken the train to London with only a tatty suitcase and a handful of banknotes hidden inside a sock. And Nicholas was not going to spoil this for her. She would defend this outing come what may.

'Pip has kindly returned the diary to me,' Evelyn continued, 'and today she is going to take me out for a walk, which I am very much looking forward to.'

Nicholas was shaking his head. 'But every time I ask if you'd like to go out, you knock me back,' he said sulkily.

This was true.

'Let me take you instead, Aunt Evelyn,' he said, although without much enthusiasm. 'We can leave a note on the door for this charity woman. Tell her that you've changed your mind.'

'But I haven't changed my mind,' objected Evelyn. 'I want to go out with Pip. And she'll be here in a moment, so if you don't mind, I'd like to get ready.'

Nicholas still looked unconvinced. 'Well, I shall stay with you until she arrives,' he said, clearly disgruntled that his half-hearted offer had been spurned. 'So I can make sure she's kosher.'

Evelyn tutted loudly. 'Of course she's "kosher", as you so indelicately put it. What do you think she's going to do? Push me off the pier?'

An expression settled on Nicholas's face that suggested this was exactly what he was thinking, but he had the good sense to keep his opinions to himself.

Evelyn pulled on her coat. It was a trench coat, the kind that had been quite fashionable some years back, but it now looked a little grubby. In the pocket her fingers found a balled-up silk scarf, which she unravelled with a flick of her wrist. She expected moths to come flying out, but there were none. Lifting the silk to her nose, she breathed in cautiously. The scarf smelled a little musty and faintly of a perfume she used to wear before such things became unimportant to her, but it wasn't bad. Standing in front of the hallway mirror, she tied it around her head and immediately felt more glamorous. She wasn't quite Audrey Hepburn, but she didn't look too unpresentable.

There was a knock on the door. Nicholas went to answer it, but she stopped him in his tracks with a glare.

'This is my house and I shall answer my own door, thank you very much.'

Nicholas fell back, admonished. Evelyn stepped to the door and opened it wide, without even using the chain. She could feel Nicholas's irritation at her flagrant breaches of his security protocol, but she didn't care.

Pip was on the doorstep dressed in her ubiquitous jeans and some sort of baggy top. Evelyn despaired of young people. Where was their sense of style? No one ever seemed to make any effort with their appearance these days, opting instead for comfort, which was all very well but not in the least attractive.

'Morning,' said Pip brightly.

Was it Evelyn's imagination or did she look a little better today? The dark rings around her eyes were still there, but her cheeks looked to have more of a bloom to them.

'Good morning, Pip,' replied Evelyn. 'Have you met my nephew, Nicholas? He seems to think that you wish me ill will.'

Pip looked confused and then horrified as she shook her head vehemently. 'Mr Mountcastle,' she began, 'I can assure you that you have no reason to . . .'

Evelyn put up a hand to stop her. 'I've told him all that,' she said. 'So, shall we go? If I don't return, Nicholas, you may assume that Philippa Rose here has buried me in a sand dune.'

'I'm just looking out for you,' said Nicholas in a tone that might have been taken for petulance.

'And I'm grateful,' Evelyn called back over her shoulder.

The sky outside was blue, but there was a bracing wind whipping up across the sea and Evelyn stood for a moment to breathe it in. It had been a while since she had had the salty air in her nostrils and her lungs, and it felt good but also a little overwhelming to be out in so much space. Was that how agoraphobia began, she wondered? Would that have been her fate? Well, she wasn't having any of it. Now that she was finally back outside, she felt neither panic nor dread. It merely reminded her of how amazing the place where she lived was, and made her feel slightly ashamed that she had forgotten. In fact, standing outside her house looking out across the wide ocean to the horizon beyond, it felt good to be alive, which was something she hadn't managed to feel for a long time.

Pip seemed in no hurry to get going and was waiting patiently at her side until she was ready to move on. Evelyn nodded at her. It seemed there was more at stake here than just a walk, but she couldn't quite grasp what it was. Tiny green shoots of something new, maybe, and not just for her. She hoped Pip was feeling this embryonic connection between the pair of them as well.

They crossed the road so they could wander along the wide promenade that ran alongside the beach.

'Shall we walk along to the pier?' asked Pip. 'Is that too far?'

Evelyn was horrified that anyone should have to ask her if she could manage the couple of hundred yards from her front door to the pier but then, when she thought about it, it wasn't such a ridiculous question. She had no idea how far her legs would carry her any more, it being so long since she had last put them to the test. That said, she was feeling confident.

'I think that'll be fine,' she said to Pip with a reassuring smile. 'And when we get there, we can have a restorative cup of tea and a sticky bun before we set out on the return journey.'

'Do you need anything else?' Pip asked tentatively. 'Would you like to take my arm?'

Bless her for offering, thought Evelyn. From what she knew of Pip so far, she didn't think arm-linking with old ladies was something that came naturally to her.

'Thank you,' she said, 'but I think I'll be all right. Isn't that breeze wonderful? I remember when Scarlet was a baby. The first time I took her outside in the wind she didn't know what to make of it at all. I don't suppose there's much weather in the womb, so it must have been a bit of a shock. The look on her face when the wind blew into her. Priceless. She couldn't work out how to breathe for a moment. It was worrying, and then extremely sweet.' Evelyn smiled at the memory, so old and yet so very fresh. It felt good to be talking about her daughter after all this time, and she resolved to do it more often.

They strolled, side by side, along the promenade towards the pier. As they walked, the sun peeped out from between the clouds and white light danced on the waves, making the sea sparkle. Optimistic holidaymakers sat in deckchairs and on towels whilst their small children, dressed in little swimming outfits that covered every inch of their bodies, scampered backwards and forwards to the water. When she had brought Scarlet to the beach she had worn her little red polka-dot costume, or sometimes just her knickers, if it was an impromptu visit. It had been, Evelyn felt now, a simpler time.

'Scarlet used to love the water,' she said to Pip. 'She was like a little seal. In and out of the waves all day long. She had even started to swim, which was early for her age, although I always made sure she had her armbands on. The tides can be brutal here.' Having rejected Pip's arm when it had been offered, she now slipped her hand in the gap made by the crook of her elbow, and continued without commenting on her change of heart. 'Looking back,' she added, 'I think Scarlet's love of water was probably what drew her to the pond in the first place. It would have been calling to her.'

But she should never have been there on her own. That's what Pip would be thinking. Evelyn knew it, because that was what everyone always thought. It was a tragedy, but why was a three-year-old child out on her own in the vicinity of a garden pond? Where was the irresponsible mother? How could she have let that happen?

Evelyn had become adept at defending herself from the ill-intentioned thoughts that came her way, bouncing them away like bullets off a shield. Pip was polite enough not to ask, but Evelyn still guarded herself against the question. She alone knew what had happened to Scarlet and what her own part in it had been. But maybe it was time to change that. Perhaps she could share the truth with Pip.

'We didn't come to the beach very often when I was growing up,' replied Pip, deftly shifting the attention away from Evelyn's drowned child. 'It seems ridiculous now, but the farm is a little way out and Mum and Dad were always too busy to bring me. And then, when I was older, I had my studies and not much time for anything else. It's a shame really. It feels like a lost opportunity now.'

'Well, when you have children of your own you can make sure they get the benefits of living by the sea,' Evelyn said.

It was mischievous of her, a statement designed to make a point to Pip, and she took pleasure in watching Pip take the bait.

'Oh, I doubt I'll be having any children,' she said flatly. 'And I don't live here, not really.'

'I forgot,' replied Evelyn, doing her best to hide her smirk. It was like a reflex in Pip, the need to deny her roots. 'You'll be back in London. Is that the plan?'

Pip cast her eyes out across the waves to the wide horizon beyond, and Evelyn saw something in her soften.

'There is no plan,' she said forlornly. 'And I don't have a home in London, not any more. And no one to have a child with, so the whole thing is pretty much immaterial.'

'Time to make some changes, then?' chanced Evelyn, casting her a sidelong glance.

Pip turned to face her and their eyes met. 'Yes,' she said. 'I think you're right.'

40

Pip loved the pier. She always had done, but somehow that had been forgotten in and amongst everything else. She used to imagine what it would be like to live in one of the little white houses that sat on the wooden boards out to sea. She could remember her disappointment when her father told her that nobody actually lived there, that they weren't real houses but little businesses. She didn't let that affect her daydream, though. She continued to picture herself existing quite independently of her family in her own world on the pier, and even under it when the tide went out.

And then one day, she just forgot. Other things took up space in her head and her childhood fantasies got left behind. How had that happened? What else had she lost sight of in her single-minded pursuit of her career? Even though she loved her job, she was beginning to wonder whether she might have made too many sacrifices along the way.

Evelyn had made a sprightly start, but was beginning to look a little jaded as they approached the pier. Should she be worried about her? Pip wasn't sure. She had no first aid skills. Girl Guides was something else that had been lost to her dogged dedication to her studies.

'I could murder that cup of tea,' she said now, hoping Evelyn didn't realise she was thinking more about Evelyn's needs than her own and take offence. 'Shall we call in here?'

She pointed to the café at the very start of the pier, and Evelyn nodded. Pip held open the door and ushered them both in.

She hadn't realised how strong the wind was until they were out of it. Evelyn shuffled towards a table and virtually fell into a chair. The walk had clearly been more demanding for her than she had let on. It wasn't surprising, given how rarely she left her house, but Pip hoped they hadn't overdone it. The nephew really would have something to complain about then.

They ordered tea and scones, sticky buns being conspicuous by their absence, then sat quietly contemplating the sea beyond the window. Pip had missed moments of peace and stillness. The pace of life was so fast in London and she loved being in the thick of it, thriving on the stress and dancing on the competitive knife-edge without losing her balance. But she had been playing the game by the wrong rules, she realised now. The lifestyle, the competition, having just the right thing or eating in just the right place – it had grown out of proportion, like a cancer that just kept multiplying until there was no room for other, less urgent things. And she hadn't made any space for quiet – had scoffed at it, in fact, as if taking time away from the cut and thrust of her London life was a sign of weakness. Now she understood that had been a mistake. She would rectify it. When her life reformed into whatever it was going to be and she got back to her work, she would make sure she found time for watching waves roll in and clouds scud across the sky.

Pip suddenly became aware of Evelyn's eyes on her, and turned her head enquiringly. The old woman held her gaze steadily, even when she had been caught staring. It felt as if she were trying to stare deep into Pip's soul. Pip stared back for a moment, but then felt forced to look down, unable to bear Evelyn's scrutiny any longer.

'Did you read my diary?' Evelyn asked abruptly. Her voice was low, but her words were very distinct.

Pip swallowed. What should she say? She could lie; Evelyn would never be able to prove the contrary was true. But where would that get her? Once she lied, she would never find out what truly happened to Scarlet and Joan. And what was the worst that could happen if she told the truth? Evelyn could clam up and refuse to see her again. That would be a shame, but there was nothing turning on it, apart from Pip's own curiosity.

'Yes,' she said simply. She offered no apology for any breach of trust.

Evelyn didn't say anything for a moment. She seemed to be considering her next move. Pip longed to say something to encourage her to open up, to tell the story, but her gut told her that staying quiet was the right thing to do.

'I thought you might have,' said Evelyn eventually. 'It's what I would have done, too. Is that why you brought it back?'

Pip nodded.

'But you didn't tell anyone else.'

Pip shook her head.

Evelyn took a deep breath, moving a stray wisp of hair away from her mouth, and then blew it all out as if she was deciding what to do next. Then she picked up her teacup, took a mouthful and placed it back down firmly.

'So,' she began. 'I'll tell you what happened, and then you can decide what you want to do next. Unless you'd rather not know, of course?'

Was Jez right? Had Evelyn really murdered Joan? The diary was ambiguous, but the 30th November entry certainly could be interpreted that way. And if that was what Evelyn was about to tell her, then where did that leave Pip morally? Would she be obliged to pass the information on to the police?

The sensible thing would be not to know, to tell Evelyn it didn't matter one way or the other, and she could take her secret with her to the grave.

But there was something about Evelyn's expression that made Pip think she really did want to tell her, that it was time for an unburdening of sorts. If she had been waiting all these years to let the truth out and had chosen this as the moment to do so, then surely Pip owed it to her to listen.

Decision made, she nodded. 'Please tell me,' she replied.

Evelyn gave a curt nod, and Pip felt that an understanding of sorts had passed between them.

'It was a Wednesday,' she began without bothering with any kind of introduction. 'On Wednesdays, Scarlet and I always went to the library to change our books, but that day Scarlet wasn't well. She had a cold starting and she was a little bit whiny, so rather than make her walk all that way, I decided to leave her at home with Joan whilst I nipped out and did it on my own. When I got home, Scarlet was dead.'

Pip's eyes widened at the abruptness of Evelyn's words, but she bit her tongue and said nothing. It felt important not to interrupt and to let it all escape at once. She watched Evelyn swallow hard, her jaw held tight. This was really hard for her, that much was obvious.

'The police were at the house when I got there. They were talking to Joan and she told them that Scarlet must have let herself out when she wasn't watching and then wandered off. They seemed to accept that, but that didn't make sense to me. Scarlet would have known not to go off without an adult. It was so out of character.

'When the police had gone, and for days afterwards, I kept begging Joan to tell me the truth, but she didn't change her story.

It was almost like she was taking pleasure in implying that I was an unfit mother, that I'd failed to bring my daughter up responsibly, and so was as much to blame for Scarlet's death as anyone else. But I knew that wasn't right, and so I kept asking her over and over to tell me the truth.' As she said the words 'over and over', she banged her palm on the table for emphasis, the snaking blue veins twisting over the back of her fragile hand.

'I had to be careful, though,' she continued. 'I knew Joan wouldn't respond well to being blamed, so even though all I wanted to do was scream at her and slap her until she told me what had really happened, I tried to keep my voice calm. The last thing I needed was for her to clam up, because then I'd never find out how it was that my precious baby had ended up outside the house and alone. I'd been over it constantly in my own head and I couldn't fit it together in a way that made it hold true. So I kept on and on.

'In the end, Joan snapped. I had been following her around the house asking my questions and we had come to a stop on the landing at the top of the stairs. She was virtually screaming at me, saying that Scarlet was a contrary little madam, just like I had been, and that I should just accept that.'

Pip noticed that Evelyn's cheeks were burning from the effort of telling her story. She wanted to reassure her, but it wasn't her place, not until she had heard it all; maybe not even then. Instead she stayed quiet and let Evelyn continue.

'So I told her that I couldn't accept it because I just didn't believe her. I knew my daughter and I knew she wouldn't just have wandered off like that. And she was ill that day. All she wanted was to sit on the sofa and have a cuddle with me.' Evelyn's eyes glazed over with tears at the thought of her unhappy little girl, wanting her mummy when her mummy wasn't there. Pip could only imagine the agony of that.

'I remember what happened next as clearly as if it were yesterday,' Evelyn said. 'It was like something out of a film. I was shouting at Joan that I didn't believe her, and Joan was shouting at me that I hadn't had to put up with Scarlet's whingeing and snivelling. I told her she was being ridiculous, that Scarlet was only three, and Joan said that was old enough to know how to behave.'

Evelyn was describing the row so clearly that Pip could imagine the scene. She pictured the two women on the landing outside Scarlet's bedroom, nose to nose as they screamed at one another.

'I could see I was getting nowhere,' continued Evelyn, 'so I made a huge effort to bring the temperature back down. I asked Joan, as calmly as I could, to just tell me the truth. She didn't have the stomach for the fight any more than I did. She said Scarlet had been moaning, that she wanted a drink, or something to eat, or was too hot or too cold, and so she had put her outside to play so she could get on with the housework without the constant interruptions, and that was when she had just wandered off into next door's garden. But, you see, that didn't make any sense to me. I knew that all Scarlet wanted was to sit quietly with a book because her head cold was making her feel so rotten.'

Pip's heart was in her throat. She was desperate for Evelyn to reach the story's resolution, but didn't dare interrupt. Instead she refilled their cups, even though Evelyn had barely touched her first one.

'And that's when it finally dawned on me what had happened,' Evelyn said, her expression suddenly steely. 'Joan must have locked her out of the house. The reason why Scarlet didn't come back inside when she'd had enough, and wandered away into next door's garden to drown in their pond, was because the door was locked and she couldn't get in.'

Pip's mouth fell open. 'Oh, my God,' she said, horrified.

If that was what had happened, if Joan really had barred the door against three-year-old Scarlet, then that was unforgivable. And if Evelyn really had killed her sister, surely that would be justification enough. Pip tried to imagine how it would feel to be Joan, knowing you had something like that on your conscience, but she drew a blank. It was, arguably, even worse than the dark shadow on her own conscience.

'So I confronted Joan with it,' Evelyn said. 'I accused her of locking Scarlet out. And as soon as the words were out of my mouth, I knew I was right. I could see it written all over her face, first regret but then defiance. "Well, you should have been here," she said, pushing all the blame on to me. "I couldn't be doing with all her coming and going. She needed to choose a place and stick to it." She seemed to think this justified what she had done. I didn't have anything else to say to her then,' said Evelyn. 'That was the end of our relationship. There could be no going back from that.'

Pip was barely breathing, and her mouth hung slack in disbelief. 'She locked her out of the house?' she repeated, although Evelyn had been clear enough.

Evelyn nodded. She held her head high, as if she were testifying in court. 'She did. My sister was responsible for the death of my only child and for that I knew I could never forgive her.'

And so, thought Pip, what happened next? She thought she knew, but she had to hear Evelyn say it. 'And then . . .' she prompted, giving Evelyn the opportunity to finish the sentence for her.

Evelyn stared straight into her eyes as if challenging her to argue with her.

'And then,' she said, 'I killed her.'

41

Evelyn had done it now. The words were out of her mouth and there was no taking them back. A chill ran down her spine as she watched the expression on Pip's face change from shock to comprehension.

Had she completely miscalculated? Had she just released her terrible secret to entirely the wrong person? What did she actually know about Pip, anyway? All she had to go on was a gut feeling that she would be on her side, nothing more. How stupid was she, that based on something as arbitrary and flimsy as a feeling, she had thrown herself entirely on to another's mercy? Until a moment ago, the only threat to her safety had been the diary and she had been planning to leave that for someone to find after her death, by which point it would be too late to do anything about what it contained.

Now she had confessed to a virtual stranger, and it was too late to go back and reclaim it.

'What do you mean, Evelyn?' Pip asked, interrupting her train of thought. 'What do you mean that you killed her?'

Evelyn hung her head. 'What I said. I was so angry. I screamed at her, she took a step backwards and she fell down the stairs.'

She could still picture the scene as clearly as if it had happened yesterday – Joan stepping back into space, her arms windmilling as she desperately tried to save herself, the sound as she tumbled down the long straight staircase and the thud when she finally landed at the bottom, her body lying, quite still, in an unnatural shape. And then the silence.

'Did you push her?' asked Pip gently.

Evelyn shook her head. 'No,' she said quietly. 'I didn't touch her.'

'Then it was an accident, surely?' said Pip.

'But if it hadn't been for us arguing she would never have fallen,' Evelyn insisted. 'It was my fault. I screamed at her and she stepped backwards and missed her step.'

'But that doesn't mean you were responsible for her death,' said Pip. 'It was just a horrible and very tragic accident, but you can't blame yourself. You mustn't feel responsible.'

Pip reached out and put a hand on her forearm, resting it there. Evelyn could feel the pressure of it through her clothes, warm, comforting, secure.

'It's all right. I've never regretted what happened,' she said, her voice and her eyes both low. 'You might be shocked by that, but it's the truth. She got what she deserved. It's always felt like a kind of karma to me. My sister took the most precious thing in my life and then fate intervened and took the most precious thing in hers.'

Pip shrugged. 'I'm not sure that's such a terrible way to look at it,' she said. 'Things have a way of working out like that. I'd agree it was the universe stepping in if I believed in any of that kind of thing. I can't say that Joan deserved to die for what she did, but I can't say that I'm sorry.'

Evelyn gave her a grateful little smile. 'She might have fallen and just walked away with cuts and bruises,' she said.

'Well, precisely,' replied Pip. 'It was an accident. Nobody's fault, and least of all yours.'

Evelyn lifted her eyes to meet Pip's. 'You know, I could say much the same to you, Pip. It was just chance that that little boy ran out in front of your car. It could have been anyone that hit him, but it just happened to be you. I suppose the only difference between the pair of us is that you are tortured by a sense of guilt about what happened, and I am not. Two sides of the same coin.'

Pip frowned and looked as if she was about to object, but then she nodded. 'I suppose so,' she said.

They sat in silence for a moment, the bustle of the café carrying on around them.

'What did you think?' Evelyn asked after a moment. 'When you read what I wrote in the diary?'

'The part about you being glad that she was dead?' Pip replied. Evelyn nodded.

Pip blew her lips out. 'I wasn't sure what to think, really,' she said. 'I heard a rumour that one of you had murdered the other, and I suppose for a moment I did wonder. The diary was quite ambiguous, but it could have been interpreted as an indication that you had killed her. It felt unlikely, though, especially after everything else that I'd read about your life and what kind of a person you are. I couldn't imagine you as a murderer!'

Evelyn gave half a smile. 'Jolly glad to hear it,' she said.

Pip put her fingers to her face and tapped a nail against her teeth as if deciding what to say next. 'There was one thing that I didn't understand, though. If I'm honest, it really confused me.' She was twisting her bottom lip between her fingers and looking straight into Evelyn's eyes, clearly uncomfortable with what she wanted to say but desperate to say it all the same.

'Go on,' said Evelyn cautiously.

'Well, I didn't realise that you had left Scarlet with Joan,' Pip began slowly. 'The diary doesn't say that. So I couldn't understand why you didn't seem to feel any remorse for what had happened. There was me, haunted by my guilt for my part in the death of a child, and yet you seemed to have none.'

Now it was Evelyn's turn to be confused. Something prickled at the back of her neck as she tried to grasp exactly what it was that Pip was saying.

'I'm not sure I follow,' she said slowly. 'Did you think I was responsible for my own child's death?'

Pip lowered her eyes to the table and nodded her head. 'Not exactly, but your three-year-old child drowned. I couldn't understand how you didn't seem to be feeling responsible for that, at least in part. From everything I read, I just assumed that Scarlet was with you when she died. But then there was nothing that suggested any guilt. I just couldn't follow it.'

Evelyn considered what Pip had said carefully. Was she saying that she thought Scarlet had died though a lack of care on her part? She felt herself bristle, but then again, she supposed that without having all the pieces of the jigsaw it wasn't an unreasonable conclusion to reach. But if that were the case, then it gave rise to a question of her own.

'So, even though you thought I might have a degree of responsibility for what happened to Scarlet, you still wanted to spend time with me?' she asked.

When Pip raised her eyes, Evelyn could see the tears welling up, her lip quivering.

'I wanted to know how you managed it,' she said, her voice faltering. 'I needed to know how you could live with that level of guilt and not let it consume you. I just can't do it. I'm crumbling under the weight of what I'm carrying. I can't get out from under it. And yet you seemed untouched by it. I just wanted to know how you coped without falling apart.'

'And now?' Evelyn asked archly. 'Now that you know I am not the panacea to all your ills?'

Pip's shoulders sagged. 'Please don't be like that,' she said. 'Of course I knew that you hadn't really been to blame. I felt it in

247

my heart. It was like I knew you, after reading so many of your inner thoughts.' Here she blushed, a pretty pink colour that washed across her face like a sunset, and Evelyn felt herself soften.

'And I knew that the woman from those pages couldn't have hurt her own child. I just didn't know what had actually happened. And now I do, now that everything makes more sense to me, I know I was right about you in the first place. Of course you couldn't have done anything that might have harmed Scarlet.' Pip bit her lip. 'And how about you, Evelyn? Do you still want to spend time with me, knowing I doubted you?'

Evelyn had to think about it for less than half a second.

'I wouldn't want to spend time with you if you hadn't doubted me,' she replied.

42

Tea and scones finished and with their relationship on a slightly firmer footing, they set back off along the prom towards the house. Evelyn reached for Pip's arm for support without comment this time, and Pip's heart warmed at the intimacy of the gesture. It felt good to be trusted like that, to be needed.

The wind was still blowing in off the water, although the sky was now a cloudless, perfect blue. Pip wished they had a kite, and then wondered where the thought had come from. She hadn't flown a kite in as long as she could remember. Was her old one still buried in a cupboard somewhere at the farm? She'd ask her mother when she got back. Hell, she might even buy herself a new one and bring it down to the beach. She pictured herself running along the beach tugging at the string, a huge brightly coloured diamond flying along behind her, its tail ribbons dancing like little butterflies. Did you ever get too old for things like that? Rose would have thought you did, but Pip definitely didn't agree.

She felt lighter than she had, knowing now that she had misinterpreted Evelyn's diary entry, and what had happened to Joan had been entirely accidental. Now she could allow herself to grow fond of Evelyn in a way she might not have done had the doubt been still hanging over her. It was also good to finally understand what had happened to Scarlet, but so unbearably sad that Pip didn't want to think about it in case it smothered the glowing embers of happiness she could feel in the pit of her stomach.

Evelyn seemed to have gained something from their conversation as well. Pip could tell from the pace of their return journey that their outing had exhausted her although she was doing her best to hide it, but she too seemed lighter in spirit. What she had said about Joan hadn't been a confession as such, but it must have been cathartic for her on some level. Despite the weariness in her step, Evelyn seemed younger than she had before.

A little girl, who must have been a similar age to Scarlet when she died, ran out in front of them and headed for the concrete steps down to the beach, her mother chasing almost immediately behind. The sudden movement made Pip jump, as all such things did these days, but Evelyn smiled, watching after the child as she made her way gingerly down the steep steps one at a time, always leading with the same leg.

'It's so lovely to be out, Pip,' she said when the child had finally reached the beach. 'Thank you for bringing me.'

'My pleasure,' Pip replied. 'Now, before we get back, tell me something about Ted. You mention him a couple of times, but not any visits. Did he come to see you?'

Evelyn's face lit up at the mention of Ted, and her eyes seemed to twinkle. 'Dear, dear Ted,' she said. 'He used to come quite often when I first moved back. And he'd ring for a chat too, when he could. He really was a good friend to me.'

Pip turned her head and eyed Evelyn quizzically.

Evelyn seemed to catch her meaning at once and she tutted and shook her head. 'Not like that, you mucky-minded pup! I don't think he was really interested in women, or men for that matter. He told me he'd been married once, but it didn't last. He devoted his entire life to caring for his mother. They were inseparable. There was such contrast there. Ted would have done anything for his mum. I couldn't get away from mine fast enough, but I suppose it takes all sorts.'

Pip thought about her own mother, how she tried so hard to do and say the right thing, always treading on eggshells around her, and her stomach tightened. She knew she'd been horribly ungrateful when she was younger. It was little wonder her parents had been upset by her airs and graces. But she'd try harder now, she decided, show her mother she really did appreciate what she had done, and was continuing to do for her.

'When Scarlet was tiny,' Evelyn said, 'Ted was about the only visitor I ever had. Peter came, of course, when she was first born, although babies really weren't his thing until he had one of his own. But Ted came whenever he could get time off and borrow a vehicle of some sort. He was great with her, used to take her for long walks in her pram so I could get some sleep. Joan would never help with her, because I'd made my own bed and all that. Sometimes Ted would come, and I'd sleep for the whole time he was here. I used to wonder what kind of conversations he and Joan might have had when I wasn't there, but actually, I think they just avoided one another.

'And then his mum fell ill and it got harder and harder for him to get away. If he rang when I was out with Scarlet, then Joan wouldn't pass the message on, so gradually we just drifted apart. He came to Scarlet's funeral, of course, but we didn't see much of each other after that. I suppose I just retreated, and he must have given up trying to help. Poor dear Ted. He didn't deserve the treatment he got.'

'He sounds lovely,' said Pip. 'I could do with a Ted in my life.'

As she said this, she realised that she had one – Jez. He'd been there for her and she had pushed him away. Pip wasn't sure if the heat in her face was the effect of the wind or her shame. She would make amends, though, with her parents and Jez, or at least she would try. She hoped she hadn't burned her bridges.

They reached Evelyn's house, dingy and unloved next to its smarter neighbours.

Evelyn stopped and looked up at it, shaking her head sadly. 'I have really let things slide, haven't I?' she said, but Pip got the impression she was talking to herself more than to her. 'But this is enough. Something needs to change here, Evelyn Mountcastle. You need to take yourself in hand.'

Pip held her tongue, but she was telling herself the same thing.

◆ ◆ ◆

Later, when she was back at the farm, Pip continued to think about Evelyn and Ted. It was obvious they'd been really close; he was perhaps the closest friend Evelyn had had. How difficult might it be to track him down? Quite hard, she concluded. She had very little to go on unless she asked Evelyn for some more details, which would give the game away. She didn't even have a surname, so the usual social media trawling wasn't an option, although she very much doubted Ted would bother with that kind of thing.

It should definitely be a surprise, she decided. If she had to bet, she would lay money on the old Evelyn, the Evelyn of the diary before Scarlet's death, being up for a good surprise. Pip felt pretty sure she would be delighted, although she supposed there was a chance she'd pegged that wrong. Still, even if it didn't work out entirely as she hoped, surely Evelyn would understand she had been trying to do something kind for her and not be too cross.

The prospect of pleasing Evelyn gave Pip a warm glow. Had it really been that long since she had done something for someone else with purely altruistic motives? It had, and she realised with more than a little shame, it went back a lot longer than just the accident. Rose Appleby wasn't big on doing kind things for other people. She had been too absorbed in making everything perfect for herself.

Well, that was going to change, Pip thought. When she finally got back to London it would be a very different Rose Appleby sitting behind her grand mahogany desk.

43

A couple of days later, Pip was changing the window display at the shop when she saw the rangy figure of Nicholas Mountcastle striding down the pavement. She hadn't seen Evelyn since their trip to the pier the previous weekend, but something about his purposeful gait made her sure that he was on his way to find her and that this visit had something to do with his aunt.

Arriving at the shop and seeing her standing in the window, trying to wrestle a naked mannequin into a bright yellow sundress, seemed to throw him off his task. He paused, staring up at her and seemingly unable to decide what to do next. Pip smiled and mouthed 'hello' through the glass. He didn't smile back at her, which didn't bode well. Pip wondered what he thought she'd done.

He stepped into the shop and loitered by the door, arms folded severely across his chest, and waited for her to emerge. It was clear he wanted a word and wasn't going to leave until she obliged him, and so she put the half-dressed woman down and extracted herself from the window display area.

'I assume you're looking for me?' she asked him, although that much was obvious.

'Indeed,' he said. Still no smile. 'I was wondering if we might have a word. In private,' he added as he caught sight of Audrey stalking across the shop towards them.

'Of course,' Pip replied as pleasantly as she could. 'Is it all right if I just nip out for a moment, Audrey? I won't be long.'

Audrey looked as though she wanted to say that that would be highly inconvenient but, as there were only the two of them in the shop, was forced to nod her agreement instead.

Pip followed Nicholas out on to the street.

'How can I help?' she asked him.

'Well, the thing is . . .' he said, his lips pursed so tightly that it must have been hard to speak. 'Please leave my aunt alone. She is a vulnerable old woman . . .'

Pip's eyebrows shot up. She could think of plenty of words to describe Evelyn, but vulnerable wasn't one of them.

'. . . and she doesn't need the likes of you preying on her, so I'd take it very kindly if you would stop calling on her.'

He spoke as if he had fallen out of the pages of a Jane Austen novel, and Pip wondered whether this was a preprepared speech rather than his natural choice of words.

'Has Evelyn asked you to come?' Pip asked. She thought it highly unlikely, particularly in light of their recent conversation, but she thought she had better check.

'No,' admitted Nicholas, 'but as her next of kin I have to have her best interests in mind.'

Pip was curious. 'And why, exactly, do you consider me to be not in her best interests?' she asked, the corner of her mouth curling up into a smirk. 'What is it that you believe I've done?'

Nicholas frowned and looked irritated at her apparent failure to take him seriously. 'I just think it would be better if you stayed away from her,' he replied tetchily.

It was obvious that he was very far from his comfort zone, that giving ultimatums to strangers wasn't something he did every day, and that it might have been funny had Pip not been genuinely concerned about what he was saying.

'Well, Mr Mountcastle,' she said firmly. 'I rather think it's up to Evelyn who she chooses to spend time with, don't you?'

'No, I do not,' he snapped. His voice was getting louder all the time, and a few people passing by turned their heads to see what was going on. 'I know your sort,' he continued. 'You see an old woman living on her own and you think that if you befriend her there might be something in it for you.'

Ah! Light dawned on Pip. He thought she was a gold-digger. That was rich. She was the only person in decades to pay any attention to Evelyn, and he immediately suspected her motives. Whatever happened to community spirit? His attitude was particularly disappointing in this small town where everybody looked out for everyone else, because she was beginning to see things in those terms now. What she had previously considered the nosiness of those around her she now understood to be a healthy concern.

'Oh, I get it,' she said slowly. 'You're worried in case I'm trying to get Evelyn to change her will.' She laughed at how ludicrous that was. 'Are you worried I might get you disinherited?'

Nicholas spluttered out an answer. 'No. Of course not. That isn't it at all,' he said, although from his demeanour it was obvious she had hit the nail on the head. 'I'm just concerned for my aunt,' he added.

'Yes, I can see that,' Pip replied pointedly. 'You leave her in that big house, drowning in dust and cornflakes. You throw away her things without asking and the first time anyone shows any interest in her for years, you try to warn them off. It's very clear just how much you care for her.'

It was harsh, Pip knew, but it seemed that her cross-examination muscles were still strong, and she was enjoying flexing them. Plus, it was fun to watch him squirming on the hook. The almost-forgotten feeling of having a witness exactly where she wanted him rose up and she welcomed it like a long-lost friend.

'You have no right . . .' he began, but Pip put up a hand to silence him.

'Listen, Nicholas,' she said more gently. 'You honestly have no need to worry. I went to the house to return the diary. Evelyn and I got chatting and discovered that we have more in common than you might think. It's as simple as that. I have no need of your aunt's money, and I would much rather have her alive and available to talk to than otherwise. So please, rest assured that all is well. There's no Machiavellian plot afoot here.'

He looked first cross, and then relieved. When he spoke again his voice was much softer, confirming her suspicion that he had built himself up to come and have it out with her.

'You do understand my position, though,' he said.

Pip nodded and gave him a little half-smile by way of peace offering, which he returned. 'I'm not sure I do,' she said, 'but it's fine. You can rest assured I'm not trying to steal any inheritance out from under your nose.'

'Well, it's good to hear that,' he said, immediately showing her all his cards.

He gave up awfully easily, Pip thought. He'd make a terrible barrister. 'Actually, now that you're here,' she said, 'there was something I wanted to run past you.'

Nicholas looked a little taken aback at the reversal of roles, but he was listening.

'Your aunt had a friend in London back in the day. Ted. I was thinking of trying to get in touch with him. I'm sure your aunt would love to see him, but I'd like to make it a surprise. Do you think she'd be up for something like that?'

Nicholas's brow wrinkled as he thought about what she'd said. 'Yes, I should think so. She's a game old bird. But she's never mentioned anyone from the old days to me, and you've only spent a few hours with her. How've you heard about him so soon?'

Pip felt her blush creep up her chest and burn her cheeks.

Nicholas was on to her straight away. 'You read her diary, didn't you?' he asked her slyly. 'The one I brought here by mistake.'

Pip could deny it, but what would be the point? 'I did,' she replied. 'I had to work out who it belonged to so I could return it.' She knew it sounded feeble, but it was the best she had.

'Well I never,' he said, looking very pleased with himself. 'Not quite as whiter than white as we'd like to make out, are we?' he said with an air of triumph.

Pip was cross to have been caught out, but there was nothing she could do about it so she tried to rise above it and pressed on. 'Anyway, I don't have much to go on, but I'll see if I can track him down.'

'Maybe we should hire a private detective,' Nicholas said. He sounded quite excited about the idea.

'I don't think we need to go quite that far,' replied Pip, bursting his bubble. 'I was thinking of placing a small ad in the *Evening Standard*. I know it's a long shot, but let's start small. If that doesn't work then maybe I'll consider your private dick.'

Nicholas looked a little disappointed, but he nodded his agreement.

'Don't tell her though, will you?' Pip checked. 'I'd really like it to be a surprise.'

'No. I won't tell her, but could you let me know if you get anywhere? If he's coming to the house, then we'll need to have a bit of a tidy up. I'm not sure Aunt Evelyn would want anyone to see the current state of the place.'

'I was thinking about that, too,' said Pip. 'I was wondering if I could help at all.'

'I'm not sure how,' replied Nicholas. 'I've tried to get her out from under all that crap, I really have. The box I brought here is testament to that.'

'And that went so well,' muttered Pip under her breath.

'But she won't have anyone in the house, and she won't let me touch anything. She can be downright difficult when she wants to be.'

Pip didn't doubt it. 'Well, maybe I could have a word with her. About the mess, I mean,' she said. 'I get the impression she's had enough of it, too, but doesn't know where to start. Maybe between the three of us . . .'

Nicholas looked unsure. It seemed that if there were sorting to be done, it would be she and Evelyn who did the bulk of the work, but she found she didn't mind the prospect. It might be good to have a project, something to really get stuck into.

Then Nicholas stuck his hand in the breast pocket of his jacket and retrieved another business card. He handed it to Pip. 'Here's my number,' he said.

Pip took it, not wanting to reveal that she had an exact copy sitting in her bedroom at home.

'Perhaps we could go out for a drink, chat it all through,' he said.

Was he coming on to her? Pip wasn't sure. She had lost all radar for that kind of thing over the last few months. She hoped not, though. He really wasn't her type. Then again, she had thought Dominic was the perfect man for her, but now she wasn't sure what she had ever seen in him.

'That would be nice,' she replied, without making a commitment. 'But now I ought to be getting back to my window.' She cocked her head in the direction of the half-naked mannequin. 'I can't leave her like that. The poor lamb has no dignity. I'll be in touch.'

And then she skipped back into the shop, leaving Nicholas looking slightly flummoxed on the pavement.

That evening at home she put together a small ad for the *Evening Standard*. She really didn't have that much to go on and she didn't want to attract the attention of all and sundry. In the end she settled for:

Looking for Ted.

Friends with Evelyn Mountcastle, 1980.

She created a new email address specifically for the purpose and added it to the message. Then she went on to the website and set the ball rolling.

44

'I hope you don't mind,' said Pip's mother over dinner the next day, 'but I told Jez you'd take him out for a drink tonight. He's so low with all that Teresa business and he just looked as if he needed cheering up.'

A month ago, Pip would have considered herself to be worse company than Jez, but over the last few weeks things had begun to change. Finding the diary and meeting Evelyn had given her something other than herself and her own misery to focus on, and that had been refreshing. But if she let herself think about her general sense of improvement, it had the reverse effect and made her guilt worse. How dare she let things move on for her when the boy's family would always be living in a half-light? As soon as she began to feel a little better, the familiar sense of self-reproach became larger and darker. It was like taking one step forward and two steps back.

However, her conversation with Evelyn had given her food for thought. Getting on with her life didn't necessarily mean she had forgiven herself or forgotten what had gone before. But it certainly went a long way to making her day-to-day existence more stable.

Jez was a friend in need and again, as with Evelyn, it was her trying to help rather than being helped by someone else. It felt good.

'That's fine,' she said to her mother. 'It'll be lovely to see him. What time did you say?'

'He'll pick you up around eight, but if that's no good you're to text him and let him know.'

Pip picked up her phone and sent a quick message confirming the plan. Already she was looking forward to the evening, even if Jez was down in the dumps and so wouldn't be on top form. She'd forgotten how well they got on, lost sight of it somehow. Spending time with him over the last few weeks had been like rediscovering a long-forgotten treasure. It was such a joy to be with someone whose company was so effortless. There was so much history between them and consequently so much that didn't need to be spoken. Their conversations worked using a type of shorthand that she just didn't have with her newer friends, and had never got anywhere close to with Dominic.

An hour later, she and Jez were in the pub again, their drinks on the table in front of them, but this time the vibe was very different. Whilst her mood had risen steadily since they had last been together, Jez's had fallen into a deep, black pit and appeared to be irretrievable.

'How's it going?' Pip asked him, deciding it would be best to start with a nice wide question that he could answer as he wished, and that would give her an idea of which way the conversation was going to flow.

'I've had better times,' he said without looking up. 'Being single is crap.'

Pip touched his shoulder gently, her palm feeling his warmth through his T-shirt.

'I'm so sorry, Jez,' she said gently. 'It's shit. Have you seen her at all?'

He shook his head. 'She came to get her stuff, but I was at the farm. She knew I'd be out, arrived then on purpose.'

Pip shrugged sympathetically, although she would probably have done the same herself.

'I went to the hotel,' Jez continued, 'to see if we could talk things through again, but they told me she was in a meeting. They were probably lying.'

'Maybe it's for the best that you haven't seen her,' suggested Pip, aware of how much she sounded like her mother. It was hard to know what to say without sounding trite or patronising. This must be what it had been like talking to her recently, not being able to find the words, worried that you would accidentally say the wrong thing and make matters worse.

He took a deep breath, sat back in his chair and looked straight at her. 'Let's just get pissed,' he said. 'Horribly, disgustingly pissed.'

Pip couldn't remember the last time she had been even tipsy, let alone the level of drunk that Jez seemed to have in mind. She had avoided alcohol since the accident, worried that if she started drinking, she might never stop, but what harm could one evening do? It wasn't as if she would be driving anywhere.

'Go on then,' she said, a broad grin creeping across her face. 'But if you puke or you start doing that stupid dance you used to do, then I'm out of here.'

With a new sense of purpose, Jez's mood seemed to improve, and by the time he began his third pint he seemed to have forgotten he had been miserable. Pip had no hope of matching him drink for drink – she was out of practice and she could never drink as much as him anyway – but she held her own. As the alcohol seeped into her bloodstream she felt an uncoupling inside her, as if someone had taken away the burden of her body and left her with just her mind, and she knew at once that she had been right not to drink her way through the last dark months.

By the time they had got to their sixth drink they had begun to play a rather raucous game of 'who would you do'. It wasn't something Pip had thought about in years, but now she remembered how much fun it was to consider a room full of people and rank them in terms of sexual attractiveness. Jez's choices didn't surprise her in the least, but her own were not what she would have predicted. Dominic was broad and dark with a patrician profile, but the men who caught her eye in the pub were quirkier, less alpha male and more cheeky-looking. In fact, they were a lot like Jez.

The second this thought crossed her mind, she knew exactly where the evening would be heading unless she did something to prevent it. It seemed as if the thought had crossed Jez's mind at almost the same moment, because he focused his slightly glazed eyes on her and said, 'And, of course, I'd always do you, Pip.'

Not having had time to work out what she felt, Pip tried to fend him off with jokes. 'Oh, you always did know how to flatter a girl, Jez. Just how far down that list did I come?' She grinned at him to show she knew he was joking and that she was, too, but instead of returning her smile he was now just staring at her as if he was seeing her for the first time.

'I'm serious,' he said, the joshing tone of the moment before now gone. 'You've always been special, Pip. You mean the world to me. You always have done, ever since we were kids.'

His words went straight to her drunken heart. Who didn't want to be told they were special? Suddenly she felt cherished in a way she hadn't for a long time. And he was right. There had been a bond between them since the first time he had led her, nervous but excited about what was to come, up the rickety ladder in the old hay barn. Sex in a hay barn was such a cliché, but no less lovely for that. It hadn't been his first time – of course it hadn't; they were seventeen – but Pip had liked to think the memory of it occupied a precious place in his heart. It certainly did in hers.

She could do it, she thought. There was nothing to stop her. They could leave the pub and walk the short distance to his tiny cottage. It would be safe and easy, and she longed for someone to take care of her, to hold her tight and let her drift away from the last few months, if only for an hour or two.

But Jez was drunk and heartbroken. The last thing he needed was a confusing night with an old flame who was barely holding it together herself. And yet . . .

Pip pushed herself up from the table and looked straight into the familiar hazel eyes.

'Come on,' she said softly. 'Let's go.'

45

Evelyn had ventured out of the house.

She had dressed with care and walked to the hardware shop to buy sturdy black plastic bags. The man behind the counter had assured her they were the strongest he stocked, although he hadn't enquired what she intended to do with them. Evelyn was tempted to hint that she had chopped up a body that she needed to dispose of. She'd had such fun with people sometimes, back when she used to have fun. They were so easy to wind up, and she was great at playing whichever part might suit her story. Perhaps she should get in touch with that Evelyn Mountcastle and invite her to come and stay.

Back at the house, she sat at the kitchen table with the bags in a heavy roll in front of her, and despaired. What had seemed like a wonderful idea first thing that morning – clearing the kitchen so she could actually function – now felt akin to climbing Everest in flippers.

She sighed, defeated before she had even begun. How had she let things get so bad? There had been a time after Joan died when she had been on top of it all. She had even thought about re-engaging the cleaner that Joan had sacked. She had always liked her, and she missed having someone around the place to talk to.

But the weeks had rolled into months and then years, and she hadn't done anything about anything. And this was the result. Chaos.

She took a deep breath, tore the first bag from the huge roll, and began. To start with, she checked each item before dropping it into the gaping mouth of the sack, but within ten minutes she took to simply sweeping the contents of each surface into the black void. It didn't take long before she was quite enjoying herself, hefting the weight of the full bin bags as if that could determine their value. Soon she had ten filled to the top, and the floor was covered in things that hadn't quite gone in the right direction when she whooshed them from the surface and into the waiting sack.

And it felt good. It was as if by clearing the backlog of stuff that had accumulated, she was also clearing her mind, her spirit. She felt lighter, less weighed down by it all. Maybe when she had the place straight, she could undertake a little refurbishment. She didn't think she could bear the upheaval of anything major, but a fresh lick of paint and maybe a new carpet or two might be nice.

This was all Pip's doing. The young woman had wandered into her life and, without meaning to, had turned something on inside her that Evelyn thought had been painted over and could never move again. Evelyn wished she could return the favour. The poor girl was in limbo, not able to move forward with her life and too scared to go back. There wasn't much she could do practically, but she could talk to her, encourage her to address the things that were haunting her. Bottling things up was no way to carry on. That way madness lay, she thought knowingly as she cast her eyes around the devastation that was her kitchen. And after all, wasn't that precisely what Pip had done for her? Talking about Scarlet for the first time in so very long had released fresh memories of her in Evelyn's mind. She had been frightened of extracting them before, worried they might have fragmented into something irretrievable, but the Scarlet who had danced into her mind had been as vivid as ever and not at all tainted by time.

Talking to Pip had also altered her feelings towards Joan, from a blind fury to something less destructive. When Pip had voiced her anger at Joan's behaviour, it had felt to Evelyn as though some of the burden she had carried for so long had been lifted. It was true what they said: a trouble shared is a trouble halved. Now Evelyn had to see what she could do to halve Pip's trouble, too.

A knock on the front door rang out and made Evelyn jump. She clutched at her heart as she waited for its pace to slow. Her newfound freedoms weren't all-encompassing yet, then. A visitor could still send her into a tailspin. She decided she would just ignore whoever it was and wait for them to leave. She made herself stand very still, even though there was no way the person at the door would be able to see her, while she waited for them to go away.

'Evelyn?' came the now-familiar voice through the door. 'It's me, Pip. Are you there?'

Evelyn let her breath out in a sigh of relief. Pip.

'Yes,' she called. 'I'm just coming.'

With a final, regretful look at the mess she had made in clearing the mess that had been there before, she hurried to the front door and opened it.

Pip looked dreadful. Her skin was sallow and there were dark stripes under either eye but she was smiling like the cat who'd got the cream.

'You look awful,' said Evelyn. Being old meant she could enjoy a degree of honesty that other, less senior people had to restrain.

'I'm hungover,' said Pip, giving a smile a mile wide that brightened her tired features no end. 'First one in as long as I can remember. I wondered if you fancied a walk, help me blow the cobwebs away.'

Evelyn cast a glance back towards the kitchen and Pip added, 'But if you're busy that's no problem. We can make it another time.' Her eyes followed Evelyn's, and when they settled on the kitchen she let out a low whistle. 'You've been hard at it,' she said.

'I'm having a bit of a clear-out,' replied Evelyn uncertainly, 'but I think I deserve a break. Let's go.'

The walk led them back to the same café as before, and Pip ordered tea for two and two slices of banana bread.

'I used to make a mean banana bread,' Pip said as she bit into her slice. 'I should do that again. Bake, I mean. There never seemed to be time before, but maybe now . . .'

They sat in companionable silence whilst the café hummed around them. It felt good to Evelyn, normal.

'Can I ask you something?' Pip asked, once her cake was gone.

A slight queasiness settled in Evelyn's stomach. This modern desire to share was all very well, but it didn't get any easier to deal with. 'All right,' she replied cagily, 'but I reserve my right to silence should I not wish to answer your question.'

Pip nodded. 'That's fine. It's just that I was wondering who Scarlet's father was. Is he still around? I mean, alive?'

So this was it. They had arrived. Evelyn had known they would get to this point eventually. It was an obvious crater in the story she had told Pip so far. But the identity of Scarlet's father was something she hadn't revealed to anyone – not Brenda, not Julian, not even Ted, bless him, although it wasn't for want of asking on his part. She hadn't even confessed it to her diary, although there was a kind of code to some of her entries that might have given a clue if anyone had read them.

Her reasons for keeping her secret were manifold and had altered with the passing years. To start with, she had worried about getting herself into trouble, then getting Rory MacMillan into trouble, although for the life of her she couldn't understand why she had ever thought that now. Then she had not wanted Joan to do anything rash. And finally she had worried that it would somehow be bad for Scarlet. And all this added up to not having ever told a living soul.

But what did she have to lose now?

'He's still alive,' she began. 'Or he is as far as I know, although I have no idea where in the world he might have settled himself. I haven't seen him since the day Scarlet was conceived.'

It had always struck her as odd that Rory MacMillan had had a daughter and then lost her again, without ever being aware that such a thing was even a possibility. Her child probably hadn't been the only one he had, in fact, given the way things worked back then. Scarlet had probably had half-siblings all over the place, although that was something Evelyn didn't like to think too deeply about.

Evelyn had allowed MacMillan to cross her mind on and off over the years. She had wondered what had become of him, and if he ever thought about her, although she doubted that very much. For a while, she had tried to keep up with what was going on in the world of television, but then she had stopped punishing herself. It hurt too much to see other people having success when hers had been stolen from her. Then she had played an imaginary game in which she confronted MacMillan with Scarlet, showed him and the rest of the world what he had done. She had gleaned a dark satisfaction from the idea that she could use what she knew to undermine his world as easily as he had undermined hers. But in the end, she had abandoned the plan. It was all so very long ago. What was there to be gained from exposing him, and who would believe her anyway? Everybody knew the score in those days. Men had the power and women understood what had to be done in order to get what they wanted. She had just been one in a very long line.

'Didn't he know about Scarlet?' asked Pip, cutting across her thoughts.

Evelyn shook her head. 'I suppose he might have worked it out. I left his film set pregnant and he'd had sex with me some months beforehand. It's hardly rocket science.'

'Was he your boyfriend? You weren't married, were you?' Pip asked.

The young could be so prudish, Evelyn thought.

'No and no, definitely not,' she replied.

Pip seemed to hesitate before delving further, as if she were fearful of crossing a line. She really did look dreadful, Evelyn thought, although there was a little more colour in her cheeks after their walk along the prom.

Then Pip gave Evelyn a smirk and raised her eyebrows suggestively. 'Was it a one-night stand?' she asked, dropping her voice to a whisper.

'More of a one-afternoon stand,' replied Evelyn coolly.

'Blimey!' said Pip, her bloodshot eyes suddenly wide. 'I would never have had you pegged as a "one-afternoon stand" kind of woman.'

Evelyn felt a little gratified at this, although she wasn't sure what she was proud of – not being thought of as that kind of woman, or the sex itself.

'I wasn't,' she said. 'This was the one and only occasion on which such a thing happened. And this one shouldn't have, either. But if it hadn't, I would never have had my darling Scarlet, and I wouldn't have been without her, no matter what I had to put up with.'

Pip's smirk slipped. 'What do you mean?' she asked. Her whole demeanour had altered. 'Was it against your will?' Her voice was so low that Evelyn could barely make out her words.

'No, no,' Evelyn replied. 'It wasn't rape. But I'm not sure I entirely agreed to it.'

'Then that's rape, surely?'

'Oh, Pip,' replied Evelyn with a sigh. 'Things are rarely ever that straightforward.'

Pip sat up straighter in her chair. 'Well, that is,' she said sharply. 'There is no doubt. You either consented or you didn't. There are no half measures.'

Evelyn wasn't at all sure she was right. 'Well, I went into his room willingly. When he suggested we had sex, I was a little shocked. It wasn't at all what I was expecting. I was more naive than anything, I suppose. I thought it was a business meeting, you see. I had no idea . . .'

Pip's mouth fell open and creases appeared across her smooth brow. 'What exactly happened, Evelyn?' she asked, her tone suddenly very serious. She shifted forward in her chair, her spine straight and her eyes boring straight into Evelyn's.

Evelyn felt a little as if she were being interviewed. Was this how Pip dealt with her clients? She shuffled a little and let her eyes fall to the Formica table between them. 'It's all such a long time ago,' she said vaguely, but Pip was having none of it.

'Come on, Evelyn. Are you seriously trying to tell me that you can't remember?'

Evelyn could see she was on a hiding to nothing taking that line. So she took a deep breath and let it out in a sigh. 'His name was Rory MacMillan and he was the producer of a television show that I'd been cast in. My agent thought I had the part in the bag, but he told me I had to go to a meeting at Mr MacMillan's hotel to go over some final details.'

Evelyn surprised herself by using such a formal description of the man. People didn't really do that these days. The use of titles had fallen by the wayside and yet, despite everything, Evelyn felt compelled to use his. Pip's expression altered minutely, but she didn't stop her.

'When I got there, he asked me if I wanted a drink, and then one thing led to another and we ended up having sex.'

'But you didn't want to?' asked Pip.

Evelyn twisted her mouth as she composed an answer. 'Well, I hadn't intended to. It wasn't what I was expecting when I walked into that room.'

'So he forced you?'

Evelyn shook her head. 'No, he didn't force me. But I didn't really have a choice. If I wanted the part – and I did, I really did – then that was the price I needed to pay. I knew that and so did he. That's how it was back then. It was just the way it worked.'

Pip sat back in her chair and shook her head slowly. 'Evelyn. Have you ever talked to anyone about this, about what happened to you?' she asked.

Her voice was quiet now, and Evelyn had the impression she had missed something that seemed obvious to Pip. She shook her head.

'And you don't keep up with current affairs? Have you seen what's been going on recently?'

Again, Evelyn shook her head. She found the news depressing and so she just watched old videos and DVDs of programmes that she enjoyed: cosy Agatha Christie mysteries and the like. And she had given up reading newspapers when they began piling up around the house. Her world was very contained, and she had seen no reason to contaminate it with things from the outside.

'Treating you like that was an abuse of power,' Pip continued. 'Plain and simple. It might have been just the way things were back then, but it's not any more. Hundreds of women have spoken out against their abusers, thousands maybe, and in all walks of life. Men have gone to prison. Famous men, high-profile ones, household names even, for things they did to women in the seventies and eighties.'

'But that can't be right,' objected Evelyn. 'It was just how things were back then. Some men were just like that. Touching your bottom when you walked past, stroking your breast in a crowded lift, having sex with women young enough to be their daughters. We all knew what was going on, of course we did, and we didn't like it, but there wasn't anything you could do about it. It was simply a fact of life for women, so we learned to avoid the worst offenders and keep our mouths shut.'

'But those men, men who behaved like that, were committing an offence,' Pip said. 'They can be prosecuted, punished.'

'Well, that hardly seems fair,' said Evelyn. 'They were just doing what everyone else did. I'm not sure many of them thought it was wrong. They imagined we'd be flattered by being wolf-whistled. Well, to be honest, we were. Who doesn't like to be appreciated?'

Pip shook her head. 'How can you defend them, Evelyn?' she said, exasperation clear in her tone.

'I'm not defending them exactly. It's just when I was your age, that kind of thing was an accepted social norm, so it doesn't seem right to punish them all this time later for something that was so common.'

'But just because it was common doesn't make it right,' Pip replied emphatically. She looked quite angry now so it was hard for Evelyn to keep in mind that it wasn't her Pip was cross with. 'What that man, Rory MacMillan, did to you, was sexual harassment at best. You can report him to the police, bring a claim against him. I bet you're not the only one. Men like him are sexual predators who deserve to be exposed. We could go to the police here in town. I can help you if you like. I could represent you, even.'

It was difficult to take in everything Pip was saying, but one thing was clear in Evelyn's bombarded mind.

'I shan't be bringing any claim against anyone,' she said firmly.

'But . . .' began Pip.

'It was all a very long time ago, a different world. Life danced to a different tune. And what possible purpose could it serve, raking it all up now?'

'He abused his position, he made you pregnant so that you lost your job, he took advantage of you when the balance of power was skewed.'

'But I could have left,' replied Evelyn. 'At any point I could have picked up my things and gone.'

'But you didn't, because you wanted what he was holding over you like a carrot. You wanted the part.'

'I did. But who's to say I wouldn't have got it anyway? We will never know.'

Pip was getting more and more agitated. 'But can't you see that . . .'

'No,' said Evelyn decisively. 'What I see is that from some random encounter in a hotel I was given the most wonderful, most beautiful, most precious gift of my life. And that is all that matters.'

Finally, Pip seemed to accept her point of view, and snapped her mouth closed before anything else could leak out. 'Okay,' she said quietly.

Evelyn was right about this, no matter what Pip said. It was in the past and best left well alone.

But later that evening, after Pip had helped her fill a few more bin liners and then said goodbye and gone home, Evelyn had searched the internet. Pip was right. Stories highlighting the abuse of young impressionable women by men in positions of authority were everywhere. Men had been prosecuted, men that she could hardly believe would be capable of such horrifying acts. Men who had been part of the fabric of society, who you thought you knew simply by virtue of the fact they were on your television set in the corner of your lounge. How wrong everyone had been.

And perhaps people thought the same about Rory MacMillan. He was personable and fun. She had enjoyed talking to him at the New Year's Eve party, had been flattered he had chosen to shine his attention down on her rather than anyone else. Even after the incident, she still couldn't bring herself to use the words that Pip had used; she hadn't blamed him, not entirely.

But how things had changed. She could hardly believe that what women of her generation had just accepted as a fact of life was now so vilified. Women had stepped forward, drawing strength and courage from one another and then from the sheer number of them. She was astonished at the men who had been brought down, men she knew about but had never been able to discuss, other than with other women and behind closed doors. It was incredible.

Evelyn sat back and stared at the computer screen until the images flicked away and the screen went black. How had she allowed herself to become so cut off from the world that she hadn't even been aware this was happening? One article said that almost five million people had put their hands up to similar abuses in just twenty-four hours. Women the length and breadth of the planet had been complaining of exactly what had happened to her. It was astounding. And yet she had known nothing about it.

Thank God, she thought, that the young women of today were protected, that society not only knew what went on but had decided it was no longer prepared to stand for it. Evelyn would never know whether she had won the part of DC Karen Walker because of her talent or because she had spread her legs for Rory MacMillan, but at least that wasn't something an actress need go through again. The thought brought hot tears to her eyes. The justice had been so long in coming but now, it seemed, it was there if you looked for it.

Evelyn lifted her hands and hovered them over the keyboard. Should she search for Rory MacMillan, to see if there was anything in the press about him? She decided not. What would be the point? That was in her past. Now she needed to look forward towards her future.

46

Pip was still reeling from Evelyn's revelations when she got back to the farm. It seemed impossible that Evelyn could think as she did, and yet it was clear she didn't seem to blame the man entirely for what had happened to her in that hotel room. She had said it didn't seem fair to prosecute men now, when what had happened had been in different times with different standards. But surely an abuse of power was an abuse of power, no matter when it occurred? Pip couldn't get Evelyn's point of view to lie straight in her head.

She had read the stories of a multitude of actors, musicians, sportswomen and others who had, empowered by the courage of a few, stepped out of the shadows and into the spotlight in order to share their dark and desperate stories. Had any of them approached what had happened to them in a similar way to Evelyn? If they had, then that wasn't the message Pip had heard, but perhaps she hadn't been listening carefully enough. Maybe some of them had also cut the men some slack, made allowances for behaviour that Pip could only see as unforgivable. Personally, she couldn't understand that way of thinking, but if her training as a barrister had taught her anything it was that issues were rarely black or white.

All that said, Pip was sure that on this occasion she was right. There were no excuses. Of course, she couldn't force Evelyn to make a complaint and she wouldn't want to. It was a personal decision for each woman to make on their own. But she had always assumed they decided not to speak out for fear that some deeply buried emotional trauma would be reborn by doing so, that it would cause them a personal psychological pain they didn't feel equipped to deal with, or that they didn't want to be cast as a victim. It had never crossed her mind that anyone could possibly believe it might be unfair to the man.

She was still pondering it when she heard the tractor in the yard. It was Jez. He bounced down from the cab and started examining one of the tyre treads. Seeing him, her stomach lurched and fizzed, as if she were suddenly seventeen again, young and in love for the very first time. It had been so long since she had last felt it, that hormone-fuelled spike of adrenaline that leaves every nerve ending buzzing at the mere sight of another person. How had she thought she was too grown up to feel that buzz when the buzz was actually what life was all about? That was how you knew you were really alive.

Losing touch with lust hadn't happened just as a result of the accident, she realised now. Whilst she had been proud when Dominic had asked her out, her legs hadn't turned to jelly every time she saw him. Instead of butterflies in her stomach, there had been an objective appreciation of a handsome man and a warm, slightly smug feeling that she had mistaken for something else. But it wasn't the same as what she felt now, not the same at all. What on earth had she been thinking back then?

But she and Jez both knew where they stood. They were neither ready for, nor even looking for, a relationship, especially not with one another. The night spent together was more about each offering something safe to their friend – a port in a storm, where they could shelter until the tempest beyond died away. They both knew that it had been lovely and welcome to spend a night together, but it wasn't a solution to either of their problems.

All that said, right now she was rather enjoying the way just looking at him in his overalls and work boots made her feel. And there was nothing wrong with a little bit of physical attraction.

She rapped on the glass, waved and smiled. He looked up and grinned back, the broad open expression she had seen countless times before. Thank God for that, Pip thought. There was no awkwardness in it, nothing that suggested he might either regret what they had done, or worse, be reading more into it than was there.

She was just contemplating this when the back door swung open and he leaned into the house to call her name, holding on to the door frame for support whilst his muddy boots remained firmly outside.

'Evening, Pipsterer. How's the head today?'

'Better than it was earlier,' she said, moving towards the door so their conversation didn't have to be bellowed. 'Yours?'

'I'm fine. I've drunk more than my fair share over the last couple of weeks. I think I'm immune,' he said, and winked at her. 'And also' – he lowered his voice a little – 'I just wanted to say how much I enjoyed myself. I assume you can remember what happened.'

Pip punched him lightly on the arm. 'I wasn't that bad,' she replied indignantly.

'Thank God for that.' He grinned. 'I wouldn't want to be accused of anything inappropriate, getting my wicked way with you when you weren't really up for it.'

In that instant, Pip's mind flicked back to her conversation with Evelyn. Of course, this was completely different, but maybe she could see what Evelyn had been getting at after all. Things weren't always cut and dried. Not that she agreed with Evelyn, not at all, but she conceded that they might look different from where she was sitting.

'But Pip. . .' Jez continued.

The grin slipped from his face and he looked hard into her eyes, making sure she was following him. She could see the dark line of chocolate brown that encircled his hazel irises and that had always fascinated her when she was young. She hadn't really looked at him for years. She regretted that now. Jez deserved far more than she had deigned to give him. They all did: her parents, her school friends . . .

'What happened last night needs to be a one-off,' he said. 'Or at least, not a regular thing.' For a moment a smirk sat on his lips, but then he was serious again. 'I'm really not ready for another relationship, and you and me, well, we're mates. I don't want anything to get in the way of that.'

Her disappointment was sharp, but slight, and then it evaporated entirely. Wasn't this the conclusion she had reached herself not moments before? No matter how safe or comfortable she had felt in his arms, it wasn't the right place for either of them to settle.

'I totally agree,' she said. 'Lovely, safe, comforting sex. Not necessarily a one-off . . .' She paused and raised an eyebrow. 'But not a state of affairs, or anything close to that.'

She reached out and gave him a hug, slightly regretful that he had agreed with her so readily, but knowing they were both right. She breathed him in as if she needed the scent to keep her going for a while. He smelled of petrol and outside and of, well, him.

'Thanks, Pip,' he said into her hair. 'I knew you'd get it.' He pulled away from her then. 'I do have one condition, though,' he said, looking a little grave and vulnerable all at once. 'Don't ditch me again, like you did last time.'

Pip was confused. When they were teenagers their relationship had come to an end by mutual decision, a situation she had considered to be particularly mature at the time. She definitely hadn't ditched Jez, and she was surprised he thought she had.

'I didn't ditch you,' she said. 'We agreed to split up.'

Jez shook his head. 'I'm not talking about the boyfriend/girlfriend thing,' he said. 'I'm talking about you and me as mates. You went off to uni and that was it. After that you never bothered to stay in touch. You didn't even talk to me when you came home for the holidays. You just dropped me, like I wasn't good enough for you any more.' His eyes met hers. 'It hurt, Pip,' he said. 'It really hurt.'

Pip didn't know what to say, other than that she was sorry. She would have liked to say she hadn't realised, that she was devastated to have caused any pain, but it wouldn't have been true, and Jez deserved the truth.

'I'm sorry I hurt you,' she said. 'I made some mistakes. But I'm trying to put them right.'

Jez nodded, accepting. 'Okay,' he said. 'Well, make sure you don't do it again!' He wagged a finger at her, grinned and then turned and went back to his tractor, leaving Pip standing on the doorstep thinking about what he had just said.

'Nice to see you getting on so well with Jez,' said a voice behind her.

It was her mother, and Pip jumped like a teenager with a guilty conscience.

'Yes,' she said as casually as she could manage. 'He's gutted about the Teresa thing. But I think he'll be okay.'

'Well, there are plenty more fish in the sea,' said her mother, and Pip stifled an eye roll.

'Oh, and a letter came for you,' her mother added. 'I put it on the mantelpiece in the lounge.'

'Who's it from?' she asked.

'No idea,' said her mother, although Pip knew she would have examined it thoroughly for clues. 'London postmark, though,' she added.

Pip made her way to the lounge and retrieved the letter. The envelope was thin with a self-sticking flap, the sort you buy in bulk from the supermarket. Her name and address were handwritten in blue biro in clear capital letters. She didn't recognise the script. She picked it up and headed towards her bedroom.

'Who's it from?' her mother asked as she walked past.

'Not opened it yet,' replied Pip without stopping.

Whatever it was, she didn't want to open it in front of her mother. She deserved some privacy.

In her room she closed the door firmly and took the letter to the bed, slitting open the envelope with her finger as she did.

The letter inside was written on a piece of lined paper torn from a ringed notebook, the top edge ragged and uneven. She opened it out and looked at the address. She didn't recognise it per se, but she knew at once exactly who had written the letter and she felt her head grow woozy as her vision blurred in and out. She thought she might faint, and she was forced to breathe deeply through her mouth the way she had been taught until she felt stable enough to read on.

The first sentence confirmed her fears.

Dear Miss Appleby,

My name is Karen Smith and I'm Robbie's mum . . .

47

Pip dropped the letter to her lap as if it were radioactive. Suddenly all the oxygen seemed to have been sucked from the room, and her head swam.

Robbie.

The boy.

The child whose life she had snatched away.

With trembling hands, she picked the letter back up and tried again.

Dear Miss Appleby

My name is Karen Smith and I'm Robbie's mum. I've been wanting to write for a bit, but it's been hard. Since what happened I haven't been much good. But I had to keep going for the other kids. It's hard for them, too. I'm on my own. Their dad left when Robbie was three. Work has been good about it. I can have time off if I need it but they don't pay me so I try to keep going. And it helps, having something to do. You don't forget. I won't ever forget. But going to work gives you something else to think about and money's tight with it being just me. I have to feed us all somehow.

Pip took a shuddering breath and wiped her eyes with the flat of her hand. She was frightened to read on, but also compelled to. What did the woman want and why was she writing now, after all this time? Pip could feel her chest grow tighter with each sentence as she waited for the letter to begin its recriminations: the anger, the blame, the sheer and unmitigated hatred the woman must be channelling towards Pip, and which only now she felt able to put into words. But she had to keep going, despite her fear of what was coming next. It was inevitable, like looking at a gory open wound, knowing that it would make you sick but at the same time finding it impossible to ignore. She read on.

I think about you a lot.

Here it comes, thought Pip: the blame. She imagined the woman lying in her bed at night, unable to find any rest or peace, and hurling curses at the woman who stole her precious child from her. It was only natural that she would do that. She must hate Pip with every ounce of her being.

Once again Pip paused. Perhaps, for the sake of her own self-preservation, she really should stop reading and not go any further. She was doing so well at the moment, could feel real progress. The panic attacks had stopped, the dreams were abating, and she was starting to feel like she might be able to enjoy life again. She didn't want to know about the mother's pain. She could imagine it for herself, had been doing that exact thing ever since the accident. What could possibly be gained from being told what she already knew and going right back to where she had been? She could just replace the letter in its cheap envelope and throw it into the fire, where it would never have to haunt her again.

But Pip knew she couldn't do that. The woman, Robbie's mother, had taken the time to put her anger and pain into a letter and the least Pip could do was to read it, absorb it, take some of it on to her own shoulders. She braced herself for what was to come and read on.

> *I've thought about what happened and how Robbie died and how you came out of it without a scratch on you. And to start with I was so angry. I really hated you. It wasn't fair that my beautiful boy had to die when you'd just walked away scot-free.*
>
> *But then I thought that you didn't walk away, did you? Not really.*
>
> *My lovely Robbie – he's gone forever. He's not coming back. I'll never see him play football for Arsenal (did you know he was a Gunners fan? He had his shirt on that day. He never took it off unless I made him). I'll never see him get a job, get married, have kids of his own. And that hurts – God, that hurts so much. But he's gone. He doesn't know any of it.*
>
> *But you. You have to live. His life was gone in a second but yours goes on and on. You have to think about what happened every day. I guess it's always in your head, like it is in mine, and it never goes away no matter what.*
>
> *The difference between you and me, though, is that Robbie was my boy. I'm going to grieve for him forever.*

*But you. You shouldn't have to spend the rest of your life
suffering. That really isn't fair.*

Pip had been bracing herself for the impact of the mother's words
to hit her between her eyes and knock her sideways, but now she
stopped in her tracks. What exactly was the letter trying to say?
She went back and reread the last two sentences. This was no con-
demnation. The mother wasn't damning her for all eternity, as Pip
had assumed she would. Cautiously now, she let her eyes trace the
rest of the letter.

*My baby is dead and he's never coming back. But your
life shouldn't be over too.*

*I know what happened was an accident. Robbie just ran
out. He was always doing it. I told him over and over,
but you know what boys are like. He thought he was
invincible and that I was stupid, fussing all the time.
When the police came to my door, I knew exactly what
had happened. I'd almost been waiting for it.*

*So, I just want you to know that I don't blame you. I did
for a while. Even after the coroner said it was an accident and the police didn't take any action, I still hated
you. I had to. I was so angry with you, with the police,
with Robbie, but mainly with myself for not keeping my
baby safe.*

*But I'm not angry now. And I know none of this was your
fault. Robbie just ran out. There was nothing you could
do. In fact, it was a miracle more people weren't hurt.*

*I don't suppose it makes much difference to you – maybe
you have forgotten all about us – but I wanted to tell you
that. I don't blame you. It wasn't your fault.*

*Please don't write back. I don't want that. But I just had
to do this for myself.*

Yours sincerely,

Karen Smith

Pip looked up from the letter, stunned. She couldn't register any
emotions at all. It was as if someone had just wiped her mind clean,
like a blackboard in a classroom. The words were clear enough; she
understood their meaning, but she was numb. She could find no
response to them.

The boy's mother did not blame her. The mother of the child
she killed could see that it had been an accident, a horrible, tragic
accident. Pip knew she would blame herself for the rest of her life,
but maybe her guilt would be easier to bear knowing that the one
person who had the most reason to blame her did not.

Suddenly, Pip needed her own mother. The desire to be with
her was so strong that she swept the letter up in one hand and ran
from her room, shouting for her as if her life depended on it. Her
mother appeared in the hallway at once, her eyes wide.

'What is it, Pip?' she asked, anxiety clipping her words short.
'What's happened?'

Pip hurtled down the stairs and threw herself into her so hard
that her mother took a few steps backwards before she could regain
her balance. She wrapped her arms tightly around Pip without
asking any further questions and Pip began to sob hard into her
shoulder. She could feel her mother's hand stroking her hair in a

gentle repetitive rhythm, like she had done when she was a little girl. There, there, Pip. There, there.

'She says it wasn't my fault,' Pip blurted through her tears. 'The accident wasn't my fault.'

'Well, of course it wasn't,' her mother replied softly. 'You know that.'

'But she said it,' Pip sobbed.

'Who said it, Pip? You're not making much sense.'

'The woman. The mother. Of the boy. Robbie. She said it. She sent the letter and she said it.'

'Ah,' replied her mother, as if no further explanation were required. 'Good.'

Pip stayed there, cocooned, until she finally stopped trembling.

48

Project Tidy Up was going rather well and Evelyn was feeling pretty smug. There was still a way to go, and the rooms she had tackled thus far were a long way from perfect, but things were definitely better. She had also figured out how to put her internet shopping on hold, so nothing new had been delivered to the house. She had missed having the delivery driver to share a few words with, but she had replaced this in a new way.

She had left the house.

She had ventured to the little supermarket at the end of the High Street and bought herself milk and bread and a rather delicious muffin. And she had spoken to the girl at the checkout. She had wanted to tell her that this was the first time she had been out and bought her own groceries in years, but that felt like too much information to share, so instead she had passed some inane comment about the weather and the girl had given an equally inane reply, and then she had left.

And it felt amazing.

Nicholas had been virtually speechless when he had made his weekly duty call.

'Can you help me get rid of these things?' she asked him as he stood, open-mouthed, gaping at the mountain of black plastic bags.

'That pile is for charity and that one for the tip. I'd do it myself, but . . .'

'Of course, of course,' he said, making a decent stab at enthusiasm, although Evelyn had seen his expression slide when he realised the amount of work that now lay ahead of him. 'What's brought this on?' he asked her.

'It's been long enough,' Evelyn replied simply.

Nicholas seemed to accept this at face value, and dutifully loaded the bags into his car and took them away over several trips.

Pip had taken to popping over in the evenings, and they shared a jug of cocoa and chatted about their lives in London. Even though Pip was a few years younger than Scarlet would have been, Evelyn couldn't help but make comparisons. If Scarlet had lived, perhaps this was what their relationship would have been like: the two of them chatting easily at the kitchen table, sharing ideas and thoughts. Evelyn couldn't imagine having that kind of rapport with her own mother, but she liked to think her Scarlet wouldn't have been as desperate to run away as she herself had been.

Evelyn told Pip about the Winter of Discontent and the freezing flat she had shared with Brenda, and Pip reciprocated with stories about the cases she had worked on. One night, after they had laughed until they cried over a calamitous show Evelyn had once been in, Evelyn sat back in her chair and licked her lips.

'You know, don't you, Philippa Rose, that there is nothing stopping you from going back to your life?'

She hadn't wanted to say it, and now, as she heard the words coming out of her mouth, she almost wished she hadn't. She loved the time she and Pip spent together and had come to rely on her company more than she would care to admit. But still, it needed to be said, and if she was to consider herself a true friend to the girl then she had to be honest.

Pip didn't seem to have caught what she said or had missed her meaning. Either way, she eyed Evelyn quizzically.

'To London,' Evelyn clarified. 'You should really be thinking about going back to London. I know you love your job so you must be missing it, and I'm certain they will be missing you. And London is where you're meant to be. It's lovely that you have been back here and that you've managed to reconcile all your old prejudices about the place, but now it's time you were getting back to your real life.'

Pip didn't speak for a long while. Instead she cupped the mug of cocoa and stared out at the street beyond the window. It was almost midsummer and the evening sky still held the last of the sun's rays. Evelyn waited. If she had learned anything in her seventy years on the planet, it was the importance of timing.

Eventually, Pip returned her focus to the room.

'I can't,' she said.

Evelyn said nothing, the obvious question hanging in the air between them. There was no need to ask. Pip would explain, given time.

'I'm scared,' she said, after a few more moments.

'Of what?' asked Evelyn.

'Oh, I don't know,' said Pip. 'Just everything. I'm scared that I won't be able to work without cracking up again. I'm scared that there won't be any work for me and my career is ruined. I'm scared that I have nowhere to live, and now that I'm single I will have no friends and no social life. I'm scared of driving. I'm scared of not driving. I'm scared that I won't be able to cope and will have to come back home. I don't think I could bear to have to do this again.'

'And you're going to let all that stop you from being where you're supposed to be?' Evelyn asked.

Pip shrugged. 'But where am I meant to be?' she said. 'I'm not even sure about that any more.'

Evelyn raised an eyebrow. The question required no further reply.

They sat in silence for a while, listening to the seagulls calling to one another.

'I always think,' said Evelyn, 'that the best way to eat an elephant is one bite at a time.'

Pip looked at her and grinned. 'And precisely how many elephants have you eaten?'

'Oh, you'd be surprised,' Evelyn replied.

'And what about you?' Pip asked. 'You're going to have this place looking tip-top pretty soon. You'll need a new project.'

'I thought I might check out the local theatre,' said Evelyn, surprising herself as this was the first time the thought had crossed her mind. 'They're bound to need volunteers to help with front of house and what have you.'

'But don't you want to be on the stage?' said Pip. 'In the spotlight?'

Evelyn thought she was probably right, but she didn't want to run before she could walk, and it had been a very long time. She wasn't even sure she could learn lines any more.

'Let's just start with selling programmes,' she said, 'and see where we get to.'

'I think that's a great idea, though,' said Pip. 'And I'm sure they'll be delighted to have a professional on their books. I can come and see you,' she added. 'I've never known anyone in a show before.'

Evelyn smiled. Pip's enthusiasm for life seemed to have grown a little each time they met. It was lovely to see.

'And I thought I might look some people up, from the old days,' Evelyn added. 'Although I've no idea who might still be alive.'

'You're not that old!' said Pip. 'You do know that seventy is the new . . .'

'Sixty-nine,' offered Evelyn, and they laughed. 'I do wonder what happened to dear old Ted, though. I really did let him float away.'

Pip opened her mouth to say something, but then seemed to think better of it.

'So, are you going to start looking for flats?' Evelyn asked.

'Maybe,' said Pip, but she didn't look as doubtful as she had moments before.

'I never got to see Scarlet all grown up,' said Evelyn, 'but if she had turned out half as well as you, Pip, then I would have been very, very proud.'

Pip looked delighted. 'Oh, Evelyn,' she said. 'That's the nicest thing anyone's said to me for ages. I'm sure Scarlet and I would have been really good friends. We might even have known each other.'

Evelyn raised a sceptical eyebrow.

'Okay,' conceded Pip. 'Given how fast I deserted Southwold I suppose that's not that likely. But if we had met, then I'm sure we would have got along.'

'I think you would have, too,' said Evelyn.

'And I think she would have been proud of you as well,' said Pip. 'The way you're turning things around, getting the house straight, joining the theatre group and all that. I think she'd have been delighted.'

Later, when Pip had gone home and Evelyn was making her way to bed, she thought about Scarlet. She liked to imagine her as an adult, maybe with children of her own by now. Until she met

Pip, she had only allowed herself to think of Scarlet as a three-year-old, preserved precisely as she had been when she died. But now she had a clearer idea of what Scarlet might have become, and it had opened up a whole new chapter for her. It was bittersweet, of course; it always would be, but she could open and close the book whenever she wanted to. And she had Pip to thank for that.

49

Pip was sitting at the kitchen table, a mug of strong tea steaming at her side and her laptop open. She scrolled down and down. All the flats she had seen thus far had either been too far out of central London or too expensive. Although she had some savings, her income had dried up once she had stopped work. Hopefully things would pick up as soon as she started again, but there was no guarantee how quickly that might happen, and she didn't want to saddle herself with a rent that would quickly become a millstone around her neck.

She was starting to think about going back. The day before, she had taken her courage in her hands and rung her clerk in chambers, the person in charge of her workflow. Matt had been her clerk from the very beginning of her career and she had always believed he had a particular soft spot for her, passing her the juiciest cases and covering up for her if she made a mistake.

'Matt,' she said when she heard his voice at the other end. 'It's me. Pi . . . Rose.'

'Rose! Hi! How are you?' He sounded so delighted to hear from her that it made her want to cry. 'Please tell me you're ringing to say you're coming back. I've got briefs coming out of my . . . Well, I've got loads of work for you. Just say the word and I'll start pushing it in your direction.'

Pip felt a little overwhelmed. This wasn't quite what she had been expecting when she'd picked up the phone, but it was so lovely to hear that she hadn't been forgotten.

'I'm not quite sure when it will be,' she said vaguely. 'But I'm hoping it won't be too long now.'

'Well, I'm thrilled to hear you're on the mend,' said Matt. 'And as I say, whenever you feel ready to come back, just let me know.'

Was she ready? A month ago, she would probably have just shaken her head in despair at the thought of returning to her old life. When her father had driven down to London to retrieve her things from Dominic's flat, she had been unable to deal with any of it and had just left it all piled up in the spare room. Then, a couple of days ago, inspired by Evelyn's sterling efforts at her house, Pip had gone into the room to sort it all out.

Dominic had clearly paid someone to pack it all up for him. Her clothes were in clear plastic sleeves, her shoes and toiletries neatly wrapped in tissue paper and boxed. It was almost like Christmas, unwrapping each item, except Pip had anticipated no joy in the task. With every unravelling, she expected to feel a little sadder, a little less in control of her future. But actually, as she held the tokens of who she had been in her hands, all she could do was marvel at how far she had come.

If you had asked her before the accident what her favourite possession was, her answer would have been quick and assured. Her first pair of Louboutins. She remembered now how she used to take them out of the box just to gaze at them and stroke their red undersides. But when she had dug them out and held them in front of her, like Dorothy with her ruby slippers, all she saw was a pair of nice but stupidly overpriced shoes, and nothing more. She could wear them in the farmhouse in full confidence that neither of her parents would have the first idea what they represented. Evelyn would be the same, and would probably have scoffed at this Rose who had attached so much significance to such status symbols. Pip thought she might think like that as well, if she were ever introduced to the person who had been Rose.

She had hung her clothes up in the wardrobe, ready for when she went back to work, and left the shoes in their boxes. Instead of being desperately sad, or even scary, she had found it cathartic. It was just stuff – nice stuff, granted, but just stuff nonetheless. None of it really mattered. None of it was actually what was important.

And now she needed to find somewhere to live. The trouble was that flats in the areas she thought she wanted to be, where she had lived with Dominic, were just so expensive. There was no way she could afford to live there on her own. She sat back in her chair and puffed out a huge and dejected sigh just as her mother walked into the room.

'What's up?' her mother asked.

'Flats in London are ridiculously expensive,' Pip said.

Her mother barely missed a beat. 'I didn't realise you were thinking of moving back,' she said, and Pip could hear she was trying hard to keep her tone neutral.

'Well, I won't be going anywhere at this rate,' replied Pip, determinedly avoiding her mother's meaning. 'I think I'm going to have to share, but the thought of trying to find the right flat and flatmate at the same time is totally hideous.'

Her mother looked over her shoulder at the flat that was currently on her screen, a new-build in Shoreditch. When she saw the rent she whistled, and then crossed the room and began to fill the kettle. 'Is that near where you lived before?' she asked. 'I'm sorry, I should know, but I get confused with how London all fits together.'

'Yes, more or less,' Pip said.

'And it's handy for work?'

'Yes. About half an hour by Tube.'

Her mother pulled a face. 'And that's handy, is it?'

Pip laughed. 'It's handy for London,' she said.

Her mother was quiet for a moment as she put teabags in the pot. 'What would happen if you drew a circle around work, on the map I mean, and marked all the places that were within say, forty-five minutes?'

Pip thought about it for a moment. She had assumed she would move back to Shoreditch. That was where she had always aspired to live. She had given her postcode proudly when she got into a taxi and she and Dominic had often congratulated each other on their excellent taste. In fact, now she came to think about it, she struggled to remember exactly how it had felt to be so pleased about something so very trivial.

But her mother was right. Why was she contemplating moving back there, to a flashy, poky, overpriced flat surrounded by people who neither knew their neighbours nor cared who they might be, when there were so many other places she could try? So what if she lived a little bit further out? Lots of people did and no one thought any the less of them.

Actually, that wasn't true, she admitted to herself. People like her and Dominic had thought less of them. Pip winced as she remembered the kinds of conversations they had had within the confines of their boxy living room, barely big enough to swing a cat in, but in the right location.

She couldn't quite picture herself cast in that role any more. It felt so long ago, almost a different lifetime. But then, when she thought about it, she supposed that was exactly what it was.

She closed down the Shoreditch search and started again.

It was a little later when she spotted a notification that she didn't recognise. It was the email account she had set up when she had posted the advert trying to find Evelyn's Ted. She clicked on it now. The inbox was full of replies.

Pip started to work her way down them. In the main they seemed to be from men who might or might not be called Ted but were still happy to introduce themselves to her. It was clear that the purpose of her email had been wilfully misinterpreted in a great number of cases, and she felt relieved that she'd had the foresight not to use her usual email address.

After scrolling through around twenty messages, a couple of which made her skin crawl, she came to one that looked more promising.

> *My name is Ted Bannister. I knew Evelyn Mountcastle in the seventies and eighties. We met at her flatmate's wedding but we lost touch after she moved to Suffolk.*
>
> *This is not me typing but a friend of mine as I do not have a computer. I do have a mobile telephone (number below). Please ring me for further details if required.*

This had to be him, Pip thought. Her initial message had been intentionally vague, but this reply had details that matched what Evelyn had told her and what she knew from the diary.

She reached for her mobile and rang the number. After a couple of rings, it was answered.

'Hello?' said a voice with a thick Cockney accent.

Pip swallowed. This had all happened so fast that she hadn't had time to prepare what she wanted to say. 'Hello. Mr Bannister? Ted?'

'Yes. What can I do you for?' came the chirpy reply.

'My name is Pip Appleby,' she said. 'You answered my advert in the *Standard*, about Evelyn Mountcastle?'

'So I did,' he replied.

Pip smiled down the line. She liked Ted Bannister already. 'I can't believe I've found you,' she said.

'Well, you have. So, what's up? Evelyn's not dead, is she?'

'No! No! She's fine!'

'Well, that's a relief at least. I was worried, when I saw your message.'

'I've recently met Evelyn and we've become friends. She's mentioned you and I just thought I'd see if I could find you. She talks about you all the time. I think she'd love to see you, so I was hoping we could arrange for the two of you to meet up, as a surprise. Evelyn's still in Southwold. Maybe you could come up here. I'd pay your fare,' she added as an afterthought.

There was a silence at the other end of the line, and Pip's heart sank. She had got it wrong. That much was clear. He didn't want to see Evelyn. Perhaps they hadn't been as close as Evelyn had suggested, or it was all too long ago. She waited, but it was fairly obvious that Ted was just working out how to turn her down.

Ted sucked his teeth. 'Well, the thing is . . .' he began.

'It doesn't matter,' interrupted Pip. 'Forget it. I'm sorry to have troubled you.'

'Hold your horses!' said Ted. 'Have I said I don't want to come? Trouble is, it's my old mum. She's ninety-seven and as blind as a bat. She's still living at home, though. We both are, as it goes. But I can't leave her. I mean, it's okay just popping out to the shops. But to come all the way up there to Suffolk – that's a no-go, I'm afraid. Shame though. I'd love to see Evie again. How's about she comes down here?'

'I'm not sure . . .' began Pip. 'She's been a bit, well, she's only recently started going out and . . .'

'She's never got that agoraphobia. A mate of mine had that. Shocking condition. Poor Evelyn.'

Pip smiled as she tried to get a word in edgeways. Ted seemed to be exactly as the diary had described him. 'No, not agoraphobia as such. But things had got a bit on top of her. She's getting better now, but I'm not sure she's ready for a long trip.'

There was another silence whilst Ted thought. 'Well, you come up with a way of getting her down here and I'll be there like a shot. I can't believe we let things drift like we have. We were best buddies, back in the day. You send her my very best regards, won't you? Right, got to go now. Mum's calling. Nice to talk to you. What did you say your name was? Pip Appleby. What a fabulous name! Your parents must have been super-smart to come up with that. Cheerio.'

And then he was gone.

What a breath of fresh air he was, Pip thought. He was exactly what Evelyn needed.

50

Pip and Evelyn stood in the middle of Liverpool Street station as what felt like the whole of London bustled around them. Evelyn couldn't believe there were so many people. They swarmed everywhere, popping up out of tunnels and shops and disappearing over bridges. She could barely see any space that didn't have people in it. Had London been as busy as this when she had lived here? It was hard to recall, but she supposed it must have been similar. She had just grown unaccustomed to crowds. It was exhilarating, though, to be in the presence of so much humanity, and she stood open-mouthed in wonder.

Pip, however, looked to be enjoying herself less. She had become very pale since they had got off the train, and her face looked clammy. Her eyes skittered about like a frightened animal's, as if she didn't know which way to run.

Evelyn decided she must take control. 'Well, if I remember correctly,' she said, trying to sound confident, 'then it's a hop along to the Northern Line and then straight up to Kentish Town. You might need to help me with the ticket though, Pip. Those barriers look terribly aggressive.'

She took Pip's arm and led her towards the sign saying Underground. Pip followed, compliant as a child. Evelyn began to worry. She could really do with Pip snapping out of it. When she had agreed to make the trip to see Ted, she had done so on the basis that Pip would look after her. She hadn't anticipated it turning out to be the other way round.

But as they walked along, jostled by the crowds of commuters, Pip seemed to find her feet and the colour began to return to her cheeks.

'I'd forgotten,' she said. 'Isn't that strange? I'd forgotten what it's like.'

'That's not so very strange,' said Evelyn in a reassuring tone. 'You've been gone eight months and you'd struggle to find many places quieter than Southwold in the winter, certainly when compared to this.' She gestured with her arms at the crowds and accidentally hit a man on his chest. He scowled at her and Evelyn laughed. 'Oh, come on. Let's get out of here and go and find darling Ted.'

Ted had told them that their café was now a fried-chicken place, and so they had opted for a Costa Coffee over the road. Pip pushed open the door and immediately Evelyn started scanning the tables for her friend. She saw him at once. His hair was white now and not toffee-coloured, but his eyes still sparkled and his smile was just the same. Evelyn had fretted that he wouldn't recognise her, but it was immediately apparent that she had been worrying for no reason.

'Evelyn Mountcastle as I live and breathe,' he said, standing up and waving his arms as if he were blessing the café. Everybody turned to see what the commotion was about, and then immediately turned back in case they made eye contact with the strangely behaving man.

'Ted!' said Evelyn. 'Oh, Ted.'

She rushed across to him and they stood, staring at one another, shaking heads and smiling.

'Just look at you,' she said. 'You haven't changed a bit.'

Ted patted his stomach sheepishly. 'Not sure I had this last time I saw you,' he said. 'But it's all bought and paid for. You look great, Evie. Absolutely tip-top. Now, how long's it been? I was trying to do the maths but it seemed like a ridiculously long time, so I gave up.'

'I think it must be about thirty-five years,' said Evelyn.

'Unbelievable,' said Ted. 'And that must be Miss Pip Appleby,' he added, looking over at Pip.

'Hi,' replied Pip. 'What can I get you both?'

'Tea,' they chorused. 'And biscuits.'

They spent the first hour or so catching up. Ted's life was much the same as it had ever been. He was still living with his mother, still wheeling and dealing like he always had done. Evelyn couldn't imagine him ever retiring. He seemed so full of life. His smile dropped, though, when she told him how she had spent the time.

'Oh, Evie,' he kept saying. 'I feel so bad. If I'd only known. I'd have been there like a shot. I assumed you'd got married or some such. I never thought of you all alone in that big old house.'

'Don't you blame yourself,' she said. 'Not for a moment. I brought it all on myself. But I'm out now, and raring to go.'

'Good job you found her then, Pip Appleby,' said Ted. 'Sounds like you pulled her out of the doldrums.'

Evelyn turned to give her a grateful smile, but Pip was shaking her head.

'Actually, Ted,' she said. 'I think it was the other way around.'

Ted looked from one of them to the other. 'Well,' he said, 'I don't suppose it matters who did what. The main thing is that you're both here now.'

And Evelyn had to agree with him.

51

Friday 21st June 2019

*Midsummer's Day. Not quite the first of January, but
halfway through the year seems like an appropriate place
to start, with half the months finished and half still to
come.*

*I found this diary on the bargain shelf in the stationer's.
I hadn't really been looking for one – it hadn't crossed
my mind to start writing a diary again – but it spoke to
me. It's not quite the same as all the others, a little taller
and thinner, but I decided that didn't matter. In many
ways it's a good thing. The shape of the diary reflects a
change in me and my life and when I look at them, all
lined up on the shelf in my now not-that-messy study, I
will know at a glance where the old life ended and the
new one began.*

*So, yesterday Pip and I took the train to London. It's a big
leap from a wander on the pier to a train ride to London
but I took it in my stride, and I was proud of myself. I*

have to confess to being more than a little nervous, not so much about the trip itself but about meeting Ted again after all these years. When Pip first told me that she'd tracked him down, I wasn't sure meeting up was a good idea. My old agent Julian used to say, never look back unless you're planning to go that way. Well, I'm definitely not. This is a fresh start for me. I know I'm an old lady, but age is just a number – you're as young as you feel and all other appropriate clichés.

Anyway, in the end I decided that no harm could possibly come from a brief stroll down Memory Lane with dear old Ted.

And I am delighted to report that he was just the same as ever. Older, of course – aren't we all? – but it wasn't hard to find the man I once knew so well in the lines and creases of his face. Our café is no more, but that was all right. Things change and move on all the time. That's just how it should be. We said we'd keep in touch, Ted and me. I think we will. I told him about wanting to get a part in a show in Southwold, and he said he'd move heaven and earth to get up to see me. Pip says she'll come, too, although I'm sure she'll be very busy when she gets back into the swing of things in London.

I've bought myself an iPad. Evelyn Mountcastle enters the twenty-first century. Nicholas said he couldn't see the point and that the old computer he gave me works perfectly well. But I told him that if I wanted to FaceTime

Pip then I needed the right equipment. I think he worries for what's left of his inheritance!

After we'd left Ted, we went to see Pip's new house. She has an apartment on the second floor of a huge Victorian townhouse in Hackney. It's not that far from where I lived with Brenda on Kentish Town Road, although the place has changed so much I didn't realise where I was until the taxi had already flown past the front door.

As we were exploring, there was a knock on the door. Pip opened it and there was a woman on the doorstep holding a lemon drizzle cake and a pot plant. Her name is Saffron, she's a midwife and she lives in the flat downstairs. Pip was delighted to have neighbours who bothered to find out who she was. I think she's going to be just fine there.

We came home together but Pip will be moving in next weekend. I shall miss her more than she knows, but I'll be up in town much more regularly from now on so it will be easy enough to get together.

And why might that be? I hear you cry. I thought you'd never ask. I have got myself an agent – not Julian, of course. I didn't even bother looking him up, although I'm sure he'll be retired by now – or dead. This one is a very keen young woman called Kate. She seems highly confident that she will be able to keep me busy. Age brings character roles, apparently, and in this brave new 'no-woman-is-invisible, age-is-no-barrier, grey-hair-don't-care' world the older actress is in great demand. If you don't believe me then just look at Dames Judy and Helen. And what about Imelda and Maggie, Diana and Celia? Honesty, the list goes on and on. I shall return to London to get some head shots done very soon, and then we shall see what I can make happen.

ACKNOWLEDGMENTS

I wanted to write a novel that examined how people can become trapped, not just by their circumstances but also by the stories they tell themselves in their minds.

Both Pip and Evelyn are desperate to break free from lives they believe they are not destined to follow, but are dragged back as a result of events they can't control. I wanted to think about how that might feel and how you could come to terms with having all your plans cast asunder.

A couple of people helped me to create Pip and Evelyn and I am very grateful to them both. Whilst my first career was as a solicitor and I dealt with barristers regularly, it was a long time ago and I needed to check how much things had changed. Kirsten Sjovoll of Matrix Chambers in Gray's Inn, London, kindly gave me some of her precious time to answer all my questions.

I knew far less about Evelyn's world and so I quizzed my good friend and actor Thomas Frere, who was able to explain how auditions and agents and such matters work.

Any mistakes or inaccuracies that I might have made in describing either world are all my own.

As ever, I want to thank the wonderful team at Amazon Publishing and in particular my editor Victoria Pepe, whose calm demeanour has seen me through many a crisis of confidence.

Thanks also to Celine Kelly who has edited all my books thus far and always steers me in exactly the right direction.

Finally, thanks to my family. I edited this book in the lockdown of 2020 with all six of us trapped in the house together, and they were all remarkably patient with me. I have to say that I was possibly less patient with them, but they took it in good spirit. The amazing support they give me carries me through the harder parts of writing books for a living, and I am eternally grateful to them all. Thanks also to my wonderful parents, and particularly my mum who is my first reader and loves everything I write (because that's what mums do).

If you have enjoyed *Reluctantly Home* then please consider leaving a review on Amazon or Goodreads. It really does help to spread the word.

Thank you so much for choosing to read my book.

ABOUT THE AUTHOR

Photo © 2020 Karen Ross Photography

Bestselling author Imogen Clark writes contemporary book club fiction.

Her first three novels have all reached the number one spot in the UK Kindle store and her books have also been at the top of the charts in Australia and Germany. *Where the Story Starts* was shortlisted for the Goldsboro Books Contemporary Romantic Novel Award 2020.

Imogen initially qualified as a lawyer but after leaving her legal career behind to care for her four children, she returned to her first love – books. She went back to university to study English literature whilst the children were at school, and then tried her hand at writing novels herself.

Her great love is travel and she is always planning her next adventure. She lives in Yorkshire with her husband and children.

If you'd like to get in touch then please visit her website at www.imogenclark.com, where you can sign up to her monthly newsletter. Imogen can also be found on Facebook, Twitter and Instagram.